The man was drop-dead gorgeous...

Six foot two...coffee brown hair with faint streaks of gray... Too bad a pair of aviator-style sunglasses hid his eyes. But there was no doubt he was the right man.

For the first time, Keri envied her sister. Why couldn't *she* ever find someone like this?

"Darling!" She affected Kim's husky voice as she threw her arms around his neck. *He would expect this,* she told herself as she pressed her mouth against his. A jolt of electricity streaked clear to her toes. Judging from the way he stiffened in her embrace before she stepped back, he felt it, too.

"Well, well, well," he said in a voice as smooth as aged cognac. "Honey, if that's how you greet your future brother-in-law, I can't wait to see how you greet your future husband."

ABOUT THE AUTHOR

Linda Randall Wisdom knew she was destined to write romance fiction when her first sale came on her wedding anniversary. A short while later she quit her job in an employment agency and became a full-time writer. She hasn't looked back since. Over forty books later, Linda has won numerous awards and been on every bestseller list. Her quirky characters and offbeat humor have become her trademarks and have made her a favorite of American Romance readers. Linda lives with her husband—and her dogs, parrots and pet turtle—in Southern California.

Books by Linda Randall Wisdom

HARLEQUIN AMERICAN ROMANCE

Linda Randall Wisdom

NAUGHTY 'N NICE

Harlequin Books

TORONTO • NEW YORK • LONDON
AMSTERDAM • PARIS • SYDNEY • HAMBURG
STOCKHOLM • ATHENS • TOKYO • MILAN
MADRID • WARSAW • BUDAPEST • AUCKLAND

For personal trainers Donna Mills and Kathy Dotto of Step by Step Fitness, Temecula, California, who showed me strength training can be fun. Even those days I was positive I would die as I discovered all those muscles I had no idea were there!
And for Debra Matteucci and a memorable line she once told me. I hope you don't mind that I used it, but I couldn't resist such temptation!

ISBN 0-373-16671-0

NAUGHTY 'N NICE

Copyright © 1997 by Words by Wisdom.

Prologue

"No, Kim."

"Please, Keri. I really need you to do this for me! It would only be for a couple of days. Think of it as a minivacation."

"I hadn't even considered taking a major vacation this year."

"You have to do this for me! You owe me, big time. You made a blood vow that if I ever needed you, you would be there to help me. You'd never abandon me. Remember? Well, I'm calling in that promise."

Keri Putnam threw up her hands in exasperation. "I was ten when I made that vow and you had only taken a math test for me," she reminded her. "Trust me, Kim, I have repaid that debt a hundred times over."

Kim pouted. "But this is so important to me. And you know very well you're the only one who can do it." She eyed her sister's casual clothing. "After some alterations, that is."

Keri stared back at her sister, which was like looking into a mirror that reflected just minor differences. Kim's honey-brown hair was the same length as Keri's but much curlier. Today, it curved around one ear and swung saucily against her opposite cheek. Her tan leather miniskirt barely covered the essentials, while her bright orange sweater showed a few inches of bare midriff every time she raised her arms the least little bit. Showstopper legs were encased in sheer nylons that ended in taupe spike heels. She waved an artfully manicured hand tipped with vivid coral nails. Her sexy attire was a direct contrast to Keri's more casual look, which consisted of black latex bike shorts, a matching crop top and a loose black-and-red tank top. Her clothing displayed a slender body glowing with good health and a gleaming coat of perspiration that covered her bare skin. Her shoulder-length hair was pulled up into a ponytail that was starting to droop.

Keri glanced at the clock and decided she could give her twin another ten minutes before she ushered her out. The moment her sister had walked into the fitness center Keri should have known she had something up her sleeve. Otherwise, Kim wouldn't have been caught dead in a place where people worked up a sweat.

"Kim, time is something I don't have. I have a client coming in at two and I will not keep her waiting just because you have a wild idea you want me to be a part of," she informed her sister.

Kim leaned forward in her chair, started to touch her sister's arm, then drew back. "I don't know why you feel you have to do something that's so physical. Honestly, if you like perspiration so much, take a sauna." Her nose wrinkled with distaste. She looked through the glass wall opposite, at people of varied ages and body types doing what was necessary in their quest for the perfect body. Her gaze lingered on one man who was running on a treadmill. A black mesh tank top and black spandex shorts showed his tanned, lightly muscled body in all its perfection. "Still, I guess there are some advantages," she murmured, offering him a bright smile when he looked her way. Her smile brightened a few more watts when he smiled back.

"Just remember, sister, dear, that those so-called advantages involve sweating, which is something you don't enjoy doing even when you're sunbathing," Keri said dryly. "You know," she drawled with just a hint of malice—after all, if anyone knew Kim's deep-seated fears, it was her twin—"it might not hurt you to think about getting into a fitness regimen before it's too late." She ran a practiced eye over her sister's form. "Gravity sets in before you know it, sis, and if a body isn't kept toned, it starts to look...flabby."

Alarm flashed in Kim's eyes. "That isn't funny, Keri."

"Neither is a sagging glute, my dear. In laymen's terms, I'm talking about your butt." She angled her gaze toward Kim's chair. "How is yours? Or are you wearing one of those special panties that firm up the rear?"

Kim's coral-tinted lips tightened. "Plastic surgery gives you the same results in a lot less time and without all the work," she said haughtily. "Keri, I'm not asking for a lot. Just a week of your time. A week at the most. Surely you can give me that."

"A week!" Keri was dismayed. "At first, you said it would only be a couple of days, now you're saying a week. I'm stashing away every extra cent I can so I'll be able to buy into the club by the end of the year. There's no way I can afford to take the time off now. I'm sorry, Kim, but this is one problem you're going to have to handle on your own." She spoke with the authority of one who was eleven minutes older. One who was tired of bailing her sister out of trouble all the time.

"This doesn't just involve me, Keri. Stuart wants to marry me, and spending this time with his family is very important to him!"

Keri paused at her sister's exclamation. "Stuart? You didn't mention any Stuart. What happened to Jean Paul?" She referred to the man Kim had declared undying love for only a few months before. "All you said was you

needed me to pretend to be you for a few days. What is
going on?'' she demanded.

"I broke up with Jean Paul," Kim explained. "The
only thing is, he doesn't know it yet."

Keri recalled meeting Jean Paul. He was very Conti-
nental, very gorgeous and very persistent in putting his
hand on her knee any time he thought Kim wasn't looking. He got the message Keri wasn't interested when she
caught hold of his fingers and squeezed so hard she almost broke a couple. She was glad to hear her sister had
called it quits with him, but she couldn't stop wondering
about the new love of her life. Sadly, Kim had the worst
luck when it came to men. Not that Keri could claim to
have any better luck; she was just more selective.

"That's why I need your help," Kim explained. "I
want to fly to France and settle things with him,"she
explained. "I want to look him in the face when I tell
him what a swine he is and that I'm in love with and
marrying a man who's worth more than ten of him."

Keri swallowed a sigh. Her sister talked about flying
to France the same way she talked about driving across
town. But then, Kim had a lucrative position with an
advertising agency. As one of their savviest account rep-
resentatives, she created award-winning campaigns that
had other agencies always actively courting her, but Dunbar Creative Associates kept her happy by giving her the
freedom she seemed to need and allowing her her quirks.
Keri wondered how a woman who was so good at business could have such a disastrous love life.

Maybe it had had something to do with their formative
years. When Keri and Kim had hit puberty, their lives
had taken opposite turns. Kim had decided boys were a
lot more fun to play with than dolls and later she had
sought the plum position as head cheerleader and the un-
divided attention of the quarterback on the varsity football team while Keri had been busy discovering athletics.

Keri had gone on to earn degrees in exercise physiology
while Kim had earned a degree in business and advertising. Keri had always wondered how her flighty sister had
settled down long enough to earn a degree in anything
other than charming the opposite sex. She loved her twin
dearly and would do anything for her. But not this!

"Trust me, after the hell Jean Paul put you through,
he doesn't deserve anything more than a phone call or a
letter," she said crisply. "You'd be lucky if he did either
if your positions were reversed. Besides, we can't switch
identities anymore. The last time I pretended to be you,
I ended up in the clutches of King Kong. The man
thought buying me dinner meant a heartfelt invitation
into my bed. Do you know what it took to get him to
realize no meant no?"

Kim shifted, looking uncomfortable at the memory.
"If I had known Lawrence was such a creep, I wouldn't
have asked you, and you know it. I understand he had to
have those two caps replaced."

"He's lucky that's all he lost," Keri said darkly.
"There's no way I can pretend to be you to your fiancé!
He's going to know the difference right away."

"No, he won't. He knows I have a sister, but I never
said you were a twin, so he won't see anything different
about me. As I told you, think of it as a vacation," she
pleaded. "He told me the island his family lives on is
beautiful this time of year. It's not far from Seattle and
very peaceful. All I need to do is zip over to Paris, tell
Jean Paul what I think of him, zip back and meet you
out there where we trade places. It's something I have to
do. Please, help me?"

Keri pressed her thumb and forefinger against the
bridge of her nose as a familiar pounding began inside
her head. She hadn't suffered a headache since Kim's
last wild scheme.

"Tell you what, you go to Stuart's family get-together

and I'll fly over to France and tell Jean Paul it's over. This way, if he tries to charm you he'll be trying to charm me and we both know that won't work," she said. "I'm sure I can tell him what a creep he is much better than you can."

"No! I want to be the one to tell him I'm finally over him," Kim said stubbornly. "It's really better if you go to Stuart's."

"It won't work," Keri insisted.

Sensing her twin's weakening, Kim zoomed in for the kill. "Keri, I am so desperate, I will do anything you want. I'll even make up any money you'd lose while you're gone." She brightened, inspired. "Tell you what, you can even torture me with all those weights and things, once Stuart and I are married. I'll probably gain weight then, anyway. I'll come in here and learn all about workouts and how to burn fat or whatever." She wrinkled her nose in distaste. "I'll never ask another thing of you again. I promise. Just please help me this one last time."

Keri swallowed her sigh. "I have to be crazy to even consider doing this for you."

Kim squealed with delight. She leaped out of her chair and hugged her sister, then drew back with a grimace. "We have no time to lose. Come over tonight and I'll get you outfitted for the weekend. Something tells me you don't have anything in your wardrobe to cover such an occasion." She grinned. "You won't regret this, I promise."

"Something tells me I already do," Keri muttered.

Chapter One

"Hey, Dad, do you think Uncle Stuart's latest girlfriend will be anything like the last one?" sixteen-year-old Jake Carson asked his father over breakfast with a great deal of enthusiasm.

Rhyder shuddered at a memory best forgotten. "I don't even want to think about it. Taffi was more woman than any one man could bear."

"Wait a minute. Taffi wasn't the last one," fourteen-year-old Lucie corrected. "She was two girlfriends ago. Uncle Stuart's last girlfriend was Cherise and Fawn was before her."

"Fawn," Jake said with the reverence only a teenage boy would use when speaking of a woman who could raise all those hormones to a high level. "She used to wear those crop tops. Man, talk about great pecs."

"She only wore crop tops so you all could see the ring in her belly button," Lucie explained, wrinkling her nose in disgust.

"From what Uncle Stuart said, that wasn't the only place she had a ring," Jake said with a lascivious lift of an eyebrow.

Rhyder raised his hands to indicate the discussion was over before it got out of hand. He'd had no idea that when his son hit the teen years, Jake would turn into a walking, talking version of a ladies' man. Rhyder figured if he accomplished nothing else in this lifetime, he would make damn sure his son didn't become a Stuart clone. One Stuart Carson in the family was more than enough.

When he received a phone call from Stuart earlier that week, he hadn't expected his brother to announce he'd finally found "the one." For well over an hour, all Stuart could talk about was Kim. Rhyder was positive he wasn't going to like her. Still, she sounded perfect for Stuart. Probably because she sounded just like him except for one important difference: she had a job.

"I don't think we need to discuss where Fawn might have had that other ring. It's bad enough he feels he has to introduce these women to the family. His idea of getting engaged is on a par with going steady," Rhyder muttered, sipping his coffee.

When he and the kids moved out to the family home on the island, he enjoyed the remoteness and peace and quiet. Since his parents and other relatives only used the main house for holidays and special occasions, he knew he and his children would have this time on their own.

He was glad he had insisted on moving into the caretaker's cottage when they first arrived here. He valued the privacy the cottage gave them any time the rest of the family showed up. It was only a short walk from the main house. He considered it a sensible distance from a family he loved dearly even if he freely admitted they usually drove him bonkers. He would still be having this time alone with the kids if his younger brother, Stuart, hadn't screwed things up by announcing that he was engaged and wanted the family to meet his fiancée. The Carsons had arrived en masse five days ago and Rhyder hadn't considered his life normal since.

And things were only getting worse.

Stuart's fiancée was arriving on the afternoon ferry and his mother insisted he accompany her and his father to the dock to greet the young woman. He had tried to get out of it, but with Stuart delayed until evening, Rhyder's excuses fell on deaf ears.

"She's not another stripper, is she?" Lucie asked, as she gathered up the lunch dishes and began rinsing them off before putting them in the dishwasher.

Rhyder winced as he thought of the stripper Stuart had brought home about a year or so ago. Lucie had taken one look at the raven-haired woman's twelve-foot python wrapped around her shoulders like a stole and broken into hysterical screams loud enough to have shattered more than a few windows. The girl had refused to leave her room for the entire weekend and two of Jake's rats had somehow disappeared. He and his son had an idea of their fate, but they had never spoke of it aloud.

"I hope not." He gazed at his firstborn, clad in a pair of cutoffs that probably should have been thrown in the trash months ago. Rhyder noticed Jake's bare chest was starting to show a bit of masculine breadth, but he hoped his son would have a ways to go before he reached physical maturity.

"You'd better change into something more presentable before we head down to the dock," he suggested.

Jake looked baffled. "Why?"

"Because if you don't, your grandma's going to bemoan the fact her baby grandson dresses like a bum and then she'll talk about taking you shopping for proper clothes."

The boy blanched. "No way." He groaned as his father just shrugged. "Fine, but I'm not wearing a tie," Jake grumbled goodnaturedly as he pushed back his chair and got up. "I just hope sister dearest did the laundry or I won't have any clean underwear."

"Try the dryer, bonehead," Lucie suggested.

Rhyder was just getting up when he heard a muffled curse and a shout from the laundry room.

"I thought you knew how to do laundry!" Jake protested, stalking into the kitchen with a handful of pale pink cotton held high in one fist.

"I do know how!" she retorted.

"You do, huh? Then tell me how the hell my white briefs turned pink?"

"There's no way," Lucie argued, backpedaling as fast as he approached her. Suddenly, she stopped. "Unless..."

"Unless this was in there, too?" He held up a pale red sweatshirt. "Come on, Luce, don't you have enough brains to figure out everything would turn pink? Even I know that!" he shouted.

Rhyder's muffled laughter was abruptly shut off when he heard his daughter's reply. "It's not as if it's all *your* underwear. Dad's is in there, too."

"What?" He shot up and stalked over to the laundry in his son's arms. A quick survey told him his white cotton briefs were now a lovely shade of pink.

"If Dad hadn't given Penny the summer off you wouldn't be complaining about the laundry," Lucie told Jake.

"Penny has the summer off to help her daughter with her new baby," Rhyder reminded her.

Jake stared at his father with eyes a stormy shade of blue-gray. "I won't wear pink underwear."

"You'll have no choice. After all, it's not as if anyone can see them."

"I'd rather go without. She's such a lamebrain she can't even do laundry right," he grumbled.

Jake let out a snort of disgust and stalked off. Rhyder turned back to his daughter, figuring she would need comfort after her brother's insults. Instead, Lucie's eyes were the same storm-colored shade as Jake's, and her lips curved in a smile that made her look a little too pleased with herself. He smothered a sigh.

"We will have a peaceful summer," he told her, as if speaking the words made it so. "Which means you will start studying the directions on the laundry-detergent box and if Jake doesn't like the way you do the laundry, he will be given the opportunity to do his own. I'm surprised it hasn't happened before now."

"Fine by me." She tossed the dishcloth into the sink and walked out of the room. In the doorway, she stopped and looked over her shoulder. "I don't know why you guys are upset. It's not as if pink isn't a good color on you."

Rhyder closed his eyes. "I'd planned a very nice, quiet summer before we go back to L.A. Where did I go wrong?"

"Gimme, gimme, gimme."

He turned toward the doorway leading from the family room. A green-winged macaw waddled into the room, heading for Rhyder. Using his beak and claws he climbed up the chair leg and settled himself on the chair back, ruffling his vivid turquoise, red and blue wing feathers back into place. Tiny red-feathered lines radiated out from his dark eyes as he gazed lovingly at his human dad.

"Gimme, Rhy," he said in his raspy voice.

"Who forgot to lock Beau's cage?" Rhyder shouted. "Lucie!"

"Are you kidding? Jake did it!"

Rhyder shook his head. "I'd get a better answer from you, wouldn't I, guy?" He used three fingers to stroke the brilliant red head feathers. "You know you're not supposed to be out of your cage without supervision."

"Ahhh." Beau closed his eyes and rested his cheek against Rhyder's hand.

"I've got enough going on without running after you, too." He edged a hand under Beau's claws and urged him onto his wrist. "Come on, I'll find you some walnuts along the way."

As Rhyder carried the large bird into the family room he silently vowed that the next time he went into the city, he would buy himself several weeks' worth of black cotton underwear. Nothing could happen to them. He hoped.

KERI FELT SO MISERABLE she wasn't sure if she was safer standing at the railing or closer to the middle of the ferry. The concession area was behind her and she quickly discovered the smell of coffee was enough to send her running to the railing. She had run in and purchased seasickness pills. The man at the counter told her they wouldn't be one-hundred-percent effective since she was taking them a little too late, but they would help settle her stomach. She sat huddled on a bench, miserable and plotting a horrible death for her sister. Why hadn't she thought to ask how people got out to this island? Even she should have known better. After all, an island was surrounded by water and didn't necessarily have a helicopter service or small airport. When she turned her head, she noticed a tiny patch of green now growing larger until she could see bits and pieces of a roof among tall trees.

"Purty place, ain't it?" one grizzled-looking old man said, coming up to stand beside her.

She nodded. "I'm staying with the Carsons," she explained.

He took a better look at her. "You Stuart's new girl? Well, of course, you are," he answered his own question. "You don't look like the others," he muttered.

Keri resisted the urge to ask about the others. At the same time, she wasn't sure she wanted to find out if his comment was meant as a compliment to her or an insult. She was already silently cursing her sister for talking her into this crazy scheme. Keri vowed that one day she would put Kim in an equally horrifying situation.

She had spent an evening at Kim's loft apartment while Kim packed an appropriate wardrobe for her stay and briefed her on the family and Stuart.

"He's funny and gorgeous and knows every five-star restaurant within a hundred-mile radius," she told Keri. "And he owns a gorgeous sailboat."

"Be still, my heart. He sounds like a prize." Keri watched with growing dismay as Kim assembled a pile of short shorts, crop tops, miniskirts and dinner dresses that either had no back or no front. While she was used to wearing next to nothing at the fitness center where she trained with her clients, Keri really preferred to wear a little more when out in public. She knew she would have to make some changes to Kim's wardrobe before leaving for Washington.

"He has a brother who's an attorney," Kim continued. "And his other brother is a financial adviser. He handles all of Stuart's investments."

"What does Stuart do?" She wandered around the area Kim laughingly called her closet. Her favorite outfits were displayed on mannequins, complete with jewelry, made up to look like Marilyn Monroe, Jean Harlow and Rita Hayworth. She examined a drop-dead sexy black evening gown on "Rita."

"I guess you'd say he does something with investments, too," Kim said airily, as she pulled out a bikini.

"Is he a stockbroker? A trader?" she asked.

"No, he just lives off them." Her twin held up a sheer tunic, debated for a moment, then tossed it into the suitcase. Keri made a mental note to find a tank top to wear under it. "When I get back from France, I'll call you to let you know. We'll arrange to meet close by and switch places." She beamed. "Stuart said his family's home is gorgeous and there's so much to do, I know you won't be bored."

"Just as long as I can go running in the mornings."

"Running?" She'd looked as if Keri had suggested climbing into a live volcano. "Stuart knows I wouldn't be caught dead running."

Keri should have considered Kim's comment her first hint that her unexpected vacation might not be as blissful as she might like. Her next hint, or warning, was the phone message her sister had left on her answering machine that morning.

"Keri, I'm at the airport and thought I'd let you know you shouldn't have to worry about you and Stuart sharing a room," she'd said airily. "I doubt he would do anything that would appear unseemly to his parents, so I'm sure he won't think anything about you having your own room."

"Terrific," Keri muttered, watching as the island grew larger the closer they got. "I don't have to worry about sleeping with him and all I know is he's a great dancer, owns his own boat and prefers play over work. I can't believe she didn't have one picture of him." Keri wasn't too happy with the brief description she had been given. Six feet two inches, coffee-brown hair, gray eyes and best of all, he was drop-dead gorgeous. As if Kim would see any other kind of man.

"You can tell he'll never lose his hair," Kim had told her. "After that one time with Adam and his toupee, I'm not taking any chances."

Keri was grateful her nausea was subsiding as the ferry prepared to dock. She doubted Stuart would be expecting to meet a seasick fiancée. After several deep breaths to settle her stomach, she looked around. A scattering of people stood on the wharf waiting for the ferry. "There can't be that many hunks there," she murmured. "It's not that big an island."

She walked back to her stack of luggage. She had made sure to add a few of her own things. One way or another, she was going to get in a few morning runs.

Keri didn't think of herself as a fitness addict, but she knew she always felt better when she worked out first thing in the morning. With the sleepy cobwebs cleared from her brain she was always ready to go to work.

The wind off the water had swept through her hair, leaving it tousled. That morning, instead of styling her hair in its usual ponytail or letting it hang loosely to her shoulders, she had run mousse-coated fingers through the strands, leaving them looking as if she'd just climbed out of bed. Her hazel eyes appeared more green than brown, thanks to the ivy-colored shadow she had applied. A bold, deep pink swept her cheeks and colored her lips. While she always kept her nails neatly manicured, her sister had insisted on taking her to her manicurist for the full treatment. She still wasn't used to the shaped nails that made her fingers look longer and almost delicate. When Keri had looked in the mirror that morning, she'd felt as if she were looking at Kim. The only difference was the reflection showed Keri's lean form and muscle definition instead of Kim's softer, less toned form. Keri doubted anyone would notice that particular difference.

So now she stood on the ferry's deck wearing geranium-pink leggings with lace edging the ankles and a short-sleeved top with matching lace hemline that revealed a hint of tanned midriff. She slightly widened her stance for balance as the ferry bumped gently against the dock.

She wondered why there were so many people waiting there since they didn't appear to be interested in boarding.

"Kim! Kim Putnam!" A silver-haired woman chirped, waving a handkerchief. "Over here!"

Keri pasted a bright smile on her face. "It's show time," she said under her breath, straightening her shoulders and heading for the ramp.

As she stepped onto the dock, the first thing she noticed was the man standing apart from the crowd. His dark gaze was intently focused on her. In a creamy beige cotton shirt with the sleeves rolled up to his elbows and brown twill pants, he looked absolutely heart-stopping.

So far, so good. He was six foot two and had coffee-brown hair with faint streaks of gray scattered through the dark strands. Too bad a pair of aviator-style sunglasses hid his eyes so she couldn't see the color, but there was no doubt he was drop-dead gorgeous. For the first time, Keri envied her sister. Why couldn't she ever find someone like that?

"Darling!" She affected Kim's equally affected husky voice as she went up to Stuart and threw her arms around his neck. *He would expect this,* she told herself as she pressed her mouth against his. The moment her lips touched his, she felt a jolt of electricity streak all the way down to her toes. Judging from the way he stiffened in her embrace, he felt it, too.

Keri was positive her body temperature would have sent any thermometer exploding. She stepped back and couldn't stop staring at him. She couldn't be this affected by her sister's fiancé!

"Well, well, well," he said in a voice as smooth as aged cognac while he offered her a crooked smile that sent her stomach tipping to one side. "Honey, if that's how you greet your future brother-in-law, I can't wait to see how you greet your future husband." It took all of her composure not to turn tail and run. He was Stuart's brother? The man whose kiss turned her into a human volcano was not Stuart!

Keri wasn't sure whether to feel relief her sister wasn't marrying the man whose touch set skyrockets off in her system, or to feel like a fool for her honest mistake. Hmm... There would be a time when she could be herself and she could suggest that they get to know each other better. She would think he would be interested. Then she heard a boy calling him Dad. As if it wasn't bad enough that she was going to have to treat him as a brother, he obviously had a wife standing nearby who probably wanted to kill her! She would make sure that particular chore was held off until she and Kim switched places. It was only fair that Kim pay for not having warned her about Stuart's equally sexy brother.

She flashed a smile she knew Kim would use—one that was alluring and asked for forgiveness even if she didn't feel she'd done anything wrong.

"I'm afraid that's something you won't be privy to since I plan to give Stuart his greeting privately," she told him in a low husky voice.

Rhyder cocked an eyebrow. "Let's hear it for blurred vision," he murmured.

"Wow, Dad! Uncle Stuart actually found someone who has a brain," Jake blurted out with great relish.

Rhyder shot him a quelling look. "My son, Jake, and my daughter, Lucie," he said to Kim. "I don't think you need to worry about greeting my son the same way you greeted me." He grinned at Jake's crestfallen look. Rhyder was fully prepared to nip those thoughts in the bud but fast!

He noticed Kim merely smiled before she walked over to Jake and placed a sedate kiss on the boy's cheek. There was no missing the light in his eyes.

"As if I'd ignore any member of the family," she murmured loud enough for Rhyder to hear.

"Kim, my dear, we are so pleased you could come out here for a visit!" The silver-haired woman practically bounced up to her. She threw her arms around Kim and hugged her tightly. "I'm Frannie, Stuart's mother."

"It was sweet of you to invite me, Mrs. Carson," she replied when she could catch her breath.

"Call me Frannie, dear," the woman insisted, tucking her arm through Keri's. "I hope you don't mind walking.

Cars aren't allowed on the island, you know. Long ago, those of us who still have homes out here, decided we'd keep it as simple as possible. I do hope Stuart explained that to you. He'll be coming in tonight. He called and said he would be delayed. But that will just give us some time together, won't it? And don't you worry about feeling bombarded with introductions down here. We can wait until we're back at the house." She barely paused for breath as she looked over Keri's shoulder. "Stu, honey, would you and Rhyder make sure Kim's luggage is brought up to the house?"

"Sure thing, sugarpop." A tall man with iron-gray hair flashed her a broad smile. "You take little Kimmy up to the house and let her get comfy. Jake, you get that bag over there while your dad and I get the others."

Keri already felt bombarded as the members of the group smiled at her in turn. She smiled back the way she knew Kim would have. The problem was she was still reeling from the kiss she'd shared with Rhyder Carson. She normally wouldn't dream of being so bold as to go up to his son and kiss him—even a sisterly peck on the cheek—but something about Rhyder's comment had sparked her into doing it. Not only his comment, but the way he watched her. She had already mentally tipped up her chin in response to the challenge in his eyes. She doubted it would take her long to show this man she could take anything he could dish out!

For now, she was eager to get to the house. Preferably to close herself away in her room. How many relatives were here this weekend? Kim hadn't been sure. How was she going to remember all their names? She would have to make up a cheat sheet for Kim. She already knew one person who would be all too easy to remember. Her next thought hit her like a lightning bolt. If Rhyder Carson could affect her so strongly, what would his brother do to her?

"A pretty little gal," Stu told his son as he hefted a suitcase. "Have to admit little Stu has good taste."

"Yeah." Rhyder tried to keep his eyes off his mother's companion. Especially her shapely bottom. From what he'd gleaned from Stuart's telephone conversation, he hadn't expected the woman who'd stepped off the ferry and given him a kiss he could still feel all the way through his bones. He was positive he could still taste her. Talk about a woman who knew just how a man liked to be greeted! He sure wouldn't mind being greeted like that again. If only she had kissed him because she'd wanted to kiss him and not because they would soon be related.

From Stuart's words, Rhyder gathered Kim preferred lounging by a pool in a bikini not meant to get wet instead of swimming in the water and yet, if he didn't know better, he would say she had pretty good muscle tone for someone who believed exercise was a four-letter word. But then, Stuart's idea of cardiovascular exercise was signing his name on a charge slip. Rhyder knew they would make the perfect couple.

"She sure smelled good," Jake muttered, then turned a bright red when his father flashed a knowing look his way.

"I suggest you not think about that," he said amiably. "Come on, her highness might need to change her clothes after the trek to the house." As the men trudged their way up the hill, Rhyder reminded himself that *he* shouldn't think about how good she smelled, either.

"I KNOW OUR HOUSE SEEMS out of the way," Frannie prattled, as she led the way down a tree-lined path. "But it's been in Stu's family for years and we've gotten in the habit of celebrating holiday and special family occasions here. Unfortunately, not everyone could make it this time." She heaved a deep sigh.

Keri stared at the group hovering together on a side terrace of a massive three-story house that looked as if it had been standing there since the late 1800s. The cream-colored exterior was simple, with French doors opening onto a balcony that appeared to surround the second story. She imagined the group as vultures waiting to pick her bones clean.

"How large is your family?" she asked, feeling panic overtake her.

"Oh, dear." Frannie tapped her chin with her forefinger. "Let's see, Uncle Winston is here. And Grandpa Harry and Grandmother Mildred. They just came over here for tonight and will be leaving in the morning. But they wanted to meet you. There's also Aunt Sylvia, Stuart's other brother, Charles, and his wife, Veronica. And, of course, Rhyder and his children. They're living in the caretaker's cottage." She lowered her voice, although Keri was positive there wasn't anyone within earshot unless she counted the squirrel in a nearby tree. "Ellen, Rhyder's wife, died two years ago. Poor dear suffered from a brain tumor. Six months ago, Rhyder decided to take a leave of absence from his law practice, so he could spend this time with the children. He thought coming up here would be good for all of them. Although I'm certain he'll be returning to Los Angeles when the new school year begins. I can tell he's finished grieving and is ready to get on with his life."

By then, Keri was positive her eyes were glazing over. Her brain already felt overloaded with information and she sensed Frannie's recitation of her son's family history was far from over. Still, one piece of information the older woman provided was very interesting; Rhyder didn't have a wife who would want to kill her for that kiss.

"Here she is!" Frannie called as she led Keri across

the terrace. "Everyone, this is Stuart's fiancée, Kim Putnam. Kim, my dear, this is Uncle Winston."

"My dear." A tall silver-haired man Keri would have sworn was Cesar Romero's twin bowed over her hand. "Stuart said you were lovely and the boy was right. I must say he always had good taste in women."

Keri smiled and nodded, then gasped as Frannie led her past the gentleman. She looked over her shoulder in time to see Uncle Winston wink at her. There was no remorse in his gaze for having pinched her on the bottom.

"And this is Aunt Sylvia," Frannie continued, oblivious to the scene behind her.

Keri's first impression of the sprite of a woman was blue-rinsed hair set in tight curls kept neat under a white straw hat decorated with spring flowers. One impossibly tiny hand held a delicate china teacup filled with tea. At least, she thought it was tea until she got a whiff of the contents and realized sweetly smiling Aunt Sylvia was drinking good old-fashioned bourbon. And before the sun was over the yardarm, no less!

"You and Stuart make such a lovely couple," she murmured before moving on.

By the time introductions were finished, Keri had each person firmly fixed in her mind. Uncle Winston was a lecher. Aunt Sylvia considered her bourbon tea. Grandma Mildred preferred the world to see her as a vague little old lady, but Keri could tell she actually was sharper than a bowie knife. And Grandpa refused to admit he was hard of hearing and shouted his words. But it was Frannie and Stu's middle son, Charles, and his cold-eyed wife, Veronica, she easily decided she didn't like. Charles looked at her as if she was that night's dessert and Veronica was openly scornful.

"And where did Stuart find you?" Veronica asked in a haughty tone. Dressed in a simple black sheath and a triple strand of pearls that Keri would bet her car weren't costume jewelry, she looked the picture of the wealthy matron. But then what she'd seen so far told her Stuart's family was most definitely old money. No wonder the man didn't have to do anything more strenuous than watch over his accounts.

Keri mentally bared her teeth at the woman. And blessed her sister for at least remembering to give her details about her and Stuart's courtship in case she was asked the clichéd questions. She also noticed Rhyder had rejoined the group and was standing just close enough to hear her reply.

"I'm with Dunbar Creative Associates. I met Stuart when he stopped by to visit an old classmate of his," she explained.

Veronica didn't look convinced. "Who?"

Keri kept smiling. "Chuck Dunbar."

"Oh, Veronica, let's not scare the poor girl right off," Frannie scolded in her airy voice. She draped an arm around Keri's shoulders. "She must be tired from all the traveling she's done today. I thought I'd take you up to show you your room," she added.

"That would be nice," Keri said with a sigh of relief.

Frannie led her through a room filled with elegant French period furniture.

"Stu's mother loves the classics," she told Keri. "Personally, I prefer Danish modern."

"Mrs. Carson, if you want dinner served on time, you're going to have to talk to Reba again."

Keri turned to see a man who could have doubled as the Incredible Hulk, except instead of torn clothing and green skin, this man was completely bald, boasted a nose that had been broken too many times, and was dressed in a worn, ash gray sweat suit. She was tempted to ask him what the other guy looked like.

"Oh, Kim, this is Ferd," Frannie said. "He's our butler."

"Pleased to meetcha." He held out his hand.

Keri hid her smile as the man squeezed her hand a little too enthusiastically, and she couldn't help squeezing back. A faint gleam of respect appeared in his faded blue eyes.

"Maybe you can last in this family, after all," he said in his booming voice. "You don't seem such a cream puff."

"My sister is a fitness trainer," Keri told him. "She doesn't allow cream puffs."

He nodded.

"Ferd, tell Reba I'll come down to the kitchen as soon as I've shown Kim to her room," Frannie said.

"Okay, boss."

"Ferd was a contender," Frannie said in a proud voice as she and Keri went up the stairs. "Unfortunately, he was hit a few too many times. Still, we couldn't ask for a better butler."

"Better than a Rottweiler," she murmured under her breath. "And I gather Reba is your cook?"

"Oh, yes, and she's wonderful. I was so glad that her appeal came through," she confided.

Keri gulped. "Appeal?"

Frannie nodded. "Rhyder found her for us. And no matter what anyone said, there was never any proof she poisoned the last family she worked for. But then, we also make sure never to anger her," she said in a low voice. "Just in case, you understand."

Keri was positive her eyes were the size of saucers.

"Good idea," she murmured.

Frannie led her down a long hallway and stopped at a door. She flashed Keri a conspiratorial smile. Keri smiled back although she wished she knew what the big secret was. And if it was something she was going to like.

"Stu and I have our suite in the other wing, as do Charles and Veronica, so you and Stuart will have all the privacy you might want,'' Frannie said, ushering her inside the room.

Keri felt another stirring of panic deep down inside as she stepped across the threshold. She was positive her smile was beginning to fray around the edges. She had no idea how she was going to get out of this, but she knew she was going to have to find a way. There might be a lot of things she would do for her sister, but sleeping with her fiancé wasn't one of them!

Frannie walked across the room to the large French doors and pulled back the drapes. Late-afternoon sunlight streamed across the carpet and fell upon a queen-size bed covered with a mint-green gingham comforter.

"This room adjoins Stuart's," she explained, gesturing toward a door on the other side of the room.

Stuart had his own room. There was a door separating them. A door with a lock. She was safe! Keri wanted to fall to the floor and scream her relief. Instead, she mustered a smile that wouldn't reveal her feelings. She decided she could collapse later when she was alone.

"Well, I'll leave you to freshen up," the older woman said briskly. "We'll be having drinks on the terrace before dinner. That's around six. And, don't worry, we're very informal here." She started across the room, stopped in front of Keri and hugged her tightly. "I am so glad we'll have this time to get to know each other," she whispered.

A moment later, Frannie was out of the room, leaving behind a cloud of Chanel No. 5. Keri collapsed onto the bed.

"When this is all over, I will no longer be a twin," she said grimly. "Because I am going to kill Kim the minute she shows up."

Chapter Two

"I gather our guest is still upstairs?" Rhyder asked Veronica. He wasn't happy that his sister-in-law was the first person he ran into; they weren't exactly enamored of each other. He had once likened their relationship to that of two junkyard dogs circling each other warily. Veronica hadn't cared for the comparison, but he thought it was a perfect description.

She sniffed. "Upstairs changing out of that cheap outfit, I hope."

"I heard she makes upwards of six figures, Ronnie," he drawled, deliberately using the nickname she detested. "You'd better be nice to her."

She narrowed her eyes. "Don't tell me she's getting to you, Rhyder. We already heard about that kiss she gave you at the dock. My, my, that must have been a surprise." Her blue eyes gleamed with a look that wasn't at all pleasant.

"I'd say it was a surprise." He thought back to her lips pressed warmly against his. Most definitely a surprise. A very nice one. Not to mention the rest of the package. When he thought about her legs, he remembered delicate ankles. No wonder Victorian gentlemen were aroused by the sight of a woman's ankle. He quickly shook himself out of his wandering thoughts.

That was very definitely not a subject that should be pursued with Veronica in close proximity. She latched onto a man's weakness with a vise grip and held on just as tenaciously. She'd had no problem figuring out Charles's weakness not long after she'd met him and keeping him on a short leash from the moment they were pronounced man and wife. Rhyder was positive the woman ruled every second of Charles's life.

"How many tattoos do you think this one has?" Veronica asked.

Rhyder's imagination went into overdrive on that question.

"Hard to say," he replied. He was eager to escape to the bar. Maybe it would be easier once Stuart showed up to lay claim to his future bride.

Veronica opened her cigarette case, plucked out a white cylinder and reached for her lighter.

"She doesn't look like any advertising hotshot I've ever seen."

"How many do you know?" he asked.

She shot him a look fit to kill. "You're an attorney. Surely, you have some nefarious contacts who could find out all about her. How do we know she isn't like the others and just after him for his money?"

"What bothers you so much, Ronnie?" he asked. "That Stuart's marriage will cut another wedge into the family fortune?"

She narrowed her eyes and blew smoke through her nostrils. "You are a very disgusting man."

"I'm an attorney. I have to be disgusting. It goes with the job description." He gave her a wolfish grin. "I think I'll get a drink."

"A good idea. I'm sure you'll need it," she called after him.

"Cute little girl, that Kimmy, isn't she?" Stu said to

his son, walking up to him as he fixed himself a splash of Scotch on ice.

Rhyder automatically poured the same for his father and handed the glass to him.

"The politically correct term nowadays is woman, Dad," he said. "There are some women who would take you out for calling them a girl."

The older man snorted his opinion of politically correct terms. "Far as I'm concerned, all people've done is change one word for another. Garbagemen called sanitation engineers. Housewives called domestic engineers. You can't tell me either one of them knows what real engineering is all about."

Rhyder remained quiet. He was used to his father blowing off steam this way and past experience told him the man would soon wind down.

"Don't go down that road again, Stu." Sylvia patted him on the shoulder and smiled at Rhyder.

Rhyder knew his aunt's vague smile wasn't due to the amount of bourbon she had consumed. It was a well-known fact the dear, sweet little old lady could drink anyone under the table. Rhyder had found that out the hard way, one long night that had left him with an extremely painful reminder the next morning. He had lain in bed begging the world to let him die while his aunt went sailing with the family.

"You'd think Stuart would have moved heaven and earth to be here to greet his lady love," he said sardonically.

Stu lifted his wrist to glance at his watch. "He should be here within the hour. He knows better than to be late for dinner." He looked around. "Where are the kids?"

"Jake's down in the gym and Lucie's with Mom," he replied, happening to glance upward and see a light come on. A light in the room he knew adjoined Stuart's. Obviously, his mother was even more open-minded than he'd thought.

Rhyder looked at his family assembled on the terrace. Not one of them could be considered even remotely normal, but dammit, they were his family. And he was more than normal enough for all of them.

KERI TOOK ADVANTAGE of her time alone by exploring the lovely bedroom suite she had been given. The mint-green color scheme was echoed in the bath with large mint towels and a decadent-looking sunken tub in one corner of the room. She picked up one of the pale green seashell-shaped soaps and sniffed. Now she knew where the fresh scent of mint came from. She made a mental note to make use of the variety of bath oils and salts in glass jars arranged on a shelf above the tub and have a good long soak before dinner. For now, she knew she had unpacking ahead of her.

Keri wrinkled her nose as she pulled out Kim's idea of casual wear. Gauzy blouses, leggings, dinner dresses a person needed a can opener to get into and out of, and shorts that barely covered the essentials. Luckily, she'd had the sense to sneak in a few of her own things.

"Maybe Kim can introduce me to her new brother-in-law at the wedding rehearsal," she mused as she hung up a skimpy red silk dress that was short enough to double as a tank top. "It would be great if he was best man, since I would be maid of honor. I already know the man can kiss the socks off me. The least I can do is show him I can do more than the same to him."

WHEN KERI STEPPED OUT onto the terrace, she instantly found herself the focus of everyone's attention.

She had chosen a pair of black silk pants with a wide cummerbund waistband and teamed them with a white blouse that wrapped around her middle, leaving a deep

V neckline with only two strategically placed hooks to keep her modest. The long sleeves were sheer and flowing, gathered into tight cuffs at the wrist. The jewelry she wore was her own—onyx earrings and an old-fashioned, Y-shaped chain with a pear-shaped onyx stone dangling from the end of the Y. Thanks to a tussle with her curling iron and hairbrush, she had been able to revive her hair into loose curls framing her face. After seeing the final product, Keri resolved that Kim wouldn't get this outfit back. She looked too good in it!

"At least you have a sense of style," Aunt Sylvia announced, walking up to her. This time her china teacup was designed with yellow flowers instead of blue and sat gently in a matching saucer. But Keri would bet good money the brown liquid contents still weren't Darjeeling or Earl Grey. "Most of the girls Stuart's brought around have worn outrageous clothing. What little they wore, that is."

"I do my best," Keri replied, still unsure of this woman.

"Aunt Sylvia, Frannie is looking for you," Rhyder's son interjected.

The woman uttered a theatrical sigh. "If it has to do with that murderous cook again, I'm sure I will scream." She walked off without another word to Keri.

"Thank you," Keri said with heartfelt gratitude.

"Aunt Sylvia's okay. She just doesn't care what she says," he explained.

"Jake, right?"

He nodded. "You weren't what we expected." He suddenly reddened. "What I mean is—"

"I'm not like the others," she said with a smile, letting him off the hook. While Kim hadn't given her a hint about Stuart's previous women, the boy's remark gave her enough of an idea. She was already sensing that what passed for normality in this family would be considered great eccentricity in another. She was also surprised to hear so much talk about Stuart's former girlfriends. How often had he been engaged? She wondered if Kim had made another mistake with a man.

"At least you don't giggle," he admitted.

"Or wear reptiles," Lucie inserted, joining the group.

Keri smiled at her. She saw Rhyder's eyes and shape of mouth in the girl's face, but felt sure the rest came from her mother. Lucie was a typical teenager in a thigh-length denim skirt and a red short-sleeved sweater. Her blunt-cut hair was brushed away from a face still bearing a trace of baby fat. Keri sensed Rhyder would be beating the boys away from the door before long.

"I gather not having a reptile draped around me is a good thing," she said to the girl.

Lucie wrinkled her nose. "She had a python with her. It was disgusting."

"Don't give away all of Uncle Stuart's secrets in one evening, kids." Rhyder walked up and draped an arm around each one. "Especially when he isn't here to defend himself. It's a hell of a lot more fun to watch him squirm his way out of embarrassing situations. You know that."

Keri hid her smile at Rhyder speaking to his children in the typical father's warning tone. "We all have little secrets we might want to hold off confessing right away," she said airily.

Rhyder's dark eyes delved into hers. "Yes, I can imagine you have a few interesting ones."

She didn't allow her panic to show on her face. There was no way he could know who she really was. He was talking about Kim's past, which was decidedly more interesting than her own. Here she was, claiming to be engaged to a man, when her last date had been more than six months ago and set up by her sister. A date that had ended in the emergency room along with the threat of a lawsuit, which was only quieted when Keri had reminded the man an attempted assault charge against him wouldn't look good to the town where he served as mayor. Dates like that she didn't need!

Rhyder was still looking at her, and Keri began to feel a familiar melting sensation take charge deep within her body.

"Would you like something to drink?" he asked her.

"A glass of mineral water is fine."

He cocked an eyebrow. "We have some excellent wines."

She shook her head. "Not before dinner."

Rhyder nodded and turned away. He had just returned with her glass of mineral water with a twist of lime when the whamp-whamp of a helicopter overhead interrupted the various conversations.

"I'd say the man in your life has arrived," he murmured. "Never let it be said that Stuart doesn't know how to make an entrance."

Keri and the others walked to the edge of the terrace and watched the helicopter hover over the expanse of lawn a short distance away before it set down. As the blades slowed, the side door opened and a man hopped out and ran toward the house.

Keri took a quick survey of Kim's fiancé. He was about the same height as Rhyder, his hair color was the same but cut shorter in what she always called a "Yuppie cut," and his skin was tanned a toasty brown from days spent on his sailboat—a boat she firmly intended to keep as far from as possible, since anything smaller than the ferry she'd forced herself on earlier that day turned her face a lovely shade of green and turned her stomach completely inside out. He looked up, broke into a smile when he saw her and lifted his arm in a wave.

"It's about time you got here," she called out gaily, walking toward the man she knew had to be Stuart. She wasn't about to make the same mistake twice! "I thought I had been abandoned." She affected the pout she knew Kim enjoyed using.

"There's no way I could stay away from you too long," Stuart Carson said, sweeping her into his arms for a kiss.

The first thing Keri noticed was that Stuart was a very accomplished kisser. The second thing she noticed was the lack of the *zing!* she'd felt when she kissed Rhyder. This time, she had to feign a desire she didn't feel.

"Sorry, darling, for being so late," he told her once he'd stepped back.

"Now that you're here, I forgive you. Just as long as you don't try to abandon me again." Keri's smile slipped a bit as she noticed the feverish glint in his eyes—a glint she doubted had anything to do with passion. "Are you feeling all right?"

He looked surprised by her question. She knew well why, too. Kim rarely noticed anything about others unless it directly affected herself.

"You feel as if you have a temperature," she explained as she pressed the back of her hand against his forehead.

He grinned and leaned over to whisper in her ear, "Just hot for you."

Don't even think about getting into my bed, lover boy, she thought to herself. *I'm sure my sister will more than make up for it when she gets out here, so you're just going to have to wait.*

Keri noticed Rhyder watching them with an intensity that was unnerving. She could have sworn he read her thoughts. Then she promptly dismissed the fanciful notion. Lawyers always did make her nervous and Rhyder, especially, made her uneasy.

"Isn't she something?" Stuart asked Rhyder, as he slipped an arm around Keri's waist.

"Oh, yes. Something, all right," he said sardonically with a wry twist of the lips.

Keri tensed, waiting for Rhyder to reveal her faux pas at the dock today, but he kept blessedly silent on that point.

"What kept you?" Rhyder asked. "Surely, it couldn't have been business?"

Stuart shrugged. "A couple of meetings. What? Don't we have any wineglasses?" He took Keri's glass out of her hand and sipped the contents, instantly making a face. "Why are you drinking this stuff? My father stocks some excellent wines."

"I didn't want any wine before dinner," she explained.

"Stuart!" Frannie called. "It's a good thing you arrived in time for dinner. You know how Reba hates for anyone to be late!" She crossed the patio to greet her son with a kiss on the cheek, then frowned as she used her thumb to rub her lipstick imprint from his cheek. "Are you all right? You feel awfully warm."

"I'm fine, Mom," he assured her with a breezy smile. "It's just all the rushing around I've done today so I could get out here to my woman."

"Now there's a Neanderthal phrase if ever I've heard one," Keri murmured.

Since Stuart's attention was taken by his mother, he hadn't heard her comment, but Rhyder had. He lifted his glass in a silent toast.

"Frannie!" Stu bellowed from the house. "I thought you came out here to tell everybody dinner's ready to be served!"

"Much better than Ferd ringing that damned gong," Stuart told Keri in an undertone as he guided her toward the house. "It usually sounds as if he's broken it."

"He does look as if he has the strength to do it," she replied.

He nodded, then chuckled. "Maybe we should introduce him to your sister. They could compare muscles."

Keri's smile froze on her lips. What all had her twin said about her? Naturally, that was something Kim hadn't told her. "I think Ferd would win," she said at last. "Wouldn't it be better to introduce her to your brother?"

He shook his head. "If Rhyder isn't with his kids, he's buried in lawbooks. I don't think even your sister has muscle enough to drag him out from under that kind of pile." Stuart partially turned away to greet Charles and Veronica.

"I wonder how long this one will last," Veronica said snootily, making no effort to lower her voice.

Stuart's smile was strained as he looked at his sister-in-law.

"Ronnie, you're showing your claws again," Rhyder inserted. "Why don't you sit beside me during dinner? We can have our poison-dart contest."

She shot him a disgusted look and stalked off.

"Sorry about that, love," Stuart apologized to Keri. "She's never been a happy woman."

"That's a kind description," Rhyder muttered, moving around to the other side of the large oval table.

Keri looked at the magnificent dining suite and had to admit she was impressed. The table and chairs looked to be antiques. China, silver place settings and crystal goblets were spaced evenly apart on a snowy-white linen tablecloth. She took the chair Stuart pulled out for her and looked up to discover Rhyder seated directly across from her.

"Reba has fixed a special celebration meal," Frannie told Keri as a stone-faced Ferd poured wine into the adults' wineglasses and mineral water into Lucie's and Jake's. "As I told you, she's a genius when it comes to the culinary arts. Rhyder was such an angel to bring her to us. Our previous cook believed everything should be either overcooked or undercooked.'' She gave a theatrical shudder.

"More like she's a genius at staying out of jail," Stuart murmured, sliding a telling glance in his brother's direction.

Keri could feel the undercurrents flowing between the two men and wondered if the cause might have something to do with Rhyder's career and Stuart's lack of direction. She'd always thought the older brother in a family was considered the responsible one. Here, it seemed to be the younger. She racked her brain to remember what Kim had said about Charles. Finally, it came to her. She leaned toward Stuart.

"Charles manages your portfolio, doesn't he?"

He nodded. "He manages Stu's investments along with mine," he replied. "Would you believe he insists on taking a percentage? All he really does is make a few phone calls."

One of Keri's clients was an investment counselor and she was well aware of the time the man put into his work. It involved a great deal more than a few telephone calls. Stress had been an active part of his life until she'd shown him how to diffuse it with his workouts.

Still, Kim would tend to agree with Stuart, wouldn't she? Or would she? Kim was flighty, but she also worked very hard and had the success rate to show it. Wouldn't she acknowledge that kind of work ethic in another? Keri couldn't understand what her sister ever saw in Stuart. Keri had known him a total of ten minutes and had decided she already wasn't all that fond of the man.

"He might be doing more for you than you realize," she settled on saying. "After all, if it wasn't for him, would you have that lovely sailboat of yours and time to spend on it?"

"You know, you might be right," he acknowledged.

"But let's not let Charles know. He might want a higher percentage."

"How long have you been in the advertising business, Kim?" Rhyder asked.

"Since I graduated from college." She turned toward him as a bowl of creamy cheddar cheese soup was placed in front of her by the somber-faced Ferd. "Dunbar was looking for new people and I happened to be there at the right time."

Rhyder nodded. "What are some of the campaigns you've worked on?"

She racked her brain. What had Kim talked about in the past? Other than her ever-changing love life, that is?

"The Soft and Sensual boutiques. They specialize in lingerie. Garden of Scents—skin, perfume and bath products in custom fragrances. Dinosaur Land."

"You came up with that cute baby-dinosaur logo for them?" Lucie asked with interest. She turned to her grandmother. "It's this really neat play school that has all these dinosaurs doubling as playground equipment. It became so popular after the TV ads ran that they've opened new schools in three counties."

Keri basked in the praise meant for her sister.

"I'm too old for the place, but I wanted to go," Lucie admitted with a giggle.

"I suggested they make it fun for the kids and luckily, we found someone who could come up with the playground-equipment designs," Keri explained, trying desperately to recall anything else Kim had told her. Which was actually precious little. Although Keri could recite the statistics for every man Kim had dated for the past five years, Kim had said next to nothing about Stuart. Keri decided she didn't mind. If she'd known in advance what Stuart looked like, she wouldn't have had the chance to kiss Rhyder!

WHAT IS IT ABOUT HER that rings false?

Rhyder consumed the creamy cheese soup, then went on to the green salad, short ribs, new potatoes and delicately spiced green beans. Kim told cute little anecdotes about her work, but he felt as if she was telling a story that had nothing to do with her.

Again, he recalled the telephone conversation he'd had with his brother. All Stuart had talked about was how sexy Kim was, the parties they'd attended during the past few weeks, how much she enjoyed going sailing with him on weekends. Except what Stuart told him didn't seem to jibe with what he was seeing. Yet he could tell that Stuart was totally enamored of her.

Rhyder wasn't sure why he felt suspicious, but over the years he had learned to trust that sixth sense of his. It sure helped in his law practice. Now all he had to do was figure out why he was feeling it now.

Unless it had something to do with the way she had kissed him that afternoon. He couldn't remember the last time a woman's kiss had just about knocked him on his ass. Even if the woman did belong to someone else.

The problem was, the next time he would have a chance to kiss her would be at her wedding, and that wasn't something he wanted to think about.

Still, there was hope. In the past eight years, Stuart had been engaged six times and no wedding had resulted from any of them.

Who knows? he thought to himself. *Maybe I'll ask her out if this engagement falls through.*

THE HEAVY MEAL LEFT KERI feeling a little sleepy and she would have loved nothing better than to go for a brisk walk to clear her head. Except Stuart knew about Kim's abhorrence of anything that resembled exercise. The only time she walked swiftly was through the mall when the stores were having major sales.

So, instead, she spent the evening listening to Frannie and Stu extol their oldest son's virtues. No matter what, she couldn't see him as that much of a saint.

She couldn't imagine Rhyder as a saint, either. Not after the way he'd watched her during dinner as if she were a fascinating specimen he wouldn't mind getting to know better. Dammit! He was a complication she hadn't counted on and didn't need!

"I'm just going to get something to drink." She smiled at Stuart as she edged her way out of his embrace. Did he have to be so touchy-feely? she fumed as she walked across the room. It wasn't until she reached the bar that she realized Rhyder was standing there. He flashed a winning smile.

"What will you have?" He gestured to the variety of bottles stashed behind him.

For a moment, she was tempted to throw him off balance and ask for something exotic like a Zambezi Virgin.

"Just club soda, please." She rested her arm on the bar. If he wanted to lay on the charm, so could she. She wouldn't do it blatantly; after all, she was Stuart's fiancée, but she wasn't going to let Rhyder have all the fun, either.

"You two make a good-looking couple," he commented, using tongs to drop ice into a glass and slowly pouring club soda over the ice. "Still, there's something that just keeps tugging at me." He squeezed a slice of lime above the glass and dropped it in. "Something that doesn't seem quite right."

"What a shame. Perhaps you should check out your shorts. They might be too tight," she said with a coy smile as she picked up her glass and walked away.

KERI WONDERED HOW LONG she would have to sit with Stuart on the love seat. He kept touching her the entire time, either by keeping an arm around her shoulder or sometimes nibbling on her ear. She hated anyone nibbling on her ear! She wanted to swat at him like a pesky fly.

Instead, she had to sit there smiling and, any time she turned her head one way, suffering Rhyder's intent gaze on her. After a while, she forced herself not to look at him because all he did was raise her body temperature. She never felt so glad as when she apologetically announced it had been a long day for her and she thought she would retire.

"I'll escort you upstairs," Stuart offered instantly.

"Don't worry, darling, I know the way," she said sweetly, then whispered, "Your parents are here, Stuart. You should spend some time with them. Not to mention you really should behave."

"That's not easy where you're concerned," he whispered back.

Keri kissed him quickly, wished the others a goodnight, and headed for the hallway, where she settled for running up the stairs.

"If Kim doesn't get out here soon, I'll end up gaining twenty pounds," she muttered, pulling off her clothing and replacing it with a nightgown. The coral silk settled over her like a sensual whisper. "Hmm, I don't think she needs this anymore, either." She picked up her book and curled up in bed with the intention of finishing the psychological thriller she had started a few days ago. She was soon so caught up in the fast-paced plot that it took her a moment to realize the persistent noise she heard was someone knocking softly on the connecting door.

Keri thought about ignoring the taps against the door until she heard Stuart whispering her name.

"This is exactly why I refuse to get into a long-term relationship," she muttered, pushing back the covers and climbing out of bed. She shrugged on the short jacket that matched the nightgown and headed for the door. "If he thinks I'm going to break down under his charm and join him for the night, he has another think coming."

"A chocolate mint for milady's pillow?" Stuart held up a gold foil square. He had dispensed with his shirt.

"What a wonderful idea." She plucked it out of his fingers. "Good night, Stuart."

His dark eyes gleamed as he took in the sexy picture standing before him. "Perhaps I should come in and make sure the room is safe. And then I could tuck you in."

"Stuart, I told you, it wouldn't be right. Your parents are here."

"Their room is on the opposite side of the house, and they're both very heavy sleepers." He leaned forward for a kiss but she adroitly sidestepped him.

"Please, Stuart, I just can't." She put on her best pleading expression. "It's only for a few days."

"Kimmy," he cajoled, reaching out to finger her hair, which billowed around her shoulders in loose casual waves. "Baby, why do you have to change your hair every time I start getting used to what you've done with it?"

"I like to change my look, you know that." She pressed her fingers against his chest. Good, definitely no zing there. "Stuart, I'm really tired. I'll see you in the morning, all right? Besides, you don't look well. I'd like you to get a good night's sleep."

He grinned and shook his head. "I'd get a better one if I were snuggled up next to you."

"I promised my sister I'd behave," she said as a last-ditch effort.

Stuart rolled his eyes. "As if you ever listened to her before. Come on, sweetheart, you know you want to be real bad," he whispered seductively. "And you do it so well."

Keri smiled even as she thought up ways to kill her sister and this man. "Oh, come on, darling," she said throatily. "If you want 'bad,' you can wait a few days. Then I'll give you so much bad you won't recover for weeks." She finished on a purr, even as she pushed him back into his room and closed the door.

"I'll be waiting," she could hear through the door.

"I just bet you will," she muttered, stomping back to the bed. "I think that's something I won't tell Kimmy about," she said, sneering her sister's name. "She may as well have a few surprises when she gets her butt here."

"WHAT DO YOU MEAN Jean Paul is in Nice?" Kim almost shrieked the question. She paced the length of her hotel suite with the phone glued to her ear. "For how long? What is his number there?" She mentally cursed Jean Paul's housekeeper. She was positive the old lady didn't like her. The woman kept repeating in French that she didn't understand, although Kim knew very well the housekeeper spoke fluent English while her own French was pretty much limited to "charge it." "His number!" she screamed. "Damn! She hung up on me!"

Kim stalked to the window that overlooked an elegant courtyard and rose garden. There she knew her sister would have imagined women in long gowns escorted by the kinds of men seen in period films. All Kim could think of was how cold it would be out there.

"How dare he go to Nice before I could get over here and tell him what I think of him," she muttered. Just as quickly, her anger evaporated as she evaluated her options. "Oh, well, I guess I could get in a little shopping while I'm waiting."

Chapter Three

"Get up, Rhy. Rhy, get up now," the raspy voice crooned in his ear.

"Some people have an irritating alarm clock. I have you," Rhyder grumbled, opening his eyes and watching a lump appear under his bedcovers at the end of his bed and work its way up until a brilliant red-feathered head popped from beneath the flowered sheet. The macaw moved up a little more until his face rested against the second pillow. Rhyder used the tips of his fingers to scratch the head feathers. Beau closed his eyes, making blissful macaw sounds. "The nice thing about an alarm clock is that I can shut it off."

"Dad, is Beau in with you?" Lucie called out from the front of the house.

"Where else but?" he called back. "We need to lock his cage."

"No," the bird protested.

"Yes," Rhyder told him. He winced when Beau leaned over and neatly plucked out a chest hair. He rubbed the sore spot. "You go in for torture, don't you?" He climbed out of bed and, on the way to the bathroom, nudged his bedroom door closed. Obviously he hadn't shut it securely the night before, which had given the macaw a way in this morning. He turned around and found Beau perched happily on the second pillow as he groomed himself.

"Beau is handsome bird," he crooned.

"Modest, too." Rhyder chuckled.

As Rhyder showered, he found himself thinking about Kim Putnam. He wondered what kind of reunion she and Stuart had shared last night. Damn, he sure knew what kind of reunion he would have had in mind for the lady.

Still... He closed his eyes against the hot spray of water and visualized Kim as he'd seen her the evening before. While she smiled constantly and cuddled up to Stuart the whole time, he felt as if she had somehow drawn a shield around herself. While she was the affectionate fiancée, he sensed that she was keeping herself somehow remote from Stuart. A few times she even looked at his brother as if she didn't know him at all. There was something that didn't seem right. He wasn't sure what, but he meant to find out.

"You know what your problem is, old man?" he said aloud, as he ran a bar of soap across his chest. "You're just envious that your brother found the lady first." Savagely, he twisted the knob to pure cold water and left it there as he finished his shower.

"Dad, Grandma called and wants us to come over for brunch," Jake hollered outside the door.

Rhyder wrapped a towel around his waist and pushed his fingers through his hair, slicking it flat against his scalp. "More family togetherness," he muttered. When he'd first learned Stuart was bringing his fiancée to the island, he'd seen it as a few days to get through. After meeting Kim, he now saw it as a few days that would seem like centuries. It wasn't so much seeing her as knowing what the lady tasted like that bothered him. Only because he wanted to rediscover that sweet taste. That did it, he decided. He'd been without a woman far too long.

"Dad?" Jake's voice rang out.

He heaved a deep sigh. "Fine. Tell her we'll be over there in about a half hour."

Rhyder dressed and carried Beau out to the family room and into the large white wrought-iron cage that the macaw called home. He issued a screeching protest as Rhyder closed the door and secured a small padlock.

"We're not going to have to spend all our time with Grandpa and Grandma, are we?" Lucie groaned as the trio took the well-worn path toward the main house. "It's not as if we know Kim real well or something. I mean, Uncle Stuart's probably going to take her out on the boat and stuff."

"Meaning you have other ideas on what you want to do. Would you care to clue your old man in?" Rhyder asked.

"Sherie Bergen and her family came out yesterday," Lucie explained, stepping carefully around a few loose rocks. "She left a message on the answering machine. They're taking their boat out and asked if I'd like to go along."

"So you'd rather go out on their boat instead of going out with the family?" he asked facetiously.

She gave the typical teenage roll of the eyes. "Get real, Dad. At least I'd be with someone my own age instead of all you old people."

"Thanks for not getting out the rocking chair for this decrepit old man, daughter," Rhyder said dryly.

"Oh, come on, Dad, you know what I mean!"

Rhyder abruptly stopped and turned to face his daughter. Sometimes he forgot his little girl was growing up. Lucie's baby fat had started to melt away, revealing the angular bone structure of her mother's face. And she had shot up two inches in the past year. He recalled when he'd stumbled his way through the talk she should have had with her mother. He'd been sweating like crazy when he finished but Lucie had kindly put him out of his misery by assuring him she understood and, yes, if he preferred that she wait until she was thirty to date she would understand, but gee, Dad, don't treat her like a baby, okay?

Rhyder would have transferred his worrying to Jake, but the young man refused to allow it.

Damn, he was feeling old!

"Let's not worry about something that might not even happen," he told Lucie. "As you said, your uncle will want to have Kim to himself most of the time."

"Yeah," Jake muttered. "No one could have missed the way he was practically inhaling her, last night. Man, talk about torture for a kid with my screaming hormones."

Rhyder muttered a curse. "Try cold showers." He playfully jabbed his son's back in an effort to get him moving. He had to admit their stay here had been good for him and for the kids. They had taken the time to air their thoughts and talk out their feelings. Especially anger at their mother for dying and leaving them. Rhyder had come to terms with Ellen's death and knew she would want him to go on, just as he would have wanted her to if their positions had been reversed. Still, there were some nights that were a hell of a lot longer and lonelier than they should have been.

By unspoken agreement, the trio bypassed the front door of the main house and walked around to the back and into the room Frannie enjoyed using as a breakfast room. Rhyder's gaze first fastened on Kim. He couldn't believe she could sit there looking so alert and lively first thing in the morning. Especially not after the hot reconciliation he'd visualized her sharing with Stuart. He took a deep breath in hopes of stopping the X-rated pictures racing through his brain. He studied the ivy wallpaper instead.

"Good morning," he greeted his mother with a kiss on her cheek. He smiled and nodded at his father before heading for the sideboard where he poured himself a cup of coffee and began filling a plate with food.

"Don't tell me you thought we were held prisoner in the house again?" Jake teased his grandmother as he leaned over and kissed her on the cheek.

She tapped him on the back of his hand with her fingertips. "There was just that one time and I said I would never do it again."

"Only because the sheriff still hasn't let you forget it," Jake insisted.

"Have you ever thought about redecorating this room to something a little less green?" Rhyder asked his mother as he sat down and picked up a green linen napkin.

She sipped her orange juice with a reflective air as she glanced around. "You know, it might be time to think about going with a brighter color." She looked down the table. "What do you think, Kim? I always did love Caribbean themes. They're so vivid."

Rhyder winced as he thought of the brilliant colors she could have chosen. Knowing his mother as well as he did, she would probably even add exotic birds for atmosphere.

Kim smiled. "I'm sorry, Frannie. I tend to trust decorators."

Veronica nibbled on her slice of toast and centered a slightly malicious gaze on Kim. "You employed a decorator for your home? Your job must pay very well for you to do that."

Kim's smile was just as frosty. She lifted her coffee cup and sipped the rich brew, then carefully set the cup down before answering. "I work very hard for what I have and I feel, therefore, I deserve the best. I also have little time to shop for furnishings, so I just leave it to the experts.''

Rhyder slathered raspberry jam on his toast and bit into it. Now why did Kim's statement sound more than a little false to him? He wondered if he hadn't been a criminal attorney too long—looking for bad where there might not be any. How could there be anything bad in such a gorgeous package? He tried to concentrate on his food, but it wasn't all that easy when he knew he would rather concentrate on Kim. Suffering was good for the soul, and if he wasn't mistaken, she was casting him a few looks, too. Maybe she would eventually decide a lawyer was better for her than a playboy. At least a lawyer could keep her out of jail.

"Kim has a great condo overlooking the bay," Stuart told Veronica, apparently oblivious to the darker undercurrents between the two women. "When I asked her to marry me, she accused me of proposing to her more for the condo than for her."

Everyone chuckled but Veronica.

"Perhaps she wanted someone to make the mortgage payments for her," she murmured, but her voice was still loud enough for everyone to hear.

"Oh, hell, Veronica," Charles muttered.

Stuart's face darkened with fury and he half rose from his chair. Frannie looked distressed, while Stu concentrated on his omelet. Rhyder and his children looked just plain curious to see how it was going to turn out.

Kim placed her hand on Stuart's arm. "No, darling," she said throatily before turning to Veronica. "I'm afraid that might be difficult to do since my condo is paid off," she informed her in an acid-sweet voice. "It's amazing how useful year-end bonuses can be."

Veronica's face turned a dark shade of purple. Without saying a word, she dropped her napkin onto her plate, stood and stalked out of the room.

"Now what is that woman's problem?" Aunt Sylvia asked, gliding into the room. "I swear she was hurrying up those stairs as if she had a bee in her pants." She shook her head as she made her way to the sideboard and poured herself a cup of coffee. She took a sip, grimaced and looked around. "Ferd!" she bellowed.

The stone-faced butler appeared with a bottle of bourbon in one hand. He poured a healthy amount into the cup, waited as she sipped and nodded her approval, then left the room as silently as he had entered.

"Is Aunt Sylvia a lush?" Lucie whispered to her dad.

He smiled as he noted the worried look on her face. "Not even close."

"Lucie, my dear, it's in the genes," Sylvia said in a haughty voice. "My father drank a quart of sour mash every day and lived until he was ninety-seven. No germ would have the nerve to invade my body."

"No kidding." Jake snickered, munching on his bacon. "I just want to know one thing, Dad. How come Uncle Stu gets all the hot women when you've got just as much on the ball as he does?"

Kim chuckled. "Yes, Rhyder, I'd love to hear the answer to that, too," she teased.

Rhyder gave his son his best "father" look while sending Kim a look that told her he wasn't going to give in to her teasing. "Forget about hot women in your life and we'll all do fine."

The boy shrugged and concentrated on his breakfast.

"I'm so sorry about Veronica, my dear," Frannie said worriedly.

Kim immediately shook her head. "That's all right. Obviously, she feels threatened."

Rhyder arched an eyebrow at her egotistical statement—something else that sounded false to his ears. He was beginning to wonder if his suspicions were getting so strong that he would see her next on "America's Most Wanted" as the woman who mated, then killed.

"Kim, what does your family think about your engagement?" he asked.

"My sister is very happy for me," she replied.

"And your parents?" he probed.

"They're on a cruise out of Hong Kong," Kim explained. "I haven't been able to get hold of them yet. But they'll be ecstatic."

He nodded. "Is your sister older or younger?"

"Older."

"When is your birthday, dear?" Sylvia asked. "I'd love to draw up your astrological chart."

"June sixth," Kim told her.

Stuart's brow furrowed. "Honey, I thought your birthday was the seventh."

She suddenly laughed. "Oh, you're right. I don't know why I get those two days mixed up."

Rhyder made a mental note. It would be interesting to find out if either date was her birthday.

Keri mentally cursed herself up one side and down the other for the mistake.

"I tend to get the date mixed up since I was born five minutes after midnight and my sister was born eleven minutes before," she continued. "Even my parents sometimes disagreed on the date. Naturally, my mother insisted she was right since she happened to be there at the time. I'm afraid I was a little young to realize which it really was," she said, flashing her most charming smile.

"Understandable," Sylvia agreed with an answering smile. "But the time of your birth is very important in working up your chart."

"Aunt Sylvia is very good at reading all the star signs," Frannie said. "I tend to stay home on the days she warns me might hold nasty surprises for me," she confided.

Keri turned to ask Stuart a question, but the words she planned to say were pushed aside for others when she noticed his hand trembled slightly as he picked up his coffee cup.

"Stuart, are you sure you're all right?" His food hadn't been touched and his face was flushed.

He offered her an apologetic smile. "I think I might've picked up a flu bug. Maybe if I take it easy this morning, I'll feel more like myself by this afternoon."

"You're not feeling well?" Frannie hopped out of her chair and hurried over to him. She placed the back of her hand against his forehead. "Sweetheart, you're burning up! I want you to go back to bed immediately. No arguments. I'll bring you some water and juice as soon as you're settled in."

"Only if Kim tucks me in," he said slyly.

Keri pushed back her chair. "Come on, Camille," she drawled, pulling him out of his chair with a great deal more ease than she knew her sister would have been able to accomplish. She ignored Stuart's look of surprise as she ushered him out of the room.

Rhyder leaned back in his chair, his arm draped along the back. "I'd say the lady has a pretty strong take-charge manner."

"Just the thing Stuart needs," Stu declared, poking through the bread basket until he found another blueberry muffin. "He tends to slide through life when what he needs is to learn how to get in there and dig out a career for himself the way you have, Rhyder." He punctuated his words with a muffin. "He's allowed his life to revolve around his toys and finding pretty women."

"Stu!" Frannie warned. "That's a horrible thing to say about your own son."

"He hasn't grown up and you know it," he argued.

"Maybe Kim is the one to give him a nudge in the right direction. She seems a bit flighty, but looks like she has more to offer than the others. At least, she has a job that doesn't involve taking her clothes off."

"Do you mean those nice girls he's brought here in the past were strippers?" Sylvia asked with interest.

"There's no other reason for a woman to have her body parts enhanced," Lucie muttered.

Rhyder nudged her into silence, then pushed back his chair. "I'll go up and see if Stuart is all right," he murmured.

He walked swiftly up the stairs and down the hallway. Before he reached his brother's bedroom door, he could hear voices filtering out.

"Stuart, behave yourself! You are sick and should rest."

"I probably got sick because you made me sleep alone last night," Stuart answered.

Rhyder should have hated himself for feeling just a tiny bit pleased to know they hadn't slept together last night, but he didn't.

"And I told you why. We are in your parents' house and I wouldn't feel right about our sharing a bed while we're here."

Rhyder liked the idea she expressed concern about others.

"Now I get it, big brother," he teased, stepping inside the bedroom. "You just wanted to be alone with your lady. Wouldn't it be easier just to take her out on the *Water Sprite* instead of chancing getting caught by Frannie?" He named the family sailboat.

"That's what I had planned for tomorrow." Stuart was sitting on the side of his bed. He wiped his forehead with the back of his hand. "I hate to think I have a temperature," he grumbled. He reached out for Kim's hand and held it against his chest. "See? You have to stay here and take care of me," he implored.

"A long nap might do you more good," she said, seeming amused with his theatrics.

"Here you are, dear." Frannie bustled in carrying a tray with two filled pitchers. "Now I want you to get undressed and climb into bed. Rhyder, dear, why don't you show Kim the rest of the house?"

"But I want her to stay with me," Stuart argued, sounding more like a petulant little boy.

"Not when your mother is here to take care of you," Frannie told him, setting the tray on the bedside table. She looked across the room. "All right, you two, scoot!"

Rhyder would have sworn Kim gave a sigh of relief before she quickly covered it with a chuckle. He followed her from the room.

"Your mother seems to have a commanding side."

"There's nothing she likes more than to have someone to fuss over," he replied, still curious about her sigh of relief—if that was indeed what he'd heard. He gestured ahead of him. "Shall we proceed with the tour?"

"Please, don't feel you have to do this just because your mother suggested it."

He grinned. "Believe me, I gave up doing everything my mother told me to years ago. Look at it this way— you could go back downstairs and finish breakfast with the family."

She didn't have to think twice when offered that option. "A tour sounds nice, thank you very much."

"I'm the first to admit my family can be a bit over-powering at times," Rhyder told her as they walked down the hallway toward the stairs. After they descended to the main floor, he added, "And now, for the tour. This house was built in 1856 when our ancestor Frederick Carson moved up here from San Francisco. This was the family's main residence until 1941 when George Carson joined the navy after Pearl Harbor was attacked. Since then, some of us have branched out to other cities and states, but we all usually find a reason to get together. The house has always been handed down to the firstborn son.''

''What if there wasn't a son in a family, only daughters?'' she asked archly.

Rhyder smiled. ''Ah, but there has always been a boy in each generation, so no one's had to worry about that problem. And I'm afraid my ancestors have always been more than a little chauvinistic.''

''And your father stayed here?'' she asked.

Rhyder opened one door and gestured for Keri to enter first. ''Dad is very family oriented. He liked the idea of having a house where he and Mom had more than enough room to entertain their children's families. They would have been ecstatic if they'd lived during the era of lawn parties, with croquet played on the grounds and tea served on the veranda.''

''Do you honestly think Aunt Sylvia would have been happy with mere tea?'' she asked, her lips curving upward.

''No, she still would have stuck with a good bourbon.'' Rhyder looked around. ''I guess you can assume this is our game room.'' He waved his hand toward the pool table and several pinball machines against one wall. A mahogany bar graced another area of the room. ''Stuart, Charles and I used to have all-night pool tournaments here during our formative years. We'd sneak a few beers and think we were pretty tough.''

He watched Kim carefully run her hand across the felt tabletop.

''Who won?'' she asked idly.

He laughed. ''Funny thing about that. We usually drank so much beer that none of us won unless you counted who was still standing by the end.''

A tiny corner of her lips lifted. "How macho."

"Yeah, well, Charles outgrew that real fast. Mainly because Veronica insisted on it," he confided.

"What a surprise," she murmured, as they left the room.

"Dad got on a fitness kick about a year ago after his doctor told him he needed to lose thirty pounds," Rhyder said, opening a door. "Since he doesn't believe in doing anything halfway, he installed a home gym."

Keri looked inside and instantly fell in love. The room contained everything a person needed to keep in excellent shape, and all the equipment was state-of-the-art. She fairly itched to get in there and try everything out.

"I guess all this fitness gear wouldn't interest you," Rhyder continued. "But there is a spa and sauna you might like to try out."

Keri stared at the computerized bicycles and treadmills and swallowed her whimper.

"Yes, my sister is the one who would love all this," she finally managed to say. "I swear she isn't happy unless she's pumping iron or something," she added, repeating one of her sister's favorite expressions.

Rhyder studied her for a long moment. "For someone who doesn't like to exercise, you look like you're in pretty good shape," he told her, openly admiring her French blue skirt topped with a cream cotton T-shirt.

"Good genes," she said glibly.

He stood looking at her so long that she felt a blush cover her cheeks.

"Something tells me that more than good genes shaped you," Rhyder murmured.

He should hate himself for wanting this woman. After all, she was engaged to his brother. And if Stuart didn't lose his nerve this time, she would be his sister-in-law before too long.

But that didn't stop him from having some feelings for

Kim Putnam that were decidedly not familial. He wondered if it wasn't wishful thinking or if there just might be a hint of returned attraction on her part. His cynical side believed she probably was the type who came on to any man who happened to be around. But something deep down told him casual flirtation wasn't her style. He wasn't sure why he thought this. He just did.

"Why don't we go outside, so you can see the grounds," he suggested, suddenly in need of some bracing fresh air. "In fact, you might like to go down to the boathouse."

"Oh goody," she murmured, not looking as happy as her words sounded. "Let me stop by my room for my sunglasses."

Five minutes later, as they headed for the door, Keri silently offered up a variety of prayers that she would only have to look at the family sailboat and not have to step one foot on it. She knew if she even boarded the boat it wouldn't be long before Rhyder, and then Stuart, would quickly learn that instead of having Kim, who lived and breathed sailing, they had Keri who upchucked if she dared sail a plastic boat in the bathtub.

Chapter Four

What does one say about a building that does nothing more important than house boats?

Keri just kept on smiling and finally settled for an inane, "It's very nice."

Rhyder smiled back and apparently took her compliment as sincere. He looked with great pride at the elongated white-painted building that sat on the edge of the water. A small dock had been placed nearby. A motorboat bobbed gently next to the planks. As Keri followed Rhyder down the rocky path, she made a show of studying the building looming before her. She immediately hung back when she realized his intention was to unlock the large padlock on a small door.

"You don't have to go to any special trouble on my behalf," she said hastily.

He looked over his shoulder as he slid the lock free. "No trouble. Stuart wanted you to see the family pride and joy, and since we're down here we may as well go inside." He pulled open one of the huge doors and stood back so she could enter first.

Keri swallowed a very large lump in her throat as she carefully stepped inside the boathouse. The first thing she noticed was the high ceiling with ropes hanging loosely from overhead beams. The second thing she noticed was the sleek sailboat before her. She knew many would ooh and ahh over the vessel. She just saw it as another way to drown.

"Don't tell me. They're for anyone who dares to mutiny," she quipped, pointing upward. "A takeoff on hanging from the yardarm."

Rhyder stared at her quizzically. "A joke, right?"

"Of course," Keri said brightly. She kept her gaze fixed anywhere but on the boat rocking gently in the water in front of her. It wasn't easy, but she managed it. After her first quick glance, her stomach had begun to feel as if it were rocking in unison with the boat. Then Rhyder crossed in front of her field of vision and she realized he must have been speaking to her. "I'm sorry, what were you saying?"

"So what do you think of the family treasure?" He waved his arm in the direction she least wanted to look.

She kept her smile pasted firmly on her face as she stared at the boat. She nodded at appropriate times as Rhyder rattled off statistics such as length, something about sails, how much water the boat could draw. She had no idea what he meant, but she pretended to look as if she did.

Keri swallowed the nausea slowly but steadily rising in her throat as she tried not to watch the sailboat bob up and down in the water. She hated this weakness of hers. It was only by the grace of the motion-sickness pills she'd picked up in the concession area and immediately downed that she'd been able to make it across the water on that ferry without embarrassing herself. But to have both feet on dry land and still get seasick just by looking at a boat in water was more than she could stand.

"Stuart mentioned he'll take you out on her one day," Rhyder concluded.

"I can hardly wait." Her tone pretty much said the opposite.

Rhyder viewed Kim through narrowed eyes. For someone who loved sailing as much as she did, he couldn't
help noticing she didn't seem all that interested in the
boat. Nor did she pester him with questions about her.
Most important, she didn't even ask if she could go
aboard. His instincts were again telling him that something about her didn't seem right. He wished he could
put his finger on the problem.

"You must go out on it a lot," Keri commented, looking at him with an ultra-bright smile.

Another mistake. Rhyder's suspicions were increasing
by the second. No avid sailor calls a boat an "it." He
wondered just how much sailing Kim had actually done.
Could it be she'd been faking her interest in the sport
just to snag Stuart? It wouldn't be the first time a woman
had looked at his brother's bank account and, after seeing
he was also good-looking, somewhat intelligent and
housebroken, would do her best to dig her hooks into
him. Rhyder decided it might be a good idea to obtain a
full report on Ms. Kim Putnam and find out just what
kind of woman she was.

Trouble was, while his left brain was viewing Kim as
a possible gold digger, the right side of his brain was
busy thinking about the attraction he felt for her. He
wasn't sure whether to hate himself for his mixed feelings
or commend himself for suddenly thinking of a way to
see just how faithful a fiancée she was.

"We all pretty much take turns. She isn't big enough
for everyone to go out on for the day. Jake is responsible
enough to take her out by himself, so sometimes he and
Lucie go out on their own or the three of us will go out
when the rest of the family isn't here," he replied, picking up a rag from the floor and dropping it on the small
workbench set against one wall. "If you'd like, we could
take her out this afternoon," he suggested, moving a few
steps closer to her.

"That's a very nice offer," she said hastily, still keeping a respectful distance from the boat as well as a safe distance from him, "but I think I should keep Stuart company this afternoon. After all, if he's sick, he might not be able to get out for a few days."

Rhyder shrugged as if it was no big deal. "No problem. We'll have plenty of days ahead of us to go sailing." He moved another step closer. Either she hadn't noticed how near he was standing to her now or she didn't mind. He wondered which. At the same time, he noticed just how good she smelled. Not like a French perfume factory the way he thought she would, but of a lighter scent that held a hint of citrus. Something fresh and clean that didn't jibe with the sophisticated advertising hotshot Stuart had talked about. "So." He idly picked up a stray strand of hair and appeared to study it closely. "What exactly does a creative genius such as yourself do when you're in your office?"

He immediately noticed Kim didn't move away from him. Instead she looked up and smiled. At the same time her smile registered with his libido, her foot landed heavily on top of his.

"She keeps everything, and everyone, in line," she said sweetly.

Not by a flicker of an eyelash did Rhyder show that he felt as if a ten-ton weight had been deposited on his foot. How did a little thing like her manage to do that?

He silently breathed a sigh of relief when she stepped back. He had to admire her less-than-subtle way of telling him she didn't appreciate his come-on. Still, he wondered what he would have done if she had flirted back. Damn! Why did she have to be engaged to his brother?

"I think I should see how Stuart's feeling," Kim said, heading for the door.

Rhyder was surprised he wasn't limping as he followed her. For a moment after she had lifted her foot off his he had been positive his foot had been neatly broken into two pieces.

"Ten to one he's being pampered to within an inch of his life. You'll soon learn Mom's a regular Florence Nightingale," he told her. "She's never happier than when she has someone to nurse." As they climbed the hill to the house, he noticed Kim's walking ahead of him gave him an admirable view of a shapely rear end and curvy legs. He pushed his hands into his pockets and decided he would just relax and enjoy the lovely picture before him. "Dad isn't one for being fussed over, so she has to take what she can, since the grandkids got too old for the kind of spoiling she likes to do."

"I can't imagine any grandchild not wanting to be spoiled by Grandma," she said.

"When said grandchild considers himself a man of the world even at sixteen, the last thing he wants is to spend too much time with his grandmother when he could be with a member of the opposite sex who's closer to his age group," Rhyder explained.

"At least he's not into older women," she teased.

Rhyder picked up his pace so he could walk beside her. "Yeah, he doesn't know what he's missing," he said, giving her a quick visual once-over so she would have no doubt he was talking about her.

KERI WASN'T SURE WHETHER to hit the man or just ignore him. What kind of man was he to flirt with his brother's fiancée! What bothered her even more was that she felt flattered by his attention. She doubted any red-blooded woman in her right mind could resist Rhyder. In fact, she couldn't imagine any woman resisting him. Who could, when the man was obviously in his prime, was described as the perfect father, and was known as an attorney who fought tooth and nail for his clients. Not to mention he was so damn good-looking, he made her teeth ache!

While Kim's social life was constantly inhabited by good-looking men, Keri's was pretty arid. Mostly by choice, since she'd spent a great deal of her time over the past years in classrooms and fitness clubs, gaining her certifications, degrees and experience.

It was only her second day here and Keri already hated herself for being a part of this deception brought on by her sister. Thoughts of her sister had her wondering what would happen if Kim were here as herself and Keri happened to stop by, able to play herself. Would Rhyder hit on Kim or would Keri have a chance with him? For now, she wasn't sure if she wanted to know the truth; she might not like the answer.

She absently scuffed her toes against the lush grass slope as she climbed it with ground-eating strides. When she reached the top, she stopped and turned in a tight circle to give herself a 360-degree view. She watched the waves lap against the narrow rock-strewn beach below. From here, she could enjoy looking at the boathouse and watching the colorful sailboats out on the water and feeling the sharp tang of the sea air tickling her nostrils. From this safe distance, she decided, she could enjoy sailboats all she wanted and not have to worry about a heaving stomach.

Actually, she'd liked everything she'd seen so far and was curious to explore the rest of the island. Except, a tiny annoying voice named Kim deep inside her head told her that the little jog up the slope would have more than tired out her twin, who would be more eager to drop into a comfortable chair and have something cold to drink. She squelched her disappointment and turned back to Rhyder.

"You know what sounds good right now?" she said brightly. "A tall glass of iced tea."

Rhyder glanced at his watch at the same time she looked at his wrist. She did a double take.

"Do a lot of attorneys wear Bugs Bunny watches?" she asked dryly.

"Bugs is only during leisure time. I keep Taz for the courtroom," he replied in kind.

Keri had to smile at his reply. "I'd say Taz is a more-than-excellent choice as co-counsel. What judge would want to go up against him?"

"When you have kids you tend to do things you might not ordinarily do," he explained.

Keri thought of her favorite T-shirt, which sported an elaborately embroidered Daffy Duck with droplets of sweat flying everywhere as he strained to lift a barbell. Below were the words I Thought Bugs Said to Pick Up the Bar Bill, not a Barbell!

"I think adults are more guilty of enjoying the cartoons than kids are," she said.

"I know I'm a sucker for the Cartoon Network." He glanced up at the house. "It should be pretty easy to find that iced tea for you, if you're willing to brave Reba."

"Considering what I've braved in the past, she'll be a piece of cake." She willingly followed him toward the rear of the house.

Rhyder reached the back door, which boasted an elaborate etched window in the top half. Keri arched an eyebrow in silent question.

"Reba saw a picture of the door in a decorating magazine and decided the kitchen out here needed sprucing up," Rhyder told her. "And what Reba wants, Reba gets." He lightly rapped his knuckles against the glass, then twisted the knob and pushed the door open. "Hey, gorgeous, think a couple of thirsty tourists could get something to drink?"

Keri found herself stepping into a kitchen that belonged in a decorating magazine and gave off the rich aroma of cinnamon and buttery pastry. All the appliances were either gleaming white or brushed steel. A work island allowed the cook easy access to any of the cabinets or the industrial-size refrigerator. She guessed that Reba was one very spoiled cook. Or a very smart one who had her employers right where she wanted them. Either way, she had to hand it to her for having the best of everything.

Reba looked up from the pastry she was rolling out. It didn't take a genius to guess she wasn't happy with the interruption.

"Do you honestly think I don't have anything better to do than crush a bunch of damn lemons to make you lemonade?" she practically barked, resting her flour-dusted hands on her bony hips. If people used her as an example for her cooking, they would worry about taking one tiny bite. Reba was medium height, her body all bones and angles. Mousy brown hair was pulled back in a tight bun pinned at her nape. Keri doubted any strand would dare stray from that coil, which looked as neat as if she had just pinned it. There was absolutely nothing attractive about her thin face with its snapping dark eyes and unsmiling mouth.

Keri was certain this was a woman who would be either a best friend or a worst enemy. She would hope for the former!

Unfazed by the cook's accusation, Rhyder hitched a hip on the counter. "Actually, I was thinking more along the lines of a couple glasses of iced tea," he said casually. "And maybe you'd even be willing to part with some of your infamous lime cookies. I doubt Kim has ever had anything as good as your lime cookies."

Reba's expression didn't change a whit as she turned to Keri.

"I suppose you'd prefer something that doesn't have any fat in it," she snorted with the scorn of one who firmly believed in real food. "I'll let you know now I don't believe in cutting corners with my cooking. When

I make cookies, I use eggs, real butter and cream cheese.''

"When I bite into one of those lime cookies will I feel as if I bit into a fresh lime?" Keri asked.

"Yep."

"Then I think you'd better bring out extras because I don't think I'll want to share any with him," she said, cocking her thumb at Rhyder.

Keri wasn't sure, but she thought the cook's expression might have lightened just a bit.

The woman turned to Rhyder. "Well? Your arms don't look broken and you know where the glasses are. I have my baking to do, still, so you can just wait on yourselves."

Keri watched Rhyder pull a glass pitcher out of the refrigerator and set it on the counter. Then he retrieved three glasses and a plate. Pretty soon, he had the glasses filled with crushed ice and iced tea and the plate loaded with powdered sugar-dusted cookies. He gently pushed one glass in Keri's direction and another toward Reba. The latter stared at the glass, then looked up at him.

"Were you raised in a barn?"

A bemused Keri enjoyed Rhyder's discomfort under the cook's feigned disgust.

He nodded his understanding and headed for a small plant in the greenhouse window. After pinching off some leaves, he returned and dropped a couple in each glass.

"'A sprig of mint makes iced tea civilized,'" he recited.

"Damn straight." Reba picked up her glass and drained half of it in one swallow. Rhyder immediately topped it off.

"Have you cooked for the Carsons long?" Keri asked. After one bite of a tart cookie, she knew she was going to find the treat addictive. She took a second bite, already wondering if she could manage to stash some upstairs in her room.

"For close to ten years now," Reba answered as she ate a cookie in one bite. "Rhyder here was my lawyer when I didn't have any money to pay for one. He heard I was a passable cook and he said I could pay the bill off by cooking for his parents. Their last cook had a habit of padding the grocery bills and buying marginal meats and produce," she said with disgust. "Talk about a person who deserves jail time."

"She paid me back every cent, too," Rhyder said with a grin.

"I'd like to remind you that was repaid with interest," Reba clarified.

"Reba, dear, could you make up a nice broth for Stuart?" Frannie bustled into the kitchen, her hands waving about.

As Keri watched Frannie seem to flutter about the large room, she finally realized the woman reminded her of Glinda, the good witch in *The Wizard of Oz*. Frannie seemed to have that otherworldly aura about her and the fluttery manner of a rare butterfly. Her white silk pants and pale pink chiffon blouse, reinforced the air of someone who might regularly consort with fairy folk.

"Kim, dear, did you enjoy your tour?" she asked brightly.

"Very much," she dutifully replied. "I'd say Rhyder showed me everything." She picked up her glass and sipped her tea, looking nothing less than angelic.

"I'm so glad." Her smile dimmed. "Poor Stuart has just felt terrible all morning. He decided to take a warm shower and I told him I'd take some broth up to him. Perhaps you'd like to do it?"

Keri mentally reminded herself that Stuart wasn't feeling well and should be somewhat harmless. As horrible as it sounded, she hoped Frannie was right about his physical state and that he just wasn't looking for a special form of sympathy from his dear fiancée, because if he had any hanky-panky on his mind, he was soon going to learn she wasn't in the mood to grant him any of his wishes.

"I'd love to," she said cheerfully, nibbling on her cookies and watching Reba warm up broth and pour it into a soup mug. The cook placed the mug on a napkin-covered tray along with a small ceramic teapot and matching cup, then added a plate of buttered toast dusted with cinnamon sugar.

"Aren't you going to give him any cookies?" Keri asked as she finished her iced tea.

Reba made a face. "My cookies don't go to anyone who doesn't appreciate my baking," she muttered.

"Oh this is lovely!" Frannie trilled as she folded a linen napkin and set it next to the mug. "I do hope the tray isn't too heavy for you, dear," she said with great concern.

Keri picked it up with ease and was ready to tell the older woman she would have no trouble carrying it. Before she could get a word out, Rhyder had relieved her of her burden.

"I'll carry it up for her, Mom," he assured Frannie. "That way I can look in on Stuart."

"I know he'd appreciate the gesture." She heaved a deep sigh. "Your father and brother are off playing golf. Who knows when they'll return. Veronica said something about meeting a friend for lunch in town." Her pink-tinted lips pursed in concentration. "She's never happy when we're out here."

Rhyder lifted the tray an inch, silently indicating for Keri to precede him. She stepped out, very much aware of him walking behind her.

As they started up the stairs, Keri noticed Ferd was in the living room, picking up porcelain figurines, carefully dusting them with a soft cloth and placing them back inside a glass-shelved curio cabinet. She was fascinated by the slow and delicate way he performed his task.

"Does Ferd enjoy doing the housecleaning?" she inquired. "Anything I've ever seen or read had the butler overseeing the household help and polishing the silver and answering the door."

Rhyder grinned. "Do you honestly think Reba would let anyone oversee her? As for Ferd, he's always marched to his own drummer," Rhyder said. "My mother has someone come in once a week to do the cleaning, but Ferd prefers to clean the Lalique figurines himself. My father gave her her first figurine on their wedding day and ever since has presented her with one for each special occasion. Ferd considers it his duty to keep them completely dust free."

A butler who dusted instead of having a maid do it? She couldn't believe what she was seeing.

This is not a normal family.

"I've always thought my family prided themselves on not being normal." It wasn't until Rhyder responded to her comment that she realized she had spoken aloud. She kept staring straight ahead in hopes he wouldn't see her mortification. Why couldn't she learn to keep her mouth shut? But a family that employed a butler who was an ex-boxer and a cook who had been in prison for poisoning a former employer wasn't exactly the Brady Bunch. Still, she was quickly learning she liked this family a great deal. And she didn't think Kim would fit in all that easily.

"Let's see how big brother is doing, shall we?" Rhyder asked.

Mouth shut, Keri nodded.

When they reached Stuart's bedroom door, she knocked softly.

"Stuart, it's Kim. I brought you some lunch," she said.

"Come in."

She noticed Rhyder arched an eyebrow at the sound of his brother's weak voice and looked as if he wanted to roll his eyes also. She wondered if Stuart was notorious for playing the part of an invalid. She twisted the knob and pushed the door open, stepping inside.

"How are you feeling?" she asked in a coo worthy of her sister, offering him a smile to match.

"A lot better now." He flashed her a killer smile as he sat up in bed. His blue silk pajama top was unwrinkled as if he had just put it on. His smile dimmed when he realized she wasn't alone. "Nice of you to carry that up for Kim," he told his brother.

"No problem." Rhyder placed the tray on his lap. "How are you feeling?"

"Other than feeling as if the heater is on in the room and a bit achy, I'm all right," Stuart answered. "It must be one of those flu bugs going around." He offered Keri an apologetic smile. "I sure hope I didn't give it to you, honey."

Keri realized by the tone of Stuart's voice, the way he worded his considerate statement and his glance at the crumpled bedclothes, that he was attempting to make Rhyder think she had spent the night in here. That was something she wanted to put straight right away but knew that no matter what she said, it would be a case of protesting too much and would only make matters worse.

"Well, here's some broth and toast for you," she told him, sitting on the edge of the bed. She figured that with his tray between them, she was perfectly safe.

She noticed Rhyder stood back a few paces, watching Stuart intently. She would swear she could hear the gears in his brain clicking madly away. Was the man suspicious of even his own brother? No wonder she'd never liked lawyers. They didn't trust anyone! Did they think everyone in this world was dishonest? If she hadn't been sitting here pretending to be her sister, she would have given him a piece of her mind.

As she gazed at Stuart, she had to admit he didn't look well. His skin was flushed and his eyes seemed cloudy.

"Perhaps you should see a doctor," she said, watching him pick up his toast.

"Reba cut it just the way I like it," he informed her delightedly, holding up his toast. "She even remembered to cut off the crust."

This time, Keri noticed Rhyder roll his eyes. With him standing off to one side, Stuart didn't see his expression of disgust.

"Men do like to be pampered when they're sick," she said. "Do you need anything else?"

"Maybe to have my back scratched," he teased. "I've been itching like crazy."

"I wonder if it could be hives," she commented, noticing red spots on his chest.

"Maybe it's something contagious," Rhyder suggested amiably.

Both sets of eyes swung in his direction.

"Contagious?" Stuart repeated with horror in his voice.

"Contagious?" Keri squeaked.

Rhyder picked up the phone on Stuart's nightstand and punched in two numbers. "Mom? Would you come upstairs, please, and confirm my diagnosis." He heaved a sigh. "No, he's not delirious. But I have a pretty good idea what he has."

"I thought you were a lawyer, not a doctor," Keri said sarcastically after he set the phone back down.

"It doesn't take a medical degree to recognize the symptoms. Just a father." He smiled and rocked back on his heels.

"Rhyder feels it's his duty to be the know-it-all around

here,'' Stuart explained to Keri as he lay back against the pillows.

A soft knock preceded Frannie's entrance into the room. ''Are you feeling worse, darling?'' she asked, placing the back of her hand against Stuart's forehead. ''You do feel much warmer than you did earlier.''

''What about that lovely rash blossoming on his chest?'' Rhyder spoke up. ''Does it look like what I think it is?''

''What do you think it is?'' Keri asked, mentally forming a list of what the bright red spots could be. Ironically, the first thing to come to mind was diaper rash and she had to swallow the laughter that started to tickle the back of her throat.

''Oh, dear,'' Frannie murmured as she studied her son's chest. ''This is the last thing I would have considered him having.''

''Something Stuart missed out on years ago,'' Rhyder said.

Frannie made soft, comforting sounds as she brushed Stuart's hair back from his forehead. ''Darling, have you been around any children for any length of time in the past two weeks?''

''What does that have to do with my being sick?'' he asked irritably. ''All right, Kim and I were at the Spencers for a barbecue a little over two weeks ago. Remember?'' He glanced at Keri who numbly nodded. ''Their son was sick, but it was one of those childhood things.''

''A childhood thing called chicken pox,'' Rhyder stated.

''Chicken pox?'' Keri repeated as the horror settled in.

Rhyder moved closer. ''And I'd say by the way they're blistering, he's in the full-blown stage.''

Keri hopped off the bed as if it had suddenly turned red-hot.

''Are you all right, dear?'' Frannie asked. ''You

shouldn't worry about Stuart. He may have a more difficult time with the virus since he's an adult, but with luck, he'll be feeling much better in a couple of weeks.''

Keri was still backing away.

She noticed Rhyder studying her as if she were an interesting art object. ''Call it a wild guess, but I'd say Kim has never had the chicken pox,'' he told his mother. ''And she must have been exposed at the same time as Stuart.''

''Oh, dear,'' Frannie murmured. ''Kim, dear, have you ever had the chicken pox?''

Keri could only whimper. If there was one thing she hated, it was being sick. Especially if that illness was accompanied by rashes and itching. Memories of a raging case of poison ivy when she was twelve still lingered.

''No,'' she said in a small voice.

Rhyder didn't waste any time in ushering her out of the room.

''It seems your visit with the Carson family has taken quite a turn,'' he commented.

Keri fumbled with the doorknob to her room. She couldn't have answered if her life depended on it. Not when she was mentally rehearsing an overseas telephone call to her sister for the purpose of ordering her back on the next jet.

When she'd agreed to do this so-called little favor for Kim, she'd figured she would be spending a couple of days enjoying the change of scenery and making sure her sister's fiancé didn't get too familiar with her.

Instead, she found herself among a family who was more than a little odd and stuck with her sister's fiancé who turned out to have a childhood disease that, with the luck she was having, she would catch, too.

The way Keri saw it, this was just one more black mark against Kim.

Chapter Five

"This can't be happening to me. Things like this don't happen to me, they happen to Kim." Keri paced the length of her bedroom with a minimum of steps. As she paced, her hands clenched and unclenched at her sides as if they were strangling someone. In her mind, she was doing just that. "I'm the one with the so-called boring life, in her eyes. I've always lived a sane life. So what do I do?" She threw up her hands as she continued pacing. "I take her name and all hell breaks loose while she's off having fun!"

She suddenly skidded to a stop, then ran for her luggage. It didn't take her long to dig Kim's cellular phone out of the side pocket. Her smile wasn't pleasant as she punched in a series of numbers. She tapped her foot impatiently as she heard several rings on the line before a woman's sultry voice with a French accent announced the name of a well-known Parisian hotel and asked how she might help the caller.

"Mademoiselle Putnam, please," Keri said crisply.

She didn't care about the time difference. If Kim was asleep, so much the better.

"Jean Paul, is that you?" Kim's voice, tinged with a hint of impatience, blared across the line.

"Jean Paul? Are you telling me you haven't talked to

that sleazy character yet?'' Keri demanded. "Kim, you
need to get back here!''

"Keri? Where are you?''

"At the Carsons'. Where else?'' she practically
growled. "But let's get back to Jean Paul. Have you, or
haven't you, talked to him?''

"Not exactly,'' Kim hedged.

"I didn't ask for 'not exactly,' I asked if you've talked
to him or not. Which is it?'' She could hear her tension
rising with every word.

"Jean Paul is in Nice and his witch of a housekeeper
won't give me the number where's he's staying, so I'm
waiting until he gets back. Oh, Keri, I found the cutest
boutique today! I bought some lovely scarves there and
an adorable sweater for you.''

Keri held the phone out at arm's length, staring at it
as if she had never seen it before. She quickly clamped
it back to her ear. "You went *shopping?*''

Even across the ocean, Kim must have heard the men-
ace in her sister's voice. "I refuse to just sit around this
hotel until Jean Paul gets back. I had to get out and do
something.''

"If you want to do something you can get your rapidly
drooping butt back here and take care of your fiancé,''
Keri retorted. "Kim, we can't keep this up! I don't know
enough.''

"I do not have a drooping butt! How can you say such
a mean thing, Keri? Besides, it sounds as if you're doing
fine,'' Kim added blithely. "Is the island pretty? You
must love all the rest you're getting.''

Keri's laughter held no humor. "Rest? What rest? I
have to constantly be on my guard so I don't make a
mistake. Kim, I want you back here! Stuart is very sick!''

"What's wrong with him?''

"He has the chicken pox.''

"Only children get the chicken pox," Kim informed her.

"No, adults can get it, too. The thing is, I've never had it and if I catch it, I will kill you," she vowed. "You never mentioned to Stuart you'd had the chicken pox, did you?"

"No. Stuart and I never bothered comparing childhood diseases. But what do you mean you never had it? We had it when we were twelve."

"No, *you* had it. I didn't because I was at summer camp while you threw the tantrum of all time because you didn't want to go," she reminded her. "That was the summer you hated anything to do with camping. You have to get back here now."

"Keri, I can't. Jean Paul might be back at any moment and I need to speak with him."

"I don't care if he's in the elevator on the way up to see you," Keri said forcefully. "I want you out of there on the next flight."

"But it's such a good time for you to get to know Stuart. What is his family like? Are they nice? He said Charles is a bit of a bore and Rhyder can be just as bad at times," she confided. "But he thinks Rhyder is too quiet because he hasn't gotten over his wife's death. Have you met him? What do you think?"

"Charles is a lech and a bore. His wife, Veronica, is a bitch of the first order and Rhyder is very nice," she replied, mentally adding a great many more adjectives to Rhyder's name such as *charming, gorgeous* and *sexy*. "Frannie, their mother is adorable in a flighty way and I haven't talked to Stu, their father, enough to know him very well. They have a cook who was in prison for supposedly poisoning someone and a butler who looks as if he's gone a few rounds with every boxer in the Northern Hemisphere. Come back, Kim. Come back now." She grimaced when she heard the panic in her voice and attempted to harden her heart. But if she were truly a hard-hearted woman, she would just pack up and leave as soon as it was dark—even if she had to row herself across the bay!

"Honey, I just told you, I can't," Kim apologized. "Now that I'm over here, I need to see Jean Paul."

"No, you don't!" Afraid her voice might carry into the next room, she quickly lowered it. "Kim, they put me next door to Stuart. We have connecting rooms, which he seems to think is an open invitation into my bed."

"But if he's infectious you won't have to worry!" Kim said brightly. "You know, if I were you, I'd just enjoy this time off. You've been working so hard you really deserve the rest. Stuart said they have a lovely sailboat. Oh, that's right, boats and you don't get along very well, do you? Well, they must have a nice beach. How's the weather?"

Keri always believed taking deep breaths could calm any internal storm. She should have known it wouldn't work with Hurricane Kim.

"On one condition."

"Anything."

Kim was always quick to jump in when she felt the situation was going her way.

"I want one of your credit cards. You can express it to me."

"My credit card?" Kim repeated.

Keri smiled. She should have known what it would take it get her sister's attention. "That's right. If I have to stay here and be you, I intend to go out and shop like you."

"But you're on an island!"

"An island that's a short ferry ride from Seattle," she told her. "Get dressed, go downstairs and send the card right out to me. Or rather, to you."

"Don't you feel as if you're blackmailing me?" Kim appealed to her sister's better nature.

Keri was beyond any appeal. "Not at all," she said cheerfully. "Think of it as insurance. If I have a credit card in your name, who is going to doubt who I am?"

"I just want you to know I'm doing you a favor by sending you up there," Kim said huffily. "Otherwise, you wouldn't have even bothered to take a vacation this year."

"Kim, this isn't a vacation. If I have to stay here, you need to give me more information about Stuart. You have to help me out."

Kim's heavily laden sigh could easily be heard. "He prefers opera to theater, enjoys sailing, has traveled extensively throughout Europe and the Caribbean. He feels Hawaii is too commercial, isn't all that fond of children, and that includes Rhyder's little ones, although he would never say so."

"Little ones? They're in their teens!"

"To him, they're little. His favorite tailor is on Savile Row and all of his ties are Italian silk. He isn't fond of Washington State and only goes up there to see his parents. He loves his mother dearly and says his father merely tolerates him since Stuart sees no need to look for a job. Plus the fact Stuart isn't fond of playing golf and his father feels his life revolves around the game."

"Kim, you can be a twit of the first order," Keri said bluntly. "At the same time, you are also one of the hardest workers I know. When you're setting up a new campaign, you've been known not to sleep for three days until everything is just right. Why would you want to marry a man who sees work as a four-letter word?"

"Because he makes me happy. Now, perhaps it doesn't matter to you, but here it's early morning and I'd like to get some sleep. I'll call and leave a message on my voice mail to let you know when I'm coming back."

"No! You need to come back now!" Keri realized immediately she was talking to dead air. Kim had already hung up. She punched the End button and slapped the phone closed.

Keri hated anger and when her temper did flare up, she preferred working it off at the fitness center. The only trouble was, she couldn't do that here. The idea of taking a run on the sand was idyllic and she cursed her luck that she wouldn't be allowed that release. As it was, she hated to think how she could continue the pretense in front of Rhyder. It was getting more and more difficult and she had only been here a day. She was positive she would be insane within the next twenty-four hours.

She settled for a hundred push-ups, a hundred stomach crunches and walking rapidly back and forth across the room. An hour later, she felt the tension start to flow away. After a quick shower, she even started feeling human again. But she still wanted to strangle her sister.

"SO, FRANNIE, DO YOU THINK tea will cure everything?" Rhyder teased, as he accepted the delicate china cup his mother had handed him. She had asked him to join her in her sitting room which he was only too happy to do.

"It certainly doesn't hurt." Frannie gave a sigh and squeezed lemon into her tea. "How everything has changed. Here we thought we would have a lovely few days getting to know each other and first Stuart comes home sick and now he's suffering from a horrible virus the poor girl might catch. I would understand her perfectly if she wanted to go home immediately."

"That might not be a good idea," he murmured. "After all, for all we know, Kim was exposed also and she could fall sick at any time. Which can be rough on a person if that person lives alone."

His mother's eyes widened with shock. "I hadn't thought about that," she said in a hushed voice.

He nodded. "I was thinking, Mom, that it might be a good idea to convince Kim to stay around longer than the few days we first planned. That way we could make sure she's all right. You understand?" He knew his mother well. There was nothing she enjoyed more than taking care of anyone who was sick. And if there was a chance Kim would become ill because of one of Frannie's children, Frannie was more than ready to wade into the fray like a modern-age Clara Barton. He hid his smile. Their guest would never know what hit her.

He wasn't too happy about Kim because he felt he didn't know enough about her. Not that she wasn't willing to respond to any questions directed to her, but he hadn't heard anything that convinced him she was truly what she claimed to be. What better way to keep her around than to sic his mother's strong maternal instincts on her!

Frannie's face lit up. "What a wonderful idea, Rhyder. I'd hate to think of the poor dear back in her home lying in her bed seriously ill with no one to take care of her. I'll talk to her about it this evening at dinner."

"Talking to her *after* dinner might be better," he said tactfully. He could imagine Veronica's reaction to Frannie's invitation for Kim to stay longer. *Ballistic* was the first word that came to mind.

"True." She looked up when the door opened to the sound of two men's voices raised in loud argument.

"I don't give a damn what you say, Charles. Your ball went into the woods. If you're going to cheat, I refuse to play with you anymore," Stu proclaimed, as he barreled into the room. His face was still screwed up into a scowl as the two men entered. Stu came forward and dropped a kiss on his wife's forehead.

"Did your golf game not go well, dear?" she asked, looking from one to the other.

"It would have been just fine if your son hadn't cheated." Stu scowled again.

"I did not cheat," Charles pronounced, dropping into the chair beside Rhyder's. "Dad is claiming one thing while I'm stating the truth. He's turned into a poor loser."

Stu's ruddy features turned bright red with anger. He fiddled with the collar of his yellow polo shirt and made a face when he noticed a grass stain on the knee of his khaki pants.

"I'm not a poor loser when my opponents play honestly," he stated between clenched teeth.

Frannie and Rhyder wisely stayed out of the fracas. Both knew Stu took his golf game seriously and woe to anyone who tried to make light of his obsession.

Rhyder wondered if the argument had begun the moment his father realized he'd lost the game. Worse yet, he knew Stu wouldn't have let up on the subject the entire trip back to the house. And knowing Charles, he wouldn't have given in, either.

That was one of the best reasons Rhyder could think of for never taking up the game.

"Stu, Charles," Frannie spoke up finally in her soft voice. She smiled at both men and reached out to place a hand on each man's arm. "With every angry word you speak you are raising your blood pressure a few more points and I would hate to think of the two of you lying in hospital beds while poor Stuart is already lying gravely ill upstairs."

Her announcement got their attention.

"What's wrong with Stuart?" Charles asked, frowning.

"How can you claim he's sick?" Stu argued. "That boy never gets sick."

"Maybe that's why he has the chicken pox now," Rhyder said lazily, tipping his head back to stare at the

ceiling. "Mom, I never knew you had nude cupids ca-
vorting up there." He gave her a quick glance. "I do
hope you don't allow my impressionable daughter to see
those."

Frannie smiled serenely. "Your impressionable daughter picked out the design, dear, when I had the ceiling
painted two years ago."

Rhyder winced.

"What do those damn flying nitwits have to do with
Stuart having the chicken pox?" Charles demanded.

"They don't have a thing to do with the chicken pox,
but it seems a safer subject," Rhyder replied. "It seems
Stuart caught it from some friends' kids when he attended
a barbecue at their house a few weeks ago. He's in bed
itching like hell and looks as if he'd make a great connect-the-dots game."

"And poor Kim is up here to spend time with her
fiancé and he's stuck in bed." Stu shook his head. "I bet
she's not too happy about that."

"I'd say if she was unhappy about anything it would
be that she's never had the chicken pox, either, and now
there's a chance she will come down with it, too," Rhyder explained.

"That's why we thought it might be an excellent idea
for her to stay here longer than the few days we all had
originally planned," Frannie said brightly. "The poor
dear shouldn't be alone if she falls ill. After all, she's
almost family."

Stu's rough features softened as he gazed at his wife.
"Did anyone tell you what a saint you are?" he murmured.

"Only every time I have to deal with you," she teased.
"But I certainly don't intend to leave here as long as
Stuart is sick, so there's no reason why Kim shouldn't
stay."

"As long as she isn't packing her bags right this minute," Rhyder murmured. He suddenly glanced at Charles. "Let's see, you've had the chicken pox, and Ronnie probably has, although I can't imagine any virus wanting to get that close to her. Your kids have had them, my kids have, so are you going to stick around? Who knows, if you lose enough golf games to Dad, he might invest in that new computer firm you talked to me about."

Charles glared at him. "I'm glad to hear you think that's amusing. I'll be staying, but not for the reason you think."

Rhyder grinned back at him, letting him know he knew exactly why his brother would stay. He glanced at his watch and pushed himself out of his chair. "Guess I'll head on back to the cottage and see if the kids have gotten home yet."

"You'll be back for dinner, won't you?" Frannie asked.

He thought of his mother's planned conversation with their guest. "Wouldn't miss it for the world."

KERI WANTED TO GO BACK to the kitchen for more iced tea and lime cookies, but she feared Rhyder might be wandering about, and dealing with him was turning out to be a great deal more than she'd anticipated. Handling Stuart was easy; she'd met many men like him at the fitness center. They liked to flex their so-called muscles and act as if they were God's gift to women. Hitting on women while working out was as natural to them as breathing.

Her biggest difficulty was the problem of her pretending to be Kim, but so far, she had been able to pull it off. Admittedly, with Stuart out of the way most of the time, her deception had been made much easier.

Then she realized that she no longer had to worry about acting in front of his family. Stuart was sick. She had flown up here to spend time with Stuart and his fam-

ily. She would have no reason to stay now! It wasn't as
if she was abandoning him. After all, she wouldn't be
allowed in to see him anyway.

There was her excuse! She could show the appropriate
amount of concern over Stuart's illness, then sadly explain it would be best if she just returned to San Diego.
After all, they would have more than enough going on
taking care of him, and she couldn't put them out any
longer. It wouldn't be right.

She brightened as she rehearsed her speech in her head
while she dropped to the floor and performed more stomach crunches. Perfect. There was no reason why, by tomorrow night, she couldn't be running on a treadmill at
the fitness center or finding a partner for a long run on
the beach. By the time Stuart was no longer contagious,
Kim should be back from Paris and she could fly up here
and take up where Keri left off.

Keri filled the bathtub with hot water and poured in
scented bath salts. She relaxed in the tub with her book,
confident her plan would work without a hitch. She
would speak to Frannie right after dinner.

"FERD, YOU DID TAKE Stuart's tray up to him, didn't
you?" Frannie asked as the butler served dinner.

"Yes, Mrs. Carson," he said in his gravelly voice.

"Uncle Stuart with the chicken pox." Lucie giggled
as she stabbed her glazed carrots with her fork. "Who
would have believed it."

"I guess it gave him a major surprise, having a kid's
disease," Jake said.

"Just be grateful you've already had it," Rhyder told
them. "The older you are, the more severe the virus is."

"And you've never had it, either?" he asked Keri.

She shook her head. "I always seemed to miss out on
it, although I was lucky enough to have everything else.
We won't even discuss the mumps." She grimaced.

Rhyder chuckled. "Lucie called it the chipmunk's disease because her cheeks were so puffed up."

His daughter playfully waved her fork at him. "Be careful, dear old Dad, or I'll start telling a few of your secrets."

Keri looked from one to the other, fascinated by the easy way father and children interacted. She had a good idea Charles and Veronica didn't view their children in the same light. She couldn't help but notice Veronica frowning at Lucie or Jake every time they teased their father. Whereas she noticed Rhyder treated his son and daughter as human beings. She was already feeling it wouldn't be easy to leave the family after they had made her so welcome. Of course, if she were honest with herself, she would admit there was one particular person she would miss. It hadn't taken her long to realize that there was something very special about Rhyder Carson.

It wasn't until Ferd had finished serving dessert that Keri broached her idea to Frannie.

"You're going to have more than enough going on, what with taking care of Stuart," she said softly. "So I think I should arrange for transportation home tomorrow. I'm sure I would have no problem changing my flight."

"Oh, my dear, no!" Frannie placed her hand on Keri's arm. "After all, you've been exposed to the virus."

"If I haven't caught it after all these years, there's a chance I might be immune," she replied, already sensing where this was going and fervently hoping she was wrong.

"But we wouldn't dream of allowing you to go home and perhaps become ill with no one to take care of you," her hostess protested. "No, you are not to worry at all. We'll be here with Stuart and the rest of us have already had the chicken pox, so there's no reason why you shouldn't stay."

Keri could think of a thousand reasons—with Kim at

the top of the list. Except she was rapidly learning that no one could say no to Frannie's gentle insistence.

"It—it wouldn't be right," she stammered.

Frannie laughed merrily at that feeble argument. "But you're practically family, my dear. And if there's one thing this family does, it's take care of each other."

Keri wanted nothing more than to thank the older woman for her lovely words and delicately refuse her invitation, but out of the corner of her eye she noticed a faint smile tipping up a corner of Rhyder's mouth. Dammit, he must have known what his mother had planned! Something about that knowing smile of his told her there was no way she could hope he might step in and give her a little assistance. She was on her own.

Come to think of it, she was on her own with more than just handling Frannie. If she ended up staying here longer than expected, with no thanks to Kim, and with Stuart sick, Keri had a dismal feeling the one spending more time with her would be Rhyder. That was the last thing she needed. Not that she ordinarily wouldn't mind spending time with him. She wasn't that crazy. But she didn't want to treat him like a prospective member of the family when she would really rather find them a nice, quiet, cozy spot and *really* get to know him! Thoughts were running through her mind at the speed of light. If only the right answer would come to her without her having to actually go insane trying to think of what to say. She opened her mouth to say she would just feel better if she went home. The only problem was, what came out was not what her mind had intended.

"Thank you, I'd love to stay," she said weakly. At that moment, she was positive she was a prime wimp.

Chapter Six

"I suppose you'll have to call your office and tell them you'll be away longer," Veronica said with her usual poison in her voice after Keri made her announcement.

"I'll just leave a message on my secretary's voice mail," Keri said, wondering what she was going to say when she called the club and explained she would be gone longer than a few days. She was positive they would never let her hear the end of it once she told them why. "Luckily, there isn't anything critical pending. That's why I was able to get away from the office right now." At that moment, she could have kicked herself. Talk about the perfect excuse! Work! No, wait. She could still salvage this. She could have someone from the club call her pretending to be Kim's secretary with important news. She kept her expression and voice neutral as she gazed at everyone. A faint narrowing of Rhyder's eyes warned her he might think something was brewing in her mind. Best she not have him getting too suspicious. She finally decided the reason he had subtly put the moves on her was to test Kim's loyalty to Stuart. She knew she would have to watch her step with him, which was going to be very draining. She was going to have to call Kim again. Perhaps if she called her enough times, Kim would get frustrated and fly back, Jean Paul or no Jean Paul.

"I thought advertising was an ongoing enterprise with something always happening," Charles said, as he reached for his wineglass.

Keri racked her brain for everything her sister has ever said about her work. "The crux of the job is creating new campaigns and then convincing the client it's just what they need, or coming up with fresh ideas for a long-term client," she replied, as she delicately cut her roast beef into bite-size pieces. If nothing else, she could thank her sister for sending her to a place that served excellent food.

"Are we going back to the course tomorrow, Charles?" Stu asked as he dropped three large pats of butter onto his mashed potatoes.

Keri mentally cringed. Clearly, the burly man thought golf was enough exercise for him to consume such quantities of rich food.

"Not if you're going to accuse me of cheating again," he grumbled. "I can find someone else to play with tomorrow if I decide I want to go back out."

Stu turned to his other son. "You should have taken up the game, Rhyder."

"Sorry, I prefer a more physical sport," he replied. "If you want to try a game of racquetball, I'm your man."

Stu shook his head. "Golf is very physical with all the walking we do."

"But dear, you always take a cart," Frannie told him. "You once told me that no one in their right mind walks that course."

Stu ignored his wife's comment. "All that fresh air for the old ticker."

"Golf might have you out in the fresh air, but it doesn't offer you any cardiovascular benefit," Keri declared. And realized her error immediately. She sincerely doubted her sister even knew there was such a word. "My sister is very vocal about that," she quickly added.

"Had a good friend who ate a low-fat diet, ran five miles every other day, lifted weights three days a week and played tennis once a week," Stu pronounced. "His doctor said he was in the absolute best of physical shape and one day he drops dead. There are people out there who do all the right things and they still kick the bucket," Stu continued. "Then there are others who drink whiskey every day, eat red meat every day, use real butter on everything and wouldn't walk any farther than from the living room to the kitchen, and they live into their nineties. Can you explain that?" He pointed his finger at Keri.

"Good genes," she said promptly. "Or just pure luck. Still, who knows? Maybe the whiskey counteracts the fat and cholesterol."

"From what you've said, you must be more like your sister than you think you are," Rhyder commented.

Whoops, she'd done it again.

"Actually, we are exact opposites," she replied. "I guess it's only natural that I would pick up some of Keri's philosophy on physical fitness. Actually, I sometimes wonder if it might not come in handy if I ever have a chance to create a campaign for a fitness center."

That's it! What better way for Kim to repay her for going through all this than to create a whole new campaign for the center! She could plan it while Keri had her stomping away on the Crossrobics equipment, belted to the seat so she couldn't escape! That way, she wouldn't have the breath to complain about the torture Keri was putting her through. Oh, yes, she could visualize it now.

Except Keri's mental picture abruptly shifted to a much more appealing scene. Instead of Kim whining about all the torture she was suffering, she could see Rhyder, in nothing more than a pair of Supplex shorts, with a bare sweaty chest. My, oh, my. She could swear he boosted the room temperature a good twenty degrees.

Keri quickly cooled down her thoughts before Rhyder read them. There was no doubt in her mind that he was adept at picking up subtle nuances and she wasn't about to give him any cause for suspicion. She'd already guessed very little got past him. She would have to constantly remind herself to be on her toes around him. Or, a tiny voice whispered, she could do a little leading around of her own, and if she was lucky, by the time he decided something was wrong, Kim would be in place and Keri would be back in San Diego where she belonged.

"So your sister's into bodybuilding like you see on ESPN?" Jake asked with more than a little interest.

"No, she's a personal trainer," she replied. "She stresses fitness and strength, not that kind of training. She helps a client build muscle, not bulk."

"Muscle-bound women with dark tans and tiny bikinis parading on a stage," Rhyder murmured. "And here I thought you only watched hockey and soccer."

Jake's face reddened. "If I'm going to go out for football next fall, I need to build some bulk in my chest and shoulders," he told his father. "Working with weights is the only way I'm going to be able to do it."

"I would think speed and agility would be just as important, not to mention I thought track was your first love."

"Track doesn't attract the girls the way football does," Lucie said with a sly smile.

"You go on the way you are, and you'll never know what a guy is interested in," Jake returned.

"Since I don't intend to allow Lucie to date until she's thirty, I'd say that's a moot point," Rhyder said calmly.

"Daddy!" Lucie cried out.

"Honestly, you're scaring the girl." Veronica

shrugged. "Our Stephanie was dating at sixteen because we made sure she only went out with suitable young men. That's all you need to do when allowing your children to go out. You just thoroughly check out her companions."

Keri finished her meal, feeling the way Alice did at the tea party. She was never so grateful as when dinner was finished and Frannie suggested they sit on the terrace and enjoy the warm night air. Keri smiled at Lucie as the girl walked outside with her.

"In case you haven't figured it out yet, this family loves to reveal all their secrets," Lucie confided in a low voice, stopping when they were a safe distance from the dining-room doors. "At least, any that they feel are safe to reveal. What gets me is Aunt Veronica tends to forget that her dear darling Stephanie, who's supposedly a grade-A student and a perfect lady, came home from her junior prom drunk as a skunk. Then, she came home from her senior prom minus her underwear. Oh, yeah, she's real trustworthy." She rolled her eyes. "That's why Gina and Scott are in boarding school."

Keri stifled her giggle. "Every family has a few skeletons in their closets," she said. "I suppose that's one Veronica would prefer to keep hidden."

"You did it, didn't you, Luce?" Rhyder came up and instantly sensed the topic of conversation. "You gave Kim the real lowdown on Stephanie, didn't you?"

"If you forget about that age-thirty rule, I won't tell her about your and Uncle Stuart's dating past," she bargained. "And believe me, thanks to Grandma, I know a lot."

He draped his arm around her shoulders and hugged her tightly. "Sweetheart, I love you more than life itself, but if you say anything about my or Uncle Stuart's past you will be lucky if I allow you to date by the time you're sixty-five."

Lucie's shoulders drooped. "I want you to say you're kidding, Dad, but I learned a long time ago this could easily be one of those times when you're not."

His smile only widened. "I have a very smart daughter."

Keri nudged Lucie. "We'll talk later," she said in a mock whisper.

Lucie grinned and nodded.

Rhyder shook his head in feigned disgust. "Threats don't work with you anymore, do they?"

"I think Kim would protect me," Lucie replied, flashing a quick grin at Keri. "And now I'm off before he thinks up something even more disgusting."

"She already knows it won't be laundry," Rhyder muttered, watching his daughter walk off. "Damn, she makes me feel old." He gave Keri a sly glance. "Have you and Stuart talked about having children?"

She hated this more and more. She was glad Kim had told her she and Stuart hadn't planned to have children. Actually, she would hate to see what kind of offspring those two would have produced! "We've decided not to have any at this time."

He cocked an eyebrow. "You sound as if you think he'll change his mind. Stuart usually referred to the kids as rugrats and that was the nicest thing he ever called them. He always said they cramped a man's style. He wouldn't even buy diapers, much less change them."

Keri had to admit Stuart was perfect for her freewheeling sister who believed children were better off with any mother other than herself. Keri loved the idea of having children, but with her lack of a social life she didn't see anything happening to change that in the near future.

She looked up to fire back a witty quip when something in Rhyder's eyes stopped the thought. Instead, she could only look up at him, lose herself in those dark brown depths, and think of a number of clichés. She felt as if time stood still around them. As if they were the only ones left on earth. The future of the universe was dependent upon them. And she could see his thoughts mirrored hers. Heat shimmered between them. All that could only mean—

"My, my, doesn't this look cozy?"

Veronica's poisonous drawl hit them like a bucket of ice water.

Taking a deep breath, Keri slowly turned her head. The older woman's smile practically sported fangs.

She itched to pull them—without novocaine, of course.

"Veronica, come join us," she urged, gesturing toward a grouping of patio chairs. "I'd love to hear more about your daughter, Stephanie. Was she ever voted prom queen?"

Veronica's lips tightened to a pale line. She looked beyond them toward Lucie who was talking animatedly to her grandmother, then turned to Rhyder.

"If you had sent her to that school I recommended, you might have ended up with a daughter displaying proper manners."

"If I had sent Lucie to that school you recommended, I could have ended up with a daughter who was pregnant at her high-school graduation," he stated flatly. "I think we'll stick with public schools, Ron. I tend to trust the students more."

Veronica favored Keri and Rhyder with an expression that promised a fiery end before she stalked off. Charles offered them an apologetic smile and ambled on behind her.

"She really needs a hobby," Keri said lightly.

When she glanced at Rhyder she could see that he was doing his best not to laugh.

"She already has a hobby. Spending Charles's money as quickly as he can make it. But her family has the kind of business connections he likes to make use of, so I guess they're happy with what each brought to the marriage. And believe it or not, sometimes she can be downright fun. Unfortunately, she's not showing that side of herself this weekend." He looked at her sharply. "At least you're sensible enough to earn the money you spend."

Keri thought of a wardrobe in her closet at home that was a bare fraction of her sister's and a loft apartment that was going to need a lot of work once she had the time and money to do what she wanted. Then she thought of Kim's credit card, which was supposed to be winging its way in her direction. She smiled.

"Yes, there are times I go a little nuts at the grocery store."

Rhyder chuckled. "Kim, you're not at all what I expected."

"Don't tell me. You thought I'd be the ultimate businesswoman who wouldn't be caught dead out of her dress-for-success suit, wore reading glasses, considered the *Wall Street Journal* necessary daily reading and would insist on drawing up an advertising campaign for you that she'd swear would turn you into the most popular attorney since Perry Mason. Or perhaps you expected a flighty female with a giggle that grates on the nerves like fingernails on a chalkboard, dragon-lady nails painted a shiny red, too much makeup and probably a cute little tattoo on her butt."

"Either one of them wear lacy underwear from Victoria's Secret?"

Her smile widened. "The former would believe in white cotton only, and the latter wouldn't wear any. Makes a body think, doesn't it?" she said huskily.

RHYDER COULD FEEL the electricity gathering around them. He knew part of it was due to her provocative words, but it was more than that. There was something about her that kept drawing him to her. He had to admire her quick wit and the way she'd taken the news that her fiancé was confined to his bed with a virus. But he felt there was a hell of a lot more than just that about her that interested him. Maybe it was wishful thinking, but he just couldn't see her as Stuart's type. Especially since he felt she was more his type.

Dammit. Now he regretted expressing that iced-tea glass down to Pete so he could run a background check on her. But he didn't regret it so much that he would call Pete and tell him to hold off the investigation. No matter what, he would prefer to be safe than sorry.

With the evening breeze came the light scent of her perfume drifting across his face and flooding his senses every time he took a breath. That was something else that didn't jibe. He could have sworn someone like her would wear a sophisticated perfume. Nor did her light hand with makeup go with the woman he had visualized from the beginning. When he'd been in visiting Stuart that afternoon, he'd casually asked his brother if he had any pictures of Kim. Stuart had laughed at his request and asked why see a picture when he had the chance to look at the real thing, which was so much better. Rhyder couldn't recall his reply, but it must have satisfied Stuart since he'd obliged him by asking him to get his wallet off his dresser.

He'd shown Rhyder not one but three pictures of Kim. The first, he explained, was taken at a charity ball they had recently attended. In the photograph, Kim wore a brilliant red satin gown that hugged her curvy body with loving care. Her hair was piled on top of her head in careless curls, and diamonds dripped from her ears and her throat. In the second, taken on Stuart's boat, she wore white shorts and a striped T-shirt, and a baseball cap that shaded her face. The third was of Kim posing on a balcony he guessed to be hers since he knew Stuart's condo didn't have an ocean view. The nightgown she wore in the photo looked like something out of a forties movie. The style would give any red-blooded man incredible fantasies about sweeping her into his arms, carrying her off to the nearest bedroom and taking that nightgown off. It was a strange thing. Rhyder looked at the pictures, yet he didn't feel the same free-falling sensation he felt at this very moment as he looked down at her face, golden in the patio lights. He was positive if he tried to figure out what was really going on with his internal system, he would never come up with a reasonable explanation, so he decided it was easier not to even try. Better he just sat back and enjoyed it while he could.

"What's wrong? Did I shock you with my answer about underwear?" Kim asked him.

He shook his head. "No, I think it was exactly what I expected. Too bad the latter Kim didn't show up. Maybe you should have been twins or triplets," he joked, ducking his head until his lips brushed against her ear. "Something tells me just one of you is more than dangerous."

He watched Kim rear back as if she had been stung. He couldn't hear what she said; only knew her lips moved as she quickly turned away and seemed almost to run into the house.

"Kim." He wasn't sure why he felt the need to say something. Hell, he wasn't even sure what he was going to say! By the time he reached the hallway, he was stunned to see she was already a third of the way up the stairs. Damn, she was fast! She didn't turn around when he called out her name again. He quickened his pace and was out of breath by the time he reached the top of the stairs and was able to catch up with her. "Kim." He grasped her arm and pulled her around to face him. "What's wrong?"

Her lips were tightly drawn. "Nothing. I'm very tired." She sagged against the wall beside them.

"It's barely nine o'clock, which must be early evening for a night owl like you."

"You know zip about me," she stated in a taut voice. "So why don't you do yourself a favor, release me and go back outside while I go on to my room and relax."

"Your room or Stuart's?" He moved closer.

She took a deep breath. "Considering I'm not into rashes and scratching myself silly, I'll be heading for my room, but then even if I was interested in the above, it wouldn't matter, since it really isn't any of your business anyway."

Instead of releasing her, he let his hand linger on her arm, savoring the silky texture of her skin. "Since he's my brother, I'd say it's more my business than you think."

He could swear fury flashed in her eyes. God, this woman was so much more than Stuart deserved! He could feel the adrenaline surging through his body. Along with something else.

"And I am engaged to the man," Kim said in low voice fairly throbbing with anger. "I'd say that gives me just a little edge over you, and don't you dare make some idiotic statement about blood being thicker than engagements." She stabbed her forefinger against his chest.

Rhyder grasped her other hand, trapping it against him. "Tell me something, Kim. Why are you marrying Stuart?"

She threw her head back in a challenging gesture. "Why do you think I'm marrying him?"

He could have sworn there was the barest hesitation before she answered.

He shrugged. "Maybe you don't want a career anymore and you figure marrying Stuart will give you an unlimited credit line and a nice cushy life-style." His fingers ran lightly up and down her arm. Funny, while her skin felt like silk, there was a tensile strength under that satiny layer that didn't fit the woman Stuart talked about. But he wasn't about to take the time to figure it out now. He kept his gaze firmly fastened on her face. He wasn't about to miss any clue her expression might give him when she lost her temper.

He should have known better.

If Kim's back hadn't already been literally against the wall, he sensed she might have stepped away from him. But then again, maybe not.

"If you think your less-than-subtle insult is going to make me so angry I'll say something I might later regret, you're very wrong, counselor," she informed him. "Stuart is a very charming, loving man whom I happen to love very much. I plan to make him a very good wife."

"Even if you're all wrong for him?"

She tensed. "What makes you say that?"

"Just that I know my brother a hell of a lot better than you do. Stuart is a great guy, I'll be the first to admit it, but he has more than his share of faults. He's proud to admit he has absolutely no ambition. He's happy with Charles playing with his stock portfolio making him enough money that he doesn't have to worry about using that business degree he got long ago. He attends all the parties he wants to, takes off for Europe at the drop of a hat and has no one to answer to but himself. He likes kids—more or less—as long as they aren't his, and the only reason he has a condo is because he needed the tax write-off."

"So he's the ultimate playboy and you don't think he can be tamed?" she drawled sarcastically. "What a wonderful picture you've painted of your own brother."

"It's only the truth," he said firmly. "Whereas it seems you're a go-getter. You enjoy the challenge your work provides for you and while you like to play, it seems you also enjoy your work.''

"Damn straight, I do,'' she retorted. "My work is what I am.''

He looked over the flirty black-and-cream print skirt that flared around her thighs and the cream-colored, short-sleeved cardigan that skimmed the skirt's waistband. Lace edging at the V neckline, the point of which was centered neatly in the faint line of her cleavage, gave the garment a decidedly feminine look. There was nothing overtly sexy about the outfit, but there was something about the way it looked on her that made it tantalizing. His fingers fairly itched to unbutton the cardigan.

He was barely conscious that he'd leaned over even more.

"I'd say there's more than your job that makes you what you are,'' he said huskily. "No wonder you do so well in your work. A man would just look at the lovely package you present and be willing and eager to sign on the dotted line.''

Her eyes narrowed to slits. "You, of all people, should know those are dangerous words, counselor,'' she purred. "If you're trying to make a good impression, you're failing miserably.''

But Rhyder was feeling reckless, a sensation he didn't encounter all that often. There was something about Kim that had him feeling not at all like his usual self. He knew he should be suspicious of her, but dammit, he also wanted her! He really had to get this straightened out in his mind.

"If I'm failing so miserably, why do you watch me so intently?'' he asked. "I wouldn't think that would be something a newly engaged woman would do. Oh, I know your fiancé isn't able to give you the attention you deserve, but is it a good idea to flirt with other men?''

"I don't flirt,'' she said slowly.

"But you're wondering, aren't you?" He leaned in even farther.

"And what exactly am I wondering?" she asked softly, meeting his heated gaze head-on.

Damn! If he didn't know any better he would swear she was issuing a challenge. Fine, he could issue one, too. There was an excellent reason for his reputation of being a coldhearted SOB in court. She would soon find out she was in over her head when it came to verbal sparring with him.

"If maybe you should try out both brothers," he told her, tipping his head to one side. Their faces were so close that he could see flecks of rust and copper in her eyes. "You might want to find out if there's any difference between us. That way, you'll choose the better man. For all you know, you might have made a bad choice with Stuart."

"Counselor, you're so full of yourself, I'm surprised you can walk upright," Kim replied in a very soft, very dangerous voice. "By all rights, I should put you through a wall. Perhaps spending some time in a body cast would give you a chance to rethink that arrogant side of your personality."

He grinned. There was nothing he appreciated more than a worthy adversary, and Kim was proving to be just that.

"I'd say the best way to prove who's right would be to put it to the test, wouldn't you agree?"

"I don't like men hitting on me. Especially at a time like this," she muttered. "Damn, I don't need this."

Rhyder wondered if she realized she was talking to herself. Her words were making her sound even more suspicious than before.

If he were honest with himself, he would admit that it didn't matter. Nothing mattered to him at this moment but discovering what she tasted like. He gave in to temptation, obeyed the devil whispering in his ear and covered her mouth with his.

At first, she froze at his touch but she didn't push him away. Feeling bolder by the second, Rhyder placed his hands on her arms and pulled her closer to him. When she didn't resist, he felt even bolder and ran his tongue along her lower lip.

He would swear she was humming! Rhyder lost track of the world around them as his tongue plunged deep into the cavern of her mouth and urged her tongue to wind around his. While he was tempted to unbutton her cardigan, he didn't want to tempt fate too much. Not yet. He was content to feel her curves flush against him.

She felt so good in his arms. Tasted like heaven and sin all at once. Rhyder found himself getting greedy. He wanted more and was contemplating just that when a searing pain in his shoulder caused him to gasp. It didn't take him long to realize the pain had to do with something Kim had done. She stepped away from him and looked ready to do battle. Her eyes fairly spit fire and her stance was that of a fighter. Rhyder had no doubt she would inflict more pain if he even tried to move closer.

"What the hell did you do to me?" he gasped.

"Just be grateful it was your shoulder and not another part of your anatomy. You are so despicable," she hissed, "it's not even funny. Here I am, engaged to your brother and you dared to do such a thing. You should be ashamed of yourself and if you ever try anything like that again, you'll find out what just happened is nothing compared to what I can do." She spun on her heel and stalked off to her room.

Rhyder stood there, rubbing his sore shoulder as he watched her open her bedroom door and step inside. He knew if it hadn't been for Stuart lying in the next room she surely would have slammed the door.

He could still feel the heat of her kiss on his mouth. No matter what, she couldn't deny she had kissed him back.

Chapter Seven

Keri learned one very important thing that night; cold showers were not as effective as books and movies always claimed they were. She stumbled shivering out of the glass cubicle, wrapped a towel around her body and another around her head as she flipped on the overhead heat lamp in an attempt to warm up.

When she turned she happened to catch a glimpse of herself in the mirror and instantly moaned. The slight redness along her jawline had nothing to do with the brisk rubbing she was giving her skin and all to do with Rhyder's beard-roughened skin as it skimmed over her while he kissed her until her toes curled, her thighs melted, her abs tightened until they seemed to nestle against her backbone, her... She settled for a mere whimper because she didn't have the strength for anything more. She grabbed hold of the counter as her knees threatened to buckle under her.

Had a man's kiss ever affected her this strongly? No way! She breathed in and out through her mouth in hopes it would help slow her racing pulse. No such luck. She was a goner.

"I am a pitiful object out of a soap opera," she told herself. "I'm pretending to be my twin sister. I am letting her fiancé think I'm my sister and I have the hots for my sister's fiancé's brother who thinks I'm my sister.'' She muffled her groan of dismay. ''Oh, my God, I'm not just out of a soap opera, I'm perfect fodder for 'Oprah'!''

A thoroughly miserable Keri cleansed her face and patted on what she hoped was moisturizer. She didn't bother to read the jar label. Afterward, she pulled on a nightgown and stumbled back into the bedroom. At the moment, all she wanted was to fall asleep.

Keri collapsed on the bed. Restless with the silence crowding around her, she switched on the television and immediately realized what a bad idea that was. The screen brightened to a scene displaying two nude lovers lying amid a tangle of bedcovers. She whispered a curse and immediately switched the channel. Her next choice turned out to be a couple kissing passionately while rain streamed down on them. The next channel proved to be no better. This time, a naked man and woman were making love with an energy that astounded even her. Keri gave up. She pulled the pillow over her head in hopes she could go to sleep. It only took her three seconds to realize the television was still on and the sounds coming from the movie were just as distressing as the picture.

When Keri finally did fall asleep, her rest was disturbed by arousing dreams all night long. Every scene she'd seen on television was transported into her dreams, with her and Rhyder as the stars.

''WAKE UP, RHYDER. Wake up and play!''

Rhyder rolled over and groaned. ''Beau, how did you get out?'' he muttered, pulling his pillow over his head.

''Rhyder, wake up!'' This time the raspy voice was more demanding as the macaw's beak found its way under his pillow.

''Ow! Dammit!'' Rhyder shot upward, rubbing his lip where Beau had nipped it. He glared at the bird who sat perched on the edge of the bed staring back at him with black eyes. "You keep up this crap and you'll end up as dinner."

Beau shook his head and ruffled his feathers.

Rhyder finally gave up and pushed his covers aside. Just as well, since he hadn't gotten more than ten minutes of sleep the last three nights. As it was, every time he did go to sleep, memories of Kim in his arms and kissing him back had been running through his mind, embellished by X-rated visions. While they had been clothed during that heated kiss, his dreams had conveniently dispensed with those items. By rights, he shouldn't hate himself for what had happened. By rights, he should be telling himself he wasn't the only one in the midst of that kiss, but he remembered only too well the tongue-lashing she had given him. He had no doubt she had liked his kiss and there was no question that she had kissed him back, but he had to admit she wasn't comfortable with it. For that, he would have given her a lot of respect—no matter how hard it was to acknowledge. Instead, he had avoided her since that night, which proved easy to do as his mother had taken her into the city for shopping the next day. He had wondered about the Federal Express envelope that had arrived for her, but she had only smiled and given no hint as to what it contained. By now, he wished he'd had word from Pete. Maybe he could handle this better if he had some of his questions about her answered.

He glanced at the clock. He doubted anyone was awake at the big house. Which meant it was the perfect time for him to sneak over and use the gym. Maybe if he had a chance to work off some of this energy of his, he would feel more like himself.

"Dad, I'm going over to Sherie's for the day," Lucie sang out. "There's waffle batter in the refrigerator if you want breakfast."

"Does your visit to Sherie's have something to do with her older brother?" he asked.

Even through the closed door he could hear her deep sigh. "Of course not," she said huffily. "She's thinking of getting her hair cut short so we're going over new styles."

"Truly a life-changing decision."

The macaw still sat perched on the edge of the bed, his brilliant red-feathered head cocked to one side.

"Want walnut, Rhyder," he rasped.

"That sure sounds easier to get than a woman," he replied, using the tips of his fingers to scratch the bird's head.

"Oh, man, you put bacon bits in the batter! I hate that!" Jake bellowed from the kitchen.

Rhyder sighed. "I should have been warned when he rarely cried as a baby," he muttered, pushing himself off the bed.

RHYDER REMAINED IN THE kitchen just long enough to receive a parting kiss on the cheek from his daughter, listen to his son mutter about bacon bits in the waffle batter and hear Beau scream until he received his walnut. By then, he was more than ready to leave the house. He ate a quick breakfast, made sure the macaw was securely imprisoned in his cage and took off for his parents' house.

"Good morning, Rhyder," Ferd greeted him the moment he stepped through the side doors.

"Ferd." He nodded his head. "I thought I'd go on down to the gym. Anyone else up yet?"

Ferd smiled. "Your father left for an early-morning golf game and your mother asked she not be disturbed unless Stuart took a turn for the worse. I looked in on him a few moments ago and he was sleeping. Peacefully."

"That'll change once he wakes up." Rhyder passed by the older man. "I'll probably be down there for an hour or so."

"Yes, sir."

If Rhyder had thought about it, he would have admitted there was something strange about Ferd's expression, but he merely put it off to his own unsettled state of mind.

The moment he opened the door to the gym, he realized he wasn't alone. The sight before him was more than his feeble brain could handle. And not at all what he'd expected.

Kim was running at what appeared to be full tilt on the treadmill. Headphones were fastened on her ears and she wore a white sleeveless T-shirt and a pair of red cotton shorts that were spotted with patches of sweat. Her tanned shoulders glistened with perspiration while her saucy ponytail was damp from her exertion. Since her back was to him, he could easily see the treadmill's display panel. He noticed the timer was showing she had been on there for well past an hour. She couldn't have been running that fast or on such an incline for that length of time—could she?

Stuart had said Kim didn't like to exercise. That she even made jokes that it wasn't one of her favorite activities. That even while she enjoyed sailing, she preferred to do it while lying on the deck. Yet, what he could see of this woman's body told him this was someone who took a great deal of time keeping herself in excellent physical condition. And such a lovely specimen she was, too.

He was thankful whatever she was listening to on the headphones didn't allow her to hear his entrance and with her back to the door, she didn't see him, either. Not taking any chances, he quietly slipped back out. And immediately headed for his father's study. He sat at the desk and picked up the phone, punching out the numbers with his forefinger. As he listened to the ringing on the other end, he relived that moment in the gym.

The woman was barely wearing anything! And what she was wearing was...

"Whoever you are, you'd better have a damn good reason for calling at this hour," Pete growled into the phone. "Otherwise, I want you to know I can break bones."

"Well, you're in a great mood," he greeted his friend.

"Rhyder, what the hell do you want?"

He grinned. This was something he could handle. "I'm fine, thank you for asking. How's Brianne?"

"She does what she does best—everything possible to make me nuts. But what else is new?"

"Hey, buddy, you start blackening my character and you will be going without for the next month," a woman's voice sounded in the background.

Rhyder burst into laughter at Pete's colorful curses.

"How does it feel being married to two women in one body?" he asked. He had met Pete's wife when she was accused of murdering her fiancé the year before and Pete had asked him to represent her. What he hadn't expected was to be told a very colorful story about a coffee-shop waitress murdered and zapped into a socialite's body, then babbled something about a voice in her head telling her what to do. Rhyder still didn't understand it all, but he knew his friend was happy and that was all that mattered.

"The two somehow merged, and we think Allie is pretty much gone," Pete replied. "Although there have been times when Allie seems to just burst out." He grew quiet. "Olivia still refuses to see Brianne. She tells everyone Bri's not her daughter. While we know it's true, there's not much we can do. Bri's story isn't exactly for public consumption."

For once, a trial had been speedy and justice equally swift, with Olivia Sinclair sent to prison. The older woman's arrogance held her family at arm's length, leaving her son, Trey, thoroughly bewildered by events. The announcement that Olivia had shot and killed Brianne's fiancé, allowing Brianne to be accused of the crime, had left him hurt and confused. After that, he had poured his energy into the family-owned department stores and to this day, couldn't understand Olivia's cold words about her only daughter. Brianne had never had another private word with the woman and had never told her the truth. That was kept between Brianne, Pete and Rhyder. The bright spots in Brianne's life were her marriage to Pete and the news that Whit, Allie's murderer, was also serving time in prison after he'd confessed to her murder, being the instigator of several major drug deals and practically begging to be sent away so she couldn't haunt him anymore. Since the prosecutors thought he was working his way toward an insanity plea, they made sure one couldn't be entered.

Brianne had truly found her niche in the store's management, and in the past year, Pete's private-investigation business had picked up. He joked that the only difference in his life-style was that he could now afford to purchase a higher grade of gasoline. Rhyder was glad to see his friend happy at last.

"Have you gotten any word on that glass I sent you?" Rhyder asked. "Your fax said the fingerprints were more than clear."

"They were no problem. The problem turned out to be the lady's name," Pete said. "Do you have to have this information now? Why don't you call me in a couple of hours when I'm at the office."

"After what you said about her name, yes, I do have to have the information now," he told him. "What did you find out?"

"Kim Putnam is the woman engaged to your brother, right?"

Rhyder picked up a pen and drew a sheet of paper toward him. "That's right."

"She's a hotshot with an advertising agency in San Diego, got a speeding ticket a year ago, pays all her bills on time, owns her own condo, has no odd habits and believes outdoor activity is best attained on a sailboat. She's never been engaged but before Stuart came on the scene she was heavily involved with Jean Paul DeVeau, a French magazine publisher, for about a year, and they fought off and on during that time. Word has it the man can't be faithful for more than three days."

Rhyder scribbled down the information he was given and frowned at what he read. He couldn't imagine Kim putting up with a man who wouldn't treat her right.

"She also left for France last week."

Rhyder's pen skittered across the paper's surface.

"What?" He heard what Pete said and he even understood what he said. A part of his brain had actually figured out why what he said was making sense. He still wanted it clarified, though.

"I said the lady left for France last week. Funny thing. She left town about the same time her identical twin, Keri, left town. Keri's a professional fitness trainer with The Fit Place, a health club on the outskirts of San Diego. She's working on buying in as a partner. Her income is a fraction of her sister's and her apartment rent was raised not all that long ago. She's pretty well-known in the fitness field down that way and highly thought of. Her clients will tease her, calling her "the master torturer" and other lovely names, but they also feel they wouldn't be in the shape they're in without her."

Rhyder thought about the body he had just seen and had to agree that if the woman looked that good, she must know what she was doing.

"In essence, Mr. Carson," Pete drawled, "the fingerprints you sent me were Keri Putnam's, not Kim Putnam's."

Now it all made sense. The way she acted toward Stuart. Warm yet not the loving fiancée. And the way she acted toward him. The attraction was there, all right, but she was being true to her sister by rejecting him. Hell! What was going on? Why was she up here pretending to be her sister?

"That's it. Ask a question I can't answer," Pete joked.

That was when Rhyder realized he'd said it aloud. "Maybe *you* can't, but I do know who *can* answer that question," he said grimly. "And I intend to see that she does."

"Do you think they're running a scam?"

"Hell if I know," he muttered. "Stuart invited Kim up here to meet the family. Now you're saying her twin sister, Keri, is the one here and Kim is in France, probably shacking up with some magazine publisher."

"And the twin is supposed to be protecting her sister's interests," Pete added, picking up the thread when Rhyder faltered.

"How much you want to bet sister number two is here in case sister number one decides Stuart's a better bet than Mr. France," Rhyder said.

"No way. The odds are on your side. What are you going to do? Are you going to tell your family?"

Rhyder looked at the notes he'd scribbled down. "I think I'll first see what sister number two has to say. But I'm not telling the others unless I absolutely have to. Stuart's down with the chicken pox and since she's never had it, she's staying away from him."

"Hey, I got a look at pictures of the two of them. Both are real lookers. How does this one look in person?"

"Let's just say sister number two is giving hot dreams a whole new meaning."

Pete uttered a low whistle. A woman's voice in the background suddenly had him laughing.

"I've been told to keep my mind off other women or I'll lose my favorite body part," he confided. "Thing is, she forgets it's also her favorite part."

"You two are very sick people," Rhyder said with mock solemnity.

"True, but the woman is hot for me and I have to admit I'm just as hot for her. Do you want me to do any more checking?"

"Only if you can find out when sister number one gets back from France."

"Can do. If this keeps up, you'll have to get back to work to pay my bill," he quipped.

Rhyder hung up and sat there, staring into space, tapping his pen against his teeth.

"So Kim is really Keri," he mused. "Which means Stuart's fiancée wasn't kissing me back, his fiancée's sister was. And there's no reason..." He pushed back his chair and stood. A tiny smile tugged at the corners of his lips. This was one confrontation he was more than ready to enjoy. As far as he was concerned, the lady wouldn't stand a chance.

Rhyder walked back to the workout room with a purpose in his walk and a smile on his lips. When he pushed open the door, she continued to run on the treadmill. He was grateful for that, since it meant she wasn't aware of his entrance. He carefully closed the door and flipped the lock. He didn't want any intruders.

Rhyder noticed she was singing under her breath. Considering the amount of time she had been running, she was having no trouble singing to herself, while he doubted he would have been able to say his own name without gasping for air.

He walked over to the treadmill, stood behind her for

a second so he could admire the view, then made his move.

KERI WAS BLISSFULLY unaware of her visitor as she happily jogged on the treadmill and enjoyed the sensation of her body working like a finely honed machine. The rock music was a perfect accompaniment to her movements. A tune she liked to sing along to.

"Born to be—wah!" she squealed when an arm snaked its way around her waist and literally jerked her off the treadmill. Before she could say one word, her mouth was covered by a man's and her body was flung intimately against a male one. Keri quickly realized the man holding her was Rhyder.

What is going on? She shivered when his tongue traveled along her bottom lip, urging her lips to part. She was helpless to resist his silent demand. Dammit, she was helpless to resist anything about this man!

Her sweat-slick body slid against him, leaving damp prints on his clothing and trails along his arms and legs, but he didn't seem to care. Neither did she. Not when Rhyder was sending such heated messages to her overloaded senses. She was positive it wouldn't be long before they exploded into overdrive.

His skin was slightly rough to the touch as if he hadn't taken extra care in shaving. And she could smell only the clean scent of soap as she buried her face against his throat. Her tongue darted out for a taste and she gloried in his groan.

"If you think you're the only one who's going to have fun at this you've got another think coming," she murmured, nipping the slightly rough skin.

"Do you hear me arguing?" he said huskily, skimming his hands down her sides. "Anyone tell you what a slippery devil you are?"

"You do some flat-out running for more than an hour

and see if you don't work up a sweat,'' Keri whispered, sliding her hands under the hem of his T-shirt and flattening her palms against the broad expanse of his back. His skin was hot to the touch and she decided touching was something she wanted to do a lot of. She was so lost in his embrace it was easy to again forget who she was and his part in this fiasco. All that mattered was that the man kissed her like no other had and she was more than willing to savor more of those kisses.

RHYDER DIPPED HIS HEAD and nuzzled her ear. Her skin was damp and tasted salty. He'd had no idea sweaty skin could taste so good, but then he hadn't met Kim/Keri yet. His mind was racing at the same rate as his libido— although, he had an idea his libido would soon win the race. He sure felt better, knowing he wasn't putting the moves on his brother's fiancée. He didn't have to feel guilty about betraying Stuart. All he had to worry about was the fact that Keri, here, was helping her sister betray Stuart. He should be angry on his brother's behalf. Except it wasn't too easy to feel angry when he had her in his arms. With the door locked, it would be so easy to lay her down on the carpet. Or urge her into the spa. His mind whirled with the possibilities as he nibbled his way along her jaw while he traced down the indentation of her spine. When he reached her buttocks, he realized just how firm the lady was. And tantalizing. She tasted like heaven, and she issued the siren's call as she kissed him back. Her trim midriff rose up and down with her labored breathing. He wanted to laugh out loud. He had been able to accomplish what the treadmill hadn't!

His logical side made an unwelcome appearance. Didn't he want to know why Keri was up here instead of Kim? Would she tell him the truth? Or were her kisses just a way to throw him off track? Had she rejected him last night as part of her attempt to keep him off guard?

"For a lady who doesn't believe in exercise, you sure were making that treadmill sing," he murmured, grazing his teeth along her earlobe. "I guess it's because you've had to stay away from Stuart, which has left you with a great deal of frustration, so you decided this was the best way to handle your problem." He deliberately spread his hand across her midriff, the thumb and forefinger brushing the edge of her breasts. He could feel her sharp indrawn breath at his intimate touch. "Of course," he murmured, "if you were feeling so horny, all you had to do was ask. I would have been more than willing to lend a hand."

She lurched out of his arms as if she had been shot from a cannon.

Rhyder had to give her credit. She didn't appear embarrassed or refuse to look at him. She faced him squarely with her head held high.

"That was absolutely disgusting," she said in a low voice. "Obviously, you don't even feel guilty about trying to seduce me."

Rhyder's stance was relaxed as he examined his nails. Idly, he brushed them against his shirtfront. His hair was tousled from her fingers, his shirt collar askew, and he didn't bother hiding his arousal from her.

"And you didn't feel guilty about deceiving your fiancé with his brother," he countered.

Her hands clenched at her sides as if she was using all her willpower not to deck him. As he studied her taut features he would say that if he didn't take care, she would lose the battle. And he could likely end up with a broken nose.

"But then I guess you can't be betraying a man you're not really engaged to, can you, Keri," he said conversationally.

Rhyder watched her face with great interest. He could

tell the moment the truth sank in. Her eyes momentarily widened, then narrowed.

"What exactly are you implying?" she asked in a low voice that could only be described as dangerous.

"That you aren't Kim Putnam, but her twin sister, Keri, and that Kim is at this moment in France with an old lover. Or maybe he's a current lover and Stuart's just sort of a standby. The trouble is, the poor guy doesn't know it. I have to say you two must be identical if even he couldn't tell the difference." He cocked his head, appearing to study her carefully. "Is there any way to tell the two of you apart?"

She straightened, shoulders thrown back, head held high. "Kim's hair is curlier right now. And for your information, we are not identical twins, we're called 'mirror image' twins. She's right-handed, I'm left-handed, and there are a few minor differences, but very few people pick up on them. How did you figure it out? Kim never said that her sister was her twin."

"There's also one very big difference between twins," he explained. "Their fingerprints. Once I sent a glass bearing your fingerprints to a private investigator he had no trouble discovering the prints belonged to Keri Jane Putnam instead of Kimberly Jean Putnam. Did your mother dress you alike when you were kids to go along with the matching monograms?"

The fire was back in her eyes now, as she realized what he was saying.

"You had me investigated?"

"No, I had Kim investigated. It just happened to be you who showed up on the computer."

She stood silent for a moment, taking several deep breaths.

"So why is it Kim is in France and you're here pretending to be her?" Rhyder asked. "I'm curious about something else. Who will show up at the wedding? Even more important, who will be there for the wedding night? Although I guess Stuart wouldn't mind as long as someone is there.''

His last comment was obviously the straw that broke her self-induced trance. Keri took one step forward with one arm swung back. Before Rhyder could protect himself, her fist was buried firmly in his abdomen. His eyes widened as pain knifed through his entire midriff. Rhyder bent forward to relieve the agony, his arms cradling his stomach.

''What the hell?'' he wheezed.

''You put the moves on me, thinking I was Kim because you wanted to prove to your brother he was marrying a tramp,'' she replied, as she calmly picked up a plastic sports water-bottle and hand towel. She dabbed her face with the towel. ''Then, when you found out I wasn't Kim, you put the moves on me, hoping I'd say something to prove my sister and I had some scam going.'' She moved toward the door. ''My sister may be flighty at times, but she is the most loyal person around and right now she's making sure there's complete closure with her past, although it's definitely not any of your business what she was doing.'' She muttered a pithy curse when she twisted the knob and nothing happened. She shot him a look that should have seared him to the bone. ''You jerk. You locked the door.'' She snapped back the lock and twisted the knob again, then glared at him one last time before snapping off a string of words in a foreign language.

He shook his head, confused by words he couldn't understand. ''Come again?''

Rhyder's first warning should have been Keri's slow smile, more dangerous than a pit viper.

''Just a lovely curse that, loosely translated, says 'May you have jock itch for the rest of your life.' Have a nice day.'' She pulled open the door and stalked out, slamming it behind her.

Rhyder flinched. "That is one woman who plays really dirty," he muttered, dropping onto the weight bench. He heaved a deep sigh. "She also has perfected a technique that will ensure she'll never be forgotten."

Chapter Eight

While Keri showered and changed into clean clothes, she was busy cursing herself. She had woken up feeling so restless she had taken a chance and gone downstairs to the workout room. She knew the residents in the house weren't early risers so she assumed she would be safe. What she hadn't counted on was Rhyder showing up. If things had turned out any other way, she knew she could have found a reason to explain her presence there. But no, she fumed, he had to be so suspicious of her that he had actually sent her fingerprints to a private investigator!

After Keri finished dressing, she dug through her suitcase for the cell phone. She started to dial Kim's hotel, then stopped.

What good would it do to tell her sister? She was thousands of miles away. No matter what, it would still be up to Keri to perform the damage control. She would have to do whatever was necessary to make things right. Although what she was going to say to Frannie or Stuart after Rhyder blew the whistle on her was another matter. Keri enjoyed reading fiction, not making up her own.

She paced the length of her room, attempting to come up with a good story.

"She's in France for a miracle cure and didn't want Stuart to know," she whispered to herself. "She's in

France because the agency sent her over there to placate a very important client. She didn't want to disappoint Stuart, since she knew how important this get-together was, so she sent me here in her place until she could return.'' She shook her head in frustration. ''She's in France because she needed to pick up a very special bottle of champagne,'' she finished on a sarcastic note. ''I swear, Kim,'' she threatened her unseen sister, ''if I had any brains at all, I would just pack up and sneak out of here and let you straighten everything out.''

''I don't think that would be a good idea.''

Keri spun around to find Rhyder leaning against the door. She wasn't certain she liked the smile on his face. He looked much too sure of himself, while she hadn't been given nearly enough time to come up with a plausible story.

''Have you ever heard of knocking?''

''Have you ever heard of telling the truth?''

She walked over and dropped onto the end of the bed. She crossed her legs, and swung her top foot gently. She noticed his gaze flicker toward her legs. Good. Something that just might keep his mind off the subject at hand. She put on her most pleasant smile and voice.

''I do hope you'll give me enough time to pack before you escort me off the island. I'm sure Stuart will understand if I don't go in to say goodbye.''

''The ferry doesn't show up until this afternoon.''

Keri nodded. ''I see. So Frannie asked you to stay in here until it was time for me to leave. Please assure her she doesn't need to count the silver. Now, if you used paper plates and plastic forks, you might have had to worry.''

Rhyder straightened and walked toward her. Along the way, he snagged a chair and swung it around before sitting down, resting his arms on the back. He gazed at her with a composed expression that was unsettling to her.

"Frannie doesn't know who you really are and neither does anyone else in this household," he explained. "Ferd saw you go into the workout room, but he isn't about to volunteer the information." He rested his chin on his laced fingers. "So what's the story, Keri? You don't mind if I call you Keri, do you? Since that *is* your real name."

She looked at him warily. "That depends on what else you'd be calling me."

Keri noticed Rhyder's expression wasn't suspicious or angry. She would have loved to know what he was thinking. Now she understood why so many people said it was difficult to read an attorney's mind. She doubted anyone could guess what went on inside this man's head. She would never play poker with him.

"I'm just curious as to why you're up here posing as Stuart's fiancée and why your sister's not here doing her duty," he replied amiably. "After all, Stuart had invited Kim to meet the family. Maybe even do some nuptial planning. Did she have second thoughts? And did you think it wouldn't hurt to come up here, maybe see if you could step into her shoes?"

"Naturally," she countered sarcastically, "I was more than willing to cancel my clients' appointments to come up here and pretend to snuggle up to Stuart since I've never even met the man."

He allowed comprehension to sweep across his face. "Which is why you threw your arms around me at the dock when you arrived. You thought I was Stuart."

Keri flushed. "All Kim gave me was a brief description, and you pretty much fit what she'd said."

"We have our similarities and I guess if all you were given was the essentials, it could have happened," he allowed. "But why you and not Kim?"

She grimaced. "It's not an easy story to tell."

Rhyder shrugged. "No problem, I have plenty of time." He settled further into his chair.

Keri took a deep breath. "Kim really does love Stuart, but she felt she needed to resolve something from her past before going forward."

"And this resolution must have something to do with a French magazine publisher she's shacked up with off and on for the past year."

She narrowed her eyes. "What did you do? Investigate Kim, too? You really are a disgusting man! And for the record, they were never shacked up off and on!"

He cocked his head. "You know, that's the funny thing about all this. In the beginning, I thought I was investigating Kim," he reminded her. "In the course of things, I found out I'm investigating you. Although I have to admit what I learned was interesting."

She didn't like the sound of that at all. She also wasn't sure she liked having him in her room. She was grateful her clothing wasn't scattered about. That had always been a fault of Kim's, not hers. Then she noticed a wisp of lace hanging off one side of the small table near where Rhyder sat. She forced her gaze away from that spot, so he wouldn't notice it.

Keri had told Kim she didn't see how this could work, but now that she had been found out she hated to think she had failed. After all, as children and teens, she and her twin had traded places many times with success. Now she knew it just couldn't work as adults.

She looked at Rhyder. She wanted to beg him not to hate her for her part in the deception. She wanted to haughtily remind him that whatever went on had nothing to do with him, ergo, it was really none of his business. She wanted not to look at him with his legs comfortably sprawled on either side of the chair. She was positive that drooling would completely ruin the proud stance she was working so hard to maintain.

It wasn't easy when she knew how he felt and how he tasted. Even worse when she reminded herself she also had the memory that when the man was aroused, he was aroused with a capital *A!* She swallowed the sigh that was threatening to travel up her throat. She hadn't really said that much but she knew she had lost all control of this conversation. She settled for staring back at him with a carefully composed expression. As she stared at him, she mentally recited body muscles. Keri always found it a good way to remain calm when she felt flustered.

"So your love for your sister had you losing good money to come up here and pretend to be her?" Rhyder was skeptical. "For someone who might be operating in the black, just barely, I'm surprised."

She flushed. "Kim offered to make up the money, but I refused. We've always been there for each other. She needed me and I gave in."

He cocked an eyebrow. "And?"

A tiny smile flickered across her lips. "And she promised to allow me to whip her back into shape. That was an offer I wasn't about to refuse."

A glint of admiration lit up Rhyder's eyes. "Why do I have the idea you're going to make sure she finds all those hidden muscles in her body?"

"Worked muscles don't scream with pain, they scream with happiness at being strengthened," she recited. "Her muscles will be ecstatic by the time I finish with her."

Rhyder shook his head. "Did you just make that up or what?"

"We find that uttering cute little sayings while the client is working on those last couple of reps makes it go easier," she explained.

"Why did you take a chance at using the treadmill today?" he asked curiously. "Weren't you afraid of getting caught?"

"I needed to do something physical." The moment she

said the word she knew she was in trouble. Rhyder's gaze slowly traveled over her body. She shored herself up and continued, "I had already learned that everyone here is a late sleeper, so I thought I'd be safe. I hadn't expected to stay on the treadmill as long as I had, but I lost track of time. I didn't expect you to show up." *Or kiss me as if there was no tomorrow.*

"We've determined that you are pretending to be your sister, that your sister is in France and that you haven't had the chicken pox." He suddenly stopped. "Or was that another ruse so you could stay away from Stuart before he found out you weren't Kim?"

She shook her head. "I've never had it. Although I got the idea it wouldn't have stopped Stuart. I think he's hoping for company in there."

Rhyder straightened as another thought occurred to him. "How did you handle lover boy that first night?" he asked, then grinned as he spied her flushed face. "Oh, come on, you can't tell me Kim and Stuart haven't been hitting the sheets together and he'd naturally expect his darling little fiancée to give him a special welcome in private."

"Judging by things Stuart has said, I'd say they've been intimate, but I would not go that far even for my sister," Keri said primly, hating the embarrassment she knew was coloring her face. "I told him that I didn't think it was right while we were in his parents' home. He didn't like it, but he honored my wishes. And my privacy," she added pointedly.

Rhyder shrugged as if that was the least of his worries.

"Stuart probably looked into those gorgeous eyes and knew he couldn't refuse you anything. I guess it's a good thing he broke out in the rash so quickly. Although," he mused, drawing out the word, "even though you weren't the one with him two weeks ago, you could still break out in two weeks. What about Kim? Has she had the chicken pox?''

Keri's mouth dropped open in shock. "Do not even go down that road." She put out her hand to ward off his prediction. "And yes, Kim's had the chicken pox. All I ask is that you do me a favor and don't give me away. I'll even go quietly. I can say the office called me back, big emergency, the boss died, whatever. I'll get on the phone to Kim, tell her to get her butt back here pronto and she can fly up later on."

"How do you know she isn't in France with the intention of having one last fling with an old lover?"

"No way!" She stopped to compose herself. "Jean Paul is very definitely a part of her past. The man is a slime. He's convinced any woman he meets, automatically wants him."

"What makes you so sure of that?" Rhyder asked.

She rolled her eyes as if to say he should already have guessed how. "I made sure he realized that the last person I'd ever want was him. Kim finally came to her senses about him, but she refused to tell him so in a letter or phone call. She wanted to tell him in person."

"Fine, so she flies over, tells the bastard off, flies back and that's that. It's been almost a week," Rhyder said. "What's the problem? She can't get a flight out of Paris?"

Keri groaned. "The problem is Jean Paul is in Nice and his housekeeper, who hates Kim, refuses to tell her where he's staying and also refuses to pass on any of Kim's messages to him. Kim's even tried calling his office but his secretary won't give her any information, either. So she's waiting until he gets back."

Rhyder closed his eyes. Keri watched him, convinced she could hear the gears whirring in his head. What was he thinking? He opened his eyes again.

"I'm not sure if you just told me one incredible story

that has the consistency of sheep dip or if you told me the truth,'' he said finally.

"It's the truth!" She was indignant that he dared accuse her of lying. Even if she had been lying for the past week. "If you knew my sister as well as I do, you'd know it was the truth. I do not lie!" She quickly backed up. "Well, only for a good purpose."

Rhyder slowly got up, pushing the chair back to where it belonged. He walked over to Keri and looked down at her.

"Have you seen Stuart in the past couple of days?"

She nodded. "I stand in the doorway every morning and blow him kisses and he blows some back. And I stop by to see him several times a day. He looks like red dotted-Swiss curtains."

He grinned. "Yeah, and his itching is driving him crazy. All right, see lover boy this morning, then you and I are going off for the day."

She was instantly suspicious. "Why?"

"Because right now, you're a bundle of nerves and if you stay around here with my family, you're going to break down and confess all."

She was mortified he could so easily read her.

"Don't worry, you're safe with me."

"I wasn't earlier today," she argued.

He traced her jaw with his fingertip. "I guess I wanted to see what kind of reaction I'd get out of you. What you're wearing is fine. Bring a swimsuit with you. We'll leave after you've had breakfast," he told her as he walked toward the doorway.

Keri flopped back on the bed. A look at the clock told her Rhyder had been in the room for only twenty minutes, but she felt as if she had been under the gun for twenty years.

"I THOUGHT I'D TAKE KIM out on the boat this morning," Rhyder announced to his brother when he stopped by Stuart's bedroom.

Stuart, covered with pastel-pink dots of calamine lotion to stop the itching, brightened. "She'll like that. I swear she's part fish."

He studied the other man. "I'm surprised you're not jealous I'll have her all to myself this morning."

Stuart chuckled. "I don't think she's your type."

He shrugged. "You never can tell," he teased.

"Then she wasn't meant for me, was she?" Before Rhyder could pounce on his cryptic remark, Stuart rushed on. "Will you do me a favor and ask Frannie if she'll bring up some tapioca for me?"

He shook his head. "You always ate gallons of that stuff when you were sick. Never got over it, did you?"

"Chewing too much makes me itch." Stuart grimaced as he started to scratch his chest, then stopped. "How did I miss all this fun when we were little?"

"Lucky, I guess. I'll have Jake drop off some of his favorite videos. That should keep you occupied for a while."

Rhyder's first stop was at the kitchen to deliver Stuart's request. Reba didn't look very happy about it.

"I hate tapioca," she said flatly. "I won't even tell you what it looks like, but it looks pretty disgusting. What the hell do you think you're doing?"

"Preparing a picnic lunch," he replied, setting a large covered basket on the table. "Don't worry, I'll make everything. I'm taking Kim sailing."

"You're not making anything in *my* kitchen." She snatched the wine bottle out of his hand and studied the label. "And there's no way you'd be serving this with the meal I'm preparing for you two. Wait a minute!"

He stopped as he reached the swing door and looked over his shoulder.

"If I'm fixing you a lunch, you can get out the ingredients for your brother's tapioca. I can't do two things at once." She bustled around the kitchen with the intensity of a mad scientist performing the ultimate experiment.

It was at times like this Rhyder would watch her and wonder whether she really was capable of poisoning a person. He silently promised himself to always stay on her good side.

KERI WAS GOING TO DIE. She was positive she was going to perish via one of the most horrible methods possible. Her stomach rolled in twenty different directions. Her head spun around clockwise, then counterclockwise. Her legs refused to support her body and she just knew if she opened her eyes she would instantly turn into a quivering mass of cooked pudding. She was positive her skin would fall off next.

"How much longer are we going to be out here?" she moaned, keeping her head and body as still as possible. Even the slightest movement brought the nausea again.

A slightly rough palm rested gently against her forehead. "Keri, we've only been out for five minutes."

She whimpered. "That's four minutes and fifty-nine seconds too long. I told you this was not a good idea, but you wouldn't listen to me. I just want you to know you're responsible for my death."

She could feel him brush a stray lock of hair away from her face. "Correction, you told me you weren't a good sailor."

Keri dared to open her eyes now. "Bad sailors don't lie on the deck just to work on their tans. What does that tell you?"

Rhyder smiled. "That a person really does turn green when they're seasick."

Keri's gaze showed an all-too-brief flash of her temper. "Come closer."

He looked puzzled by her request. "Why?"

"So I can throw up on you."

RHYDER STEERED the sailboat around the island to a cove he was familiar with. Keri still lay on the deck looking as movable as a stone statue. He regretted his quip about her looking green, but when he had seen the verdigris tint to her skin he couldn't resist it.

Once he'd dropped anchor, he walked over to her and crouched down.

"Hey." He gently rubbed his forefinger against her forehead.

"Please tell me we're back at the house," she begged, not opening her eyes.

"No, but we're anchored."

Keri's face scrunched up in a grimace. "We can't be. The boat is still moving."

"It's only moving a little because of the waves," he explained. "I thought you might like to take a swim and we can eat on the beach."

Slowly she turned her head to one side. "You expect me to get up, change my clothes and swim away from this torture chamber? You really are sadistic, aren't you?"

"Eating a little something will help your stomach," he explained.

Keri moaned. "I don't have a stomach. I have a roller coaster in the middle of my body. It absolutely refuses anything solid."

Rhyder shook his head, dismayed by what he saw. "I can't believe the seasickness patches didn't work."

"I didn't use them. They always made me more sick than I am without them." She rolled onto her side. "I'll be honest with you. I don't think it would be a good idea for me to go down inside your boat to change into my suit."

Rhyder took a good look at her face and knew she spoke the truth. "Then change up here. There's no one else around."

She rose carefully, straightening as if her spine were composed of eggshells. Her bag had been left nearby. She started to bend over but swayed a bit on her feet, so Rhyder waved her off and dug into the bag, pulling out a brilliant coral bikini. He handed the skimpy pieces to her. She started to unbutton her camp shirt, then realized he was looking at her.

"Turn around."

Rhyder turned, but the picture of that bikini sliding through his fingers remained clear in his mind. Was such an item of clothing legal to wear in public? In his hands, it had appeared to be all skinny straps. What was it going to look like on her body? Would she have trouble putting it on? Find the strings all tangled? Would she need help untangling them? He stared ahead at the horizon. The sounds of seagulls overhead and the breeze blowing through his clothing did nothing to calm the thoughts racing through his mind.

"All right," Keri said quietly.

He took his time turning around and once he did, he realized the wait was more than worth it.

The bikini that appeared all straps in his hands indeed covered Keri in the essential areas. And left even more of her bare. Triangular cups barely concealed her firm breasts and a triangle held up by two straps covered her lower body. He promptly decided this item of clothing was his favorite.

Keri raised her arms to pull her hair up into a ponytail. Rhyder watched her, positive he would never be the same again.

"If your stomach's still bothering you, take a deep breath," he suggested. "It will help ease it until you can get some food into it."

"I doubt there's anything that can do that after the watery roller-coaster ride I've been on," she retorted.

"And do us both a favor. Do not mention food again or I will show you pain like you've never endured before."

He winced, knowing she spoke the truth. "Well, sweetheart, you're too late since the food is definitely going with us." He picked up the picnic basket before climbing to the base of the ladder, where a small flotation device was attached to the bottom rung. He set the basket on top and extended a hand to her. "Come on. I'll help you down."

Keri stopped on the first rung, looked down at the water below and moaned softly.

"Wait a minute." Rhyder suffered a disquieting thought as he noticed her expression. "You can swim, can't you?"

"Of course, I can swim," she snapped. "It's boats I can't handle. Swimming in a nice pool is a wonderful form of exercise."

"I'd think an athlete like you would be into everything."

"I am, as long as it's on dry land. Don't try that kind of psychology crap on me, mister. I meant it about the pain." She carefully made her way down the ladder. When she reached the bottom rung, she slipped into the water. And promptly shrieked. "Why didn't you tell me the water was this cold?"

Rhyder looped the rope to the flotation device around his wrist and struck out. "Start swimming and you'll warm up in no time."

"Easy for you to say," she said between chattering teeth as she pushed herself off.

Within a few moments, they had reached shallow water where they could stand. The moment she was on dry land Keri danced up and down.

"Obviously, your stomach has recovered," Rhyder said dryly, as he hauled the flotation device and basket onto the sand.

"I am on dry ground again and I'm celebrating." She continued to dance, waving her hands over her head.

He watched her antics, amused by her renewed vitality. Not to mention what her lean body in that bikini did to his own vitality.

"Let's hear it for physical fitness," he murmured.

KERI FINISHED HER impromptu dance and turned back to Rhyder. What she saw took her breath away.

A man wearing trim-fitting black trunks should be considered illegal. Or at least, require that the woman looking at him have a permit allowing her to drool. She privately thought he didn't have the build of a man who spent long hours behind a desk or in a courtroom. His shoulders were broad, tapering to a narrow waist. But what she noticed most was the dark brown hair dusted across his chest and arrowing down to his navel and beyond. She wasn't about to think about "beyond." If she did, she would dive back into the cold water for a much-needed shock. She wondered what he would say if she told him he also had a pretty good pair of legs.

At the moment, Keri could have cared less if a permit had been required since she was with an attorney and she was positive he could get her off.

In more ways than one.

She giggled.

Rhyder stared at her. "Are you all right?"

She grinned. "Just fine. At least I will be as long as you don't force me back on that floating bathtub. How about you sail back and I'll hike back. I love to go hiking, so it's no problem."

"I'm afraid it is." He jerked his thumb upward.

Keri tipped her head back and stared straight up a sheer slab of rock. She couldn't imagine anyone trying to climb that wall.

"I guess there's no elevator," she said hopefully.

"Stairs?" She paused a beat. "Holes in the rock to use for climbing?"

He shook his head. "This part of the island is uninhabited because it's so rocky up there. Actually, I'd say the island is as strange as its inhabitants."

She dropped gracefully to the sand and leaned back, resting her weight on her elbows. "Your family included?"

"My family especially." A rueful smile touched his lips. "Not that I don't love them all, wild as they may be at times. And you haven't even met all of them."

"All right, tell me about some of the other residents and other members of your family," she invited.

Rhyder dropped to the sand beside her, sitting cross-legged. "No problem. First, the residents. There's Plato. No relation to the well-known Plato. He changed his name several years ago because he thought it sounded more appropriate for a writer of incredibly bad poetry." He paused as she giggled. "Then there's Madelaine who was a stripper back in the forties. She claims she was good friends with Gypsy Rose Lee and had more than one mobster as a lover."

"I'll bet she has some stories to tell," Keri commented, taking the towel Rhyder handed her and shaping it into a roll and sliding it under her head.

"Yeah, but none I'd care for Lucie or Jake to hear for at least the next twenty years," he muttered.

She laughed. "Ah, there speaks the father of teenagers. All right, who else?"

"Last but not least, there's Claude and Claudia."

"Claude and Claudia. Catchy." She offered him a smile loaded with innocence. "And what do they do?"

"They met forty years ago, decided their names proved they were meant to be together and married immediately. Thing is, they quickly discovered they weren't exactly the perfect couple," he explained. "She's a night person, he's day. She's artistic and a dreamer, he's very logical. So she paints and sculpts at night and he plays with the stock market during the day. They've come to the conclusion that they're better off than most couples.''

"That's not all that odd," Keri protested.

"It is, since Claudia is also a practicing nudist and believes being nude when working frees her creativity. While Claude refuses to leave the house without wearing a tie."

Keri laughed and shook her head. "And you have relatives who are worse?"

"I have a great-aunt who refuses to play bridge but can clean your clock at stud poker. I also have an uncle who's positive his ancestors come from another world," he said amiably as if he were saying nothing more than that his relative lived out of state.

She straightened. "Another world? Do you mean...?" She pointed upward.

He nodded. "He's just waiting for the mother ship to come back for him." Rhyder grimaced. "You probably hate the idea of your sister marrying into this family now that you've heard what they're like."

"It seems like one that Kim would fit into just fine. Especially after spending the day shopping with your mother." Keri heaved a deep sigh. "The woman is inexhaustible and she wields those charge cards like a sword."

"Mom is a champion shopper," he agreed.

She lay down again, content to allow the midday sun to bake into her skin. "Wait until she meets the real Kim. I doubt there's any store my sister doesn't know."

"But it's not your idea of fun," he guessed.

She shrugged. "I go when I need to and even then it's with a lot of reluctance. I think the only reason I enjoyed the trip with your mother was because I was using Kim's Visa." She grinned, then went on to explain, "When I phoned her about Stuart's chicken pox, I told her the only way I'd stay was if she'd send me one of her credit cards.''

Rhyder now understood. "The Federal Express package you received."

"That's right. I could have made an even larger dent than I did, but I went easy on her."

He picked up a handful of sand and cupped his hand around it, allowing it to fall in a steady stream. "I still can't believe you let her talk you into impersonating her. I could understand if you were kids, but not as adults."

"Which goes to show you're not a twin." She rolled over onto her stomach, then bent one leg at the knee and kicked it backward. "They pretty much think alike, act alike and have been known to practically share the same heartbeat. While Kim and I have differing life-styles, we feel the same about many other things. One is that we are always there for each other. My sister may appear selfish and flighty to many, but she has a heart of gold. I guess I said yes because I hoped this time might be it for her. Maybe she'd found the right man and would finally settle down." Keri absently pushed together damp sand and fashioned a small castle.

"Why haven't you settled down?" He found himself unable to keep his eyes off her shapely rear end.

"I've been too busy getting my certifications and working to pay off school loans," she replied. "My degree in exercise science and nutrition didn't give me an instant job at a club, but it helped, along with the experience I'd gained on the way. But I knew from the beginning what I really wanted was to work strictly for myself, not for someone else. Now, I can see that dream come true since I have a chance to buy into a friend's fitness center. More people are looking for personal training but at an affordable price, and we're hoping to offer exactly that in our club. We won't be catering to the serious bodybuilder types, but to those who want to keep themselves in top physical condition. For the past few years, I've been able to slowly but surely build up a nice clientele. I have until the end of the year to buy in.''

"Sounds like a pretty big undertaking," he commented.

She shot him a sly look tinged with humor. "Look at it this way, once I'm part owner of Fitness Plus, anytime you're in San Diego, you can stop by and I'll see what you can do with some free weights."

Rhyder couldn't keep his eyes off her mostly bare back. His fingers itched to trace the line down her spine. "That just might be an offer I'll accept." He regained sanity by turning away. His gaze fell on the picnic basket. "Think you can eat something now? Reba's known for packing a great lunch."

She rolled over and sat up. "Now that we're on solid ground and my stomach has finally come to know it, I think I could."

Rhyder got to his feet and held out his hand, helping Keri up. For a moment, their fingers lingered until she moved away. He walked over to the basket and picked it up, carrying it a little farther inland where the rock wall afforded them scant shade and they were out of the breeze. The cloth Reba had used to cover the food was laid over the sand and he started pulling containers out of the large basket and placing them on the cloth.

Keri didn't hesitate in opening the containers to investigate their contents. "Croissants stuffed with chicken salad, raspberries." She popped one into her mouth. Her eyes closed as she bit into the tart fruit. "Mmm, good. Let's see, what else do we have?" She started pulling out napkins and several bottles of chilled sparkling water. "What, no champagne?" she teased.

"Good thing she didn't pack any alcohol. I don't think

your stomach would have appreciated it," he teased in return.

"Drunk *and* seasick. Not my idea of fun," she admitted.

Vicki Lewis Thompson

They knew it would have approached like he would in the secure.

Drink now she felt. Between he was fully. Are same

143

Chapter Nine

"I don't think it would be any fun, either," Rhyder murmured, staring at her.

Keri looked up, captured by the intensity of his gaze. *Not a good idea* kept running through her mind. Still, how many times had she ever listened to her good sense? Especially when the sun was shining, the beach was deserted and she was alone with a good-looking man who made her hormones sizzle. *Not a good idea.* She took a deep breath and quickly looked away.

"You know this is all so crazy," she said, once she could speak again. "What we have here is the makings of a soap opera. Man out with brother's fiancée except fiancée is actually fiancée's sister. All we need is for either sister's supposedly dead husband to show up and we've got a hit."

"It sounds more like a comedy of errors to me." He breathed a silent sigh of frustration and willed his racing pulse to return to normal. It wasn't easy—especially since the heated look they'd just exchanged gave him ideas he really shouldn't be having. Even if he could now pursue Keri with a clear conscience.

Rhyder was taken aback by his line of thought. Dating hadn't been uppermost on his mind for a number of years. After Ellen's death, he had gone through the usual phases of the newly widowed, just trying to make it through each day. He hadn't even missed the sex. Well, if he were honest, he would have to say hell, yes, he did miss the sex, but he had two kids to raise and couldn't worry about it. Except on those long nights after the kids were in bed, when he would lie awake and think of other nights when he and Ellen would curl up under the covers. Now, after this time here on the island where he felt he had started to find himself again, he was discovering that all of him was most definitely returning to life. He blinked when he saw a croissant under his nose.

"Feed those brain cells you're burning at such an incredible rate," Keri advised, dropping the sandwich into his automatically outstretched hand.

"Sorry, guess I zoned out for a minute." He bit into his croissant.

"Reba knows how to make great chicken salad. I'll have to ask her for the recipe." Keri had polished off one sandwich and was happily munching on a second.

"Trust me, Reba doesn't share anything," he replied. "She believes everything she cooks is a government secret. One of Ronnie's guests once asked for her recipe for borscht and Reba let the woman know that in no uncertain terms. Needless to say, Ronnie's friend has never come back." He watched Keri eat, impressed by her hearty appetite. "Obviously, your earlier bout with seasickness is over."

"Obviously." She popped a raspberry into her mouth, then dug into another container and brought out tiny meringue cookies. "I'm going to have to sneak into the gym again to burn all this off, but it's worth it."

"And here I thought you'd only eat greens or lecture people on the dangers of fat and cholesterol," he joked.

Keri gazed at him with a keen eye. "You're in danger of going a little soft around the middle if you don't catch it soon, but otherwise, I don't see any problems."

Rhyder frowned and looked down. He would have sworn his midriff looked as flat as when he had been in law school. Was there a chance it was suddenly losing its battle with gravity?

"I'm in terrific shape," he said defensively.

"You handled the boat, sure, but how often do you sail ordinarily?"

"Maybe once a week."

"And the other days, what do you do? Laze in a hammock in the backyard with a beer and a good book?" Her smile said she knew she'd hit it right on the head.

"I'm on vacation."

"Vacations are generally for two weeks," she told him. "How are you going to be your best in court if you're not at your physical peak?"

Rhyder shifted uneasily under the truth of her words. "Is this how you get your clients?" he demanded peevishly.

She grinned. "It works every time. You know, if you'll keep my secret and make sure no one finds me in the gym, I'll work up a program for you."

"I'm very familiar with the equipment in that room and I use it."

Keri didn't argue. She settled for grabbing another cookie. "I was merely offering."

"You must be a terror in the weight room," he groused.

"I've been called a few names but my clients have always assured me they were all meant in an affectionate way," she said solemnly.

Rhyder decided observing Keri in a bikini had to be a million times better than seeing her in workout wear. He reached for one of the meringue cookies. He was beginning to understand why it was said some people substituted food for sex. Food was looking better to him all the time.

Keri found herself enjoying the day. She knew it was because she was off the boat and she dreaded the moment when she would have to step back on board. She was tempted to find out if she could swim back. While her stomach had recovered from the sail out, she wasn't looking forward to that form of torture again.

She was also enjoying Rhyder's company.

She had been torn between anguish and relief at his finding out her identity. After Rhyder had left her room, she'd told herself she should call Kim and tell her the game was over, but she hadn't. She thought a chance to get to know Rhyder better might be to her advantage. One thing that had surprised her from the first was that he had shown no anger about the deception. If anything, he seemed amused. She couldn't imagine any other man reacting the way he had—coming in and kissing her senseless.

The sun beating down on her seemed to have suddenly gotten even hotter. She opened a bottle of the sparkling water and drank deeply of the cold liquid flavored with lime. It seemed to do little to soothe her dry throat.

"So, Keri Putnam, what do you do when you're not whipping clients into shape?" Rhyder followed her lead and picked up one of the other bottles.

She shrugged. "The usual. Running errands, catching up on housework, going out with friends."

He suddenly took an interest in digging through the basket. "Any in particular?"

Keri stared at the top of his head. "By in particular, do you mean male?"

He looked up. "Okay, yes, I do. What I'm asking is if some muscle-bound hulk will come up here and beat the crap out of me for kissing you." His eyes bored into hers.

Her smile widened. "I have some very good friends you would probably describe as muscle-bound hulks who

would defend my honor if they felt it was besmirched."
Rhyder winced. "Although I would strongly advise you
never to use those words to their faces. One has a doc-
torate in psychology and is a practicing clinical psychol-
ogist. Another owns a chain of health and fitness stores
throughout the state, and another is a lawyer."

He perked up. "What's his name?"

"Bill Castle."

"Now I know why he always looked so imposing in
the courtroom," he murmured. "I gather this means there
is no one in your life?"

"I thought about buying a cat, but it seemed so cli-
ché." She leaned in his direction. "Rhyder, if you
thought there was someone significant in my life, why
did you kiss me the way you did in the workout room?"

He took a moment, apparently composing his thoughts,
before replying. "I guess it seemed like the thing to do.
Especially because it was something I'd wanted to repeat
since that day at the ferry." He suddenly grinned. "Plus
you looked so damn cute I had no choice but to kiss
you."

"Cute?" she scoffed. "That's a new one."

He shook his head. "What can I say? You did look
cute!"

"I was dripping with sweat," Keri protested. "It
wasn't exactly one of my most attractive moments."

His gaze was steady and in some ways, illuminating.
"For me, it was."

She looked down at her hands, which were methodi-
cally tearing tiny pieces of meringue away from the
cookie she held.

"I had to burn up my excess energy somehow. I felt
so much guilt that I was attracted to my sister's fiancé's
brother while I was playing the part of my sister that it
was eating me up inside," she said quietly. With her head
downcast, she didn't see him move closer to her, but she

sensed him sitting beside her. She carefully lifted her head and turned in his direction.

"You can't stop playing the part now," he murmured.

She nodded. "I know."

"Did you let your sister know what's happened?"

She mutely shook her head.

"Are you going to tell her?"

"What good would it do?" she whispered. "She's still thousands of miles away."

When Rhyder reached out to touch her face, his gesture was hesitant as if he were unsure how she would accept it. When she didn't shy away, his touch grew more certain as his fingertips lightly traced the curve of her cheek.

"Do you think this is a good idea?" Keri murmured, reaching up to cover his hand with her own.

"Would you rather we didn't?" he countered.

She took so long in answering, there was a question as to what her response would be. Her smile was equally long in coming but no less welcome.

"I don't think either one of us would want to back off now, would we?" She twisted around to face him. She straightened out her legs until one rested on either side of his hips. Her movement was graceful and natural as she lowered herself back onto the sand with Rhyder following.

Their legs tangled together as their bodies molded from two to one.

If Keri had thought Rhyder's kisses were lethal before, she was quickly finding out that they'd been mild compared to the way he kissed her right now. She felt as if he were consuming her with flames.

His firm lips skated over her cheeks and along the corners of her mouth, nipping gently until her lips parted under his silent entreaty. He tasted of lime and raspberries. She doubted there was a better combination anywhere.

"If I may invoke a note of sanity here for just a moment," she gasped, pulling her mouth from his and smiling when she realized he was eagerly following her. "What if another sailor comes along, intent on using this beach for a picnic?"

"No one in their right mind would come along now," he murmured, nuzzling the side of her neck.

"Still, it's something to think about," she persevered breathlessly.

"We're far enough from the water that we'll see them before they'll see us." He gently bumped his hips against hers. There was no doubt he was aroused.

Keri was pleased that Rhyder didn't try to take his seduction a step further. She'd always felt that the combination of sand and naked bodies wasn't as sexy as it looked. Not when sand had an unfortunate ability to end up in delicate places. He seemed content with their kisses. She couldn't find any complaint with that. Not when he was whispering some pretty outrageous suggestions at the same time. She could feel her head spinning again. She gripped his shoulders, finding them sun-warmed to the touch.

"Where does a lawyer learn all about this?" she demanded, once she had caught her breath.

"It's easy when one of his clients ran a phone-sex operation," he replied, gently licking her bottom lip.

"I don't even want to think about it," she mumbled.

Rhyder chuckled.

When he licked her bottom lip again, she parted her lips, allowing him entrance. Their tongues danced, winding around each other in a parody of the motions they longed for their bodies to make but knew now wasn't the time. Instead, she settled for running her fingers down his spine to his tight buttocks while he used his fingertips to stroke her shoulders. Her bikini-top straps fell down her arms but he made no move to lower them farther.

Keri enjoyed the leisurely kisses and slow caresses they shared. She felt as if they were two teenagers away from the all-seeing eyes of adults. In this case, it was the rest of the Carson family. As it was, she would have to return to the house acting as if this had been nothing more than a platonic picnic. She was going to have to give the acting performance of her life!

"Whew!" Rhyder pulled away and rolled over onto his back. His chest rose and fell with his rapid breathing. "For a minute I thought it was the Fourth of July."

"For a minute I was convinced I'd die a very happy death." She was breathless herself. She extended her arms over her head and stretched. She couldn't miss the hot and hungry look in Rhyder's eyes and gloried in the fact that she had caused it.

"Are you sure you didn't deliberately choose that bikini to drive me out of my mind?" he asked in a rough voice.

"Hmm." She pretended to ponder his question. "Sorry, but I only brought two with me and I figured I'd have a better chance to work on my tan with this suit."

His gaze seared into her. "Considering I haven't seen much in the way of tan lines, I was wondering. Although I am surprised that someone into fitness would tan."

"One of my vices," she admitted. "You'll notice most of us have a habit of tanning, one way or another."

He eyed her with a leer. "I'd say you've done a great job of it."

She couldn't resist it. She leaned over and kissed him, but what started out as a teasing gesture ended as a heated exchange.

"This is not a good idea!" she wailed, drawing back. Turning around, she grabbed her bottle of water and drank deeply until it was empty. She jumped when a pair of hands settled on her shoulders. She tried to pull away, but her heart wasn't in it, so it was easy for him to keep hold of her.

"This is the way I see it." Rhyder knelt behind her, wrapping his arms around her waist and resting his chin on top of her head. "Until your sister shows up and/or Stuart's over the chicken pox, Mom is going to expect me to entertain you. Unless, of course, you'd prefer to play with Ronnie." Her dramatic shudder was answer enough. "Okay, we just take it as it comes. At least you've gotten over your seasickness, so we can take the boat out more."

Keri groaned. "Let's not make any statements that can't be backed up just yet, shall we? After all, I haven't gotten back on that floating horror chamber yet. I may take one step on board and immediately throw up all over you."

He chuckled. "Then I guess I'd better make sure I stay a safe distance from you." He stood and held out his hand. "How about a swim?"

She placed her hand in his and allowed him to pull her to her feet. "Fine with me." She slid her fingers free of his light grip and ran down to the water's edge, then waded in until she could safely make a shallow dive.

Rhyder watched her in admiration as she swam with smooth strokes.

"This could be the start of something fantastic," he muttered just before he ran in after her.

KERI'S PREDICTION PROVED to be wrong. She was able to take *two* steps onto the boat before her stomach started rolling. Rhyder wasted no time in getting the boat under sail and steering it around the island.

"No dance now that you've reached solid ground again?" Rhyder asked after he'd secured the boat and helped her onto the dock.

Her reply was a deadly glare. "If you value your life you will not make jokes."

She was relieved he was smart enough to immediately back off. He grabbed the picnic basket and followed her up to the house.

She noticed the family gathering on the patio and merely settled for a wave of the hand as she veered around to the side of the house.

"How was your sail?" Frannie called out.

"Wonderful!" Keri called back with an enthusiasm she didn't feel.

"Well, change and come out for a before-dinner drink," she invited.

Keri nodded and headed for the kitchen door with Rhyder right behind her.

Reba was in the midst of stirring the contents in a large iron pot when the couple stepped into the kitchen. The cook looked up and frowned at the intruders.

"What the hell did you do to her?" she demanded, stalking over and peering closely into Keri's face. "You look somethin' worse than the cat would ever drag in."

Keri grimaced at her apt description. "I'm fine. Maybe I had too much sun today," she said, hoping to sidestep any more questions.

It appeared Reba was having none of it. She shook her head. "I thought they all said you loved sailing. You look as if you just went through a major bout of seasickness. I should know. I have it bad."

"Maybe it's that time of the month," Keri mumbled.

"Or maybe you don't like sailing as much as you claim to." Reba returned to her pot, checked the contents, gave it a few quick stirs, then turned back to Keri before she could sneak out. "You go on upstairs and change your clothes. I'll send something up to you that will help."

The idea of any food or drink passing her lips was enough to bring the nausea on again.

"I don't know," she hedged.

"No talking back, miss. I know what I'm talking about." The cook unceremoniously pushed them both out of the kitchen.

"No one wins an argument with Reba," Rhyder confided as he followed her up the stairs and into the hall.

Keri eyed him skeptically. "Even you?"

"Especially me."

She stopped a few feet away from her bedroom door. "I'm sure I can find my own way from here."

"I don't know," he muttered. "You were pretty sick out there. You might suddenly faint and require mouth-to-mouth resuscitation."

She placed her hand squarely against his chest. "Trust me, that won't happen. You go downstairs and make nice with your family. I'll look in on Stuart and change."

Rhyder looked as if he was going to steal a kiss, but instead he turned away. Then, just as suddenly, he spun and kissed her quickly.

"I didn't want you to forget," he murmured, before he took off.

As Keri knocked on Stuart's door, she idly ran her tongue across her lower lip. She could imagine she tasted Rhyder there. The last thing she wanted to do was stand here and talk to her sister's fiancé, but she knew Stuart would expect Kim to see him first thing upon her return to the house.

"Come in."

She mustered a bright tone as she opened the door but remained in the doorway. "Hi."

He frowned. "You look pale. Are you all right?"

"It's just the lighting," she replied. "How do you feel?"

"Still itchy but not as bad as before," he told her. "What did you think of my dad's boat?"

"She's gorgeous." She was secretly glad Rhyder had reminded her to refer to the boat in the feminine form when she would happily have called it a floating hell. "We sailed around the island."

He smiled. "I'd hoped we could have done that."

Something else for which Keri was secretly grateful. Stuart would have known right away he wasn't sailing with his fiancée and the hoax would have ended.

"If you don't mind, I'm going to take a shower. I feel itchy from all the salt water."

"I wish you could come in for a while, but I don't want you to get this."

"I'll stop in again after dinner," she assured him before closing the door.

Keri had barely reached the door of her own room when she heard her name called out. She turned her head to see Lucie walking down the hallway carrying a glass.

"Reba sent me up with this. She said your stomach needed settling," she explained.

Keri opened her door and gestured for the young girl to enter. As Lucie stepped inside, she handed the glass to Keri, who eyed the contents with the caution of one looking into a bubbling, disgusting mess.

"Please tell me I'm supposed to rub this on my stomach."

Lucie giggled. "Believe me, it tastes a lot worse than it looks, but it works."

Keri hesitated.

"If you dump it, she'll know," the girl warned. "I don't know how she will, but she always does."

For a moment, Keri was willing to risk the older woman's wrath. Then she decided it wasn't worth it. She took a deep breath and drank deeply, not stopping until she'd finished. When she lowered the glass she was choking.

"That is horrible!" she wheezed.

Lucie ran over and grabbed the glass before she dropped it. "I warned you it would be. But after a couple of minutes your stomach will be good as new." She looked at Keri curiously. "I thought you loved sailing."

"There're certain times of the month I don't have as good luck," she murmured.

"Well, I'll take this back down to Reba. I hope you feel better soon."

"I guess I should thank you for bringing this up to me, but right now, I'm not all that sure I'm grateful," Keri said as she walked her to the door.

Lucie nodded. "She took care of me when I had the flu last winter. I wasn't sure which was worse, the flu or the horrible stuff she made me take. See you at dinner."

By the time Keri walked into the bathroom and turned on the shower, she realized that she *was* feeling better.

"Thank goodness her meals don't taste like her concoctions," she said reverently, shedding her clothing and stepping into the shower.

Chapter Ten

"Kim, did you enjoy your day out on the boat?" Veronica asked at dinner with an outward show of friendliness Keri hadn't experienced from the woman before.

"Yes, it was very nice," she said pleasantly, remaining wary of the woman's amiable manner. She had been relieved that while Reba's concoction had tasted vile, it had allowed her to look at food without turning green again. She had a good idea a change in skin tone would have given her away. "Rhyder took me on a tour around the island. It was a lovely trip," she lied.

"With your love of sailing, I'm surprised you don't own your own boat," Veronica continued.

"I don't have a boat for the same reason I don't have a pet. I don't have the necessary time to give to either one," Keri explained.

She hid her smile when she noticed Rhyder's subtle thumbs-up gesture.

Veronica's smile tightened as her gaze wandered from one to the other. She narrowed her eyes a fraction.

"I'm just glad Rhyder was up here so he could take you out for the afternoon," Frannie bubbled. She reached for her glass of wine. "While the children have always enjoyed sailing, it was never one of my favorite pastimes."

"You wouldn't get me out on one of those floating coffins," Aunt Sylvia murmured, holding her china tea-cup in a protective gesture. She sipped the contents daintily.

"Mom likes to pretend she's one of the Southern ladies of old," Rhyder teased his mother. "She enjoys spending afternoons in her parlor where she can embroider throw pillows."

"I also took up knitting a few years ago," she reminded him.

"Grandma broke her leg two years ago and we all had hand-knit sweaters in every color you can think of," Jake added. "Trouble was, none of the sleeves were the same length."

"I never could understand how I misread that part of the instructions." Frannie gave a deep sigh.

"What did you do all day while your father and I were out on the boat?" Keri asked Jake.

The boy grimaced. "I was in the gym. I want to try out for football next fall, but I need more upper-body strength. I asked Ferd for advice, but he keeps talking about fighting strength, not muscle strength."

Keri knew exactly what he needed, but with her pretending to be Kim, there wasn't any way she could help him. She couldn't let anyone else in on the secret. It was difficult enough to keep now, with the wonderful way Frannie had treated her. It was rougher when she was near Rhyder. She was amazed that she could act so naturally around him as if nothing had happened in that cove. She put it down to the way he was treating her, as if she were nothing more than his prospective sister-in-law.

She savored the chicken in wine sauce Ferd served and inwardly sighed at the thought of going back to her own cooking. Even at her best, she had never been this good!

"I meant to ask you before, Kim," Charles spoke up.

He topped off his glass of wine. "What kind of portfolio do you have? You do diversify your income, don't you? After all, you don't want the government to get too much of your money." He chuckled.

"I have a broker who takes care of all that for me," she replied, hoping he wouldn't ask any more technical questions. The only way she diversified her income was by deciding what part of her paycheck went for rent and what part went for food!

He nodded as if, naturally, she would have a professional handle her money.

"But you still keep on top of everything, don't you? Make sure he's doing everything he can for you? You can't be too careful nowadays."

"Actually, my broker is a she and Bette does a wonderful job for me."

Charles looked a bit confused for a moment.

"Well, I guess she probably knows what she's doing," he muttered, returning to his meal with a decided lack of interest.

"I've never been sure women in business was a good idea," Stu blustered, waving his fork for emphasis.

Keri sincerely wished her sister were sitting here right now to hear her future father-in-law's sexist statement. She knew Kim would make mincemeat of the man with a few choice words, but would do it in such a way he would have no idea how well she'd filleted him. Keri wanted to do just that, but decided she would leave that pleasure to Kim.

"Bette Long has always done very well for me."

Charles's face turned a dull red. "Bette Long? She's your broker?" She nodded. "She was written up in the *Wall Street Journal* about a month ago."

Keri nodded again. Luckily, she was aware of the article since Kim had mentioned it.

"My, my, you are a bundle of surprises, aren't you?"

Veronica drawled. "Pretty soon, we're all going to think you might be too good for our Stuart."

"Then I guess it will be nothing more than Stuart's good fortune he has me, won't it?" she said cheerfully.

Lucie looked from one woman to the other to see what would happen next. Jake choked and had to reach for his water glass. Frannie looked bewildered, Stu seemed to be debating whether an insult had been given, Charles pretended to concentrate on his meal, Veronica was stunned to have it turned so neatly against her, and Rhyder merely smiled. Keri decided Aunt Sylvia had the right idea. She smiled and continued drinking her "tea."

Keri was never so grateful as when dinner was finally over. She stood, positive the raspberry shortcake was sitting a bit too heavily in her stomach. She didn't blame her condition on the food because she knew it had everything to do with the company.

When the family headed outside for the patio, which was their usual after-dinner destination, Keri felt fingers circle her upper arm and she was pulled to one side.

"You're being kidnapped," Rhyder whispered in her ear. "If you're smart, you won't cry out for help."

"And if I do?" she whispered back, intrigued by his theatrics.

"I wouldn't try that if I were you. You'd have to spend the evening with them." He jerked his thumb toward the patio.

Keri slid her arm out of his grasp and replaced it with her hand, curving her fingers around his. "I'm your more-than-willing hostage."

Rhyder gave her hand a brief squeeze, then quietly led her down the dark hallway. They careened to a halt when a dark figure seemed to materialize in front of them.

"Mr. Rhyder," Ferd said in a deep, raspy voice.

"Ferd, I'm taking Ms. Putnam for a walk to help her settle her dinner," Rhyder said, unperturbed at getting caught sneaking out of the house like a teenager trying to escape his parents.

"Mr. and Mrs. Carson will expect both of you on the patio," the butler explained, not budging an inch. "Mr. Carson didn't have a good day playing golf and he isn't too happy with Mr. Charles for beating him again, so everyone is needed to keep them from furthering the argument they brought home with them this afternoon."

Keri looked at the man and realized that trying to move him would be as successful as moving a tank.

"I'll let you in on a secret, Ferd. My father can't play golf worth a damn," Rhyder confided.

"Yes, sir, we all know that," he replied. "That's why you should be out there."

"Ferd." Keri laid a hand on his beefy arm. It felt like a tube of iron. She had a pretty good idea he made frequent use of the gym. "You wouldn't really tell Mr. and Mrs. Carson that Rhyder and I decided to go for a walk instead of sitting out there with them, would you?"

"You're not what I expected Mr. Stuart to come home with," he said solemnly.

"I hope that's good."

He looked from one to the other. "Just as long as you remember you're engaged to Mr. Stuart."

"You don't have to worry about that," Rhyder assured Ferd. "I promise I will not make any improper advances toward Kim."

"I am very glad to hear that, Mr. Rhyder." He stepped to one side and allowed them to pass.

"Did you get the feeling he was watching out for Stuart's fiancée in a big way?" she asked when they had escaped outside.

Rhyder took possession of her hand and pulled her away from the house. "Ferd is very protective of all of us. He's going to make sure I behave myself while Stuart's sick and unable to spend any time with you."

"And if you misbehaved?" she asked.

"He'd beat the crap out of me on Stuart's behalf," he said candidly. "Just as he'd do to Stuart if the situation were reversed." He glanced at the white top of her dress. "You almost glow in the dark."

She gave him a droll look. "Not even close, buster."

Keri had to admit she had liked the dress the moment she saw it in the store that day when she and Frannie had gone shopping.

The white knit top with its scoop neck and short sleeves was attached to a red-and-white gingham ankle-length skirt with small white buttons down the front. She had left the bottom four buttons undone, which left the skirt flying in the evening breeze and baring her legs to the knee. With it, she wore simple red flats. It wasn't an outfit she ordinarily would have bought herself, but since she was using her sister's credit card, she had happily grabbed the dress and, later, the shoes when she realized how well they matched the outfit.

They walked down the path silently, content with each other's company.

"I guess you know Stuart's getting better every day. Pretty soon he won't be contagious," Rhyder said suddenly.

Keri looked up, surprised by this out-of-the blue statement. "Yes, I guess that time is coming, isn't it?" she said quietly. "I'll have to call Kim again and tell her she needs to get back here as soon as possible, whether she's talked to Jean Paul or not. There is no way he can mean as much to her as Stuart does."

"Tell me something. Do you honestly think she loves him? I can't imagine any woman talking her sister into impersonating herself, so she could fly to another country to break it off with an old lover," he said.

She heaved a deep sigh. "If you knew Kim, you'd know once she gets something in her head, she doesn't stop to consider anything, or anyone, else. She just goes off and does it. Once she'd decided this was what she had to do, nothing was going to stop her."

"And in doing that, she left you to clean up the mess."

She grimaced at his apt observation. "Don't worry, I always get even."

"You can't tell me you've been able to exact revenge before?"

A smile hovered on her lips. "When we were juniors in high school she knew she was going to flunk her geometry exam and begged me to take it for her. Math was always very easy for me. I thought she had an excellent reason for asking me until I found out the real reason she hadn't studied was because she had been out with my boyfriend. By the time I finished with her, she not only flunked the exam, she had to take the course over again during the summer. She wasn't happy about it, but she also wasn't going to squeal on me because she knew it would get her in even more trouble. So I worked as a lifeguard at our parents' club and she slaved away in summer school."

Rhyder laughed. "That is really cold."

"I don't know. I could have done much worse if I thought about it long enough," she said darkly.

"Remind me not to get you mad at me." He stopped, and pulled her toward him.

Keri didn't hesitate as she walked into his arms and tipped her face up for his kiss. It was as if they'd always known this would happen and they were powerless to prevent it. With the darkness as their protection, they didn't worry about anyone back at the house seeing them.

He already felt familiar. Tasted familiar, as he stroked her parted lips with his tongue before dipping inside. She immediately wrapped her tongue around his, tempting him to play. Tempting him to do much more. His hands were equally busy as they gripped her hips, stroking in a circular motion that pulled her dress upward until the hem drifted around her knees. He inserted his knee between hers, snugging up tightly against her at the same time his hand cupped her breast through the cotton fabric. She gasped against his marauding mouth as she felt his arousal.

"That's what you did to me the first time I saw you," he whispered in a rough voice. "I watched you get off the ferry and I didn't want to believe you were engaged to my brother. Then you threw your arms around me and kissed me and I was positive my brother couldn't have you. Not when I wanted you all to myself."

She giggled softly and rested her forehead against his chin. "I have to admit that wasn't one of my better moments," she replied. "When I first saw you I didn't want to think you were going to marry Kim. Then I decided if you were, I may as well do it up big, so I kissed you. I just didn't expect to feel a lightning bolt when I did it. After you told me who you were, I wasn't sure whether to be relieved you were someone I could chase after or to curse Kim because I couldn't do any chasing for a while."

"Ah, a nineties woman." His breath ruffled her bangs as he spoke. "You weren't going to wait around for me to make the first move, were you?"

"Hell, no." She tucked her fingers into the back of his waistband. "Of course, I was also worried that you wouldn't like me as Keri."

"Why? Because you're not in big business like your sister?" he teased. "Or because you obviously have a more level head."

"All of the above and more." She uttered a soft sigh. "I'm very pragmatic. I lead a very boring life."

"I'd say you haven't been all that pragmatic for the past week."

"That's true. I haven't acted at all like myself, so

you've never seen the real me. Makeup isn't a daily thing with me and my working wardrobe usually consists of bike shorts and a T-shirt and I hate to tell you what my hair looks like by the end of the day. I'm not a pretty sight.''

He shook his head. ''Do you think all I care about is what's on the outside? Keri, Stuart had told me enough about Kim to make me believe I was going to meet some cute little piece of fluff who just happened to know how to set up a crackerjack advertising campaign. From the first minute of meeting you, I felt he was wrong. I could sense that there was much more to you than he talked about.'' He suddenly grinned. ''Now I know why. So let's return to our earlier conversation.'' He pulled her back against him.

''We weren't conversing,'' she reminded him.

''I know,'' he murmured, tilting his head in her direction.

RHYDER SHOULD HAVE known he was in trouble the first time he kissed Keri. He knew he was in trouble now. He just didn't care! He hadn't expected a woman to knock him off his feet so easily. Admittedly, he didn't like the idea that they would have to sneak around to be together. He had enjoyed their afternoon even if Keri was a disgusting shade of green for a good part of it. But their lunch on the cove had made up for it.

He had only come up here to spend the extra time with the kids and find himself again. Which he had done. He just hadn't thought he would also find a woman who would affect him so deeply.

Rhyder reminded himself that once he was back in Los Angeles and Keri was home in San Diego, they would be living a couple of hundred miles apart and nothing would be the same again. For all he knew, they might not even see each other again until their siblings' wedding. Not unless they made plans to get together before then.

For one moment, he wondered what he was getting himself into. Then he inhaled the scent of her perfume and he knew.

He kissed her the way a drowning man inhaled air. He held on to her as if she were his lifeline. At that moment, that was exactly what she felt like.

Rhyder was known as a man who weighed all his options. A man who looked at both sides of the issue before he made a decision. Not this time, it seemed. No, he was well and truly hooked.

He was brought back to earth when he felt her shiver. He realized the air was rapidly cooling.

"Come on," he murmured, pulling her along.

"Where are we going?" She was still dazed by his last kiss.

"My place."

"Uh, wait a minute." She skidded to a stop, pulling on his hand so he was forced to stop also. "I'm not so sure that's a good idea."

He grinned. "Don't worry. Beau is an excellent chaperon."

She allowed herself to be pulled along. "Who?"

"You'll find out soon enough."

It was too dark to see the color of the small caretaker's cottage—only that it was the clapboard style that made her think of Grandmother's house in a fairy story. An amused voice inside her head asked if it wasn't more the Big Bad Wolf's house instead of Grandmother's.

"Is this house big enough for all three of you?" she asked as they walked up to the front door.

"Luckily, it has three bedrooms. We wanted our own space instead of staying at the main house where the rest of the family could drop in at any time." He opened the door and guided her inside.

"Where's Rhyder?" a raspy voice called out.

"What was that?" Keri looked around.

"The other member of the family. Come on." He led her into the small living room, which was dominated by a large black wrought-iron cage. A brilliant red-and-turquoise macaw was climbing large branches that had been set inside. "Keri, meet Beau. Beau, say hello."

The macaw looked up at her. "Hello."

"He's gorgeous!" she enthused, stepping a bit closer but wise enough to give the bird his space. "What a gorgeous guy you are," she told him.

The macaw seemed to purr as he ducked his head in apparent shyness.

"Careful, he accepts all flattery as fact," Rhyder said dryly. "Come on, you ham."

Beau's head shot up, and with typical macaw disdain, he turned his back on his usually favorite human.

Keri burst into laughter.

"I told you he was a ham," Rhyder said, walking past her. "Okay, big guy, time for bed." He draped a light-weight blanket over the cage until it was fully covered.

"Mean Rhyder!" Beau squawked.

"We go through this pretty much every night," he explained. "How about some wine along with a nice view, even if it's not as nice as the one you'd have at the big house?"

"Sounds fine." She followed him into the kitchen.

Rhyder winced at the sight of the breakfast dishes still sitting in the dish drainer. He mentally reminded himself that at least they were clean.

Keri looked around the small kitchen. While the counters had been wiped, she could see crumbs on the little round table and a box of cereal on the counter by the refrigerator. The appliances were probably a good fifteen or twenty years old and the cabinets even older, but there was a homeyness about the room, with its green print curtains and green towels hanging on a rack.

"The kids have a list of chores they're supposed to do, but getting them accomplished on time isn't always guaranteed," he explained, following her line of sight.

"I'm not exactly known as the neatest person in the world, either," she assured him, accepting the glass of wine he'd poured.

Rhyder guided her out the back door and onto a large open porch that overlooked a stretch of lawn that led down to the water.

"The caretaker thought the view out here was better than the one on the front porch," he explained, pulling two lawn chairs forward. "Actually, he liked to smoke and his wife hated him smoking, so he was banned from the house whenever he wanted to light up. He came out here to smoke his cigars while she relaxed in the clean air on the front porch."

"Are you sure you aren't talking about another set of relatives?" Keri asked, sitting back and curling her legs under her.

He thought about it for a moment. "Come to think about it, they could have been cousins several times removed. It's not all that easy to keep them straight."

She shook her head. "How did a lawyer end up with a twisted sense of humor?" She sipped her wine and found it dry and light, just the way she preferred it. "I didn't think it was allowed."

"I didn't always have one, but after Ellen died I decided that being serious all the time didn't improve my life any. At first, all I did was work." He looked pensive. "She used to say I needed to lighten up, but after spending the day with some of the clients I defended I couldn't see what was so funny in the world. When I realized I was continuing with my old habits, I decided to take a leave of absence and see if I could find humor in life. Luckily, I did.''

She half turned in her chair so she could see his profile in the fading light. ''You must have loved her a great deal,'' she said softly.

He stared at the water. ''She was a good wife and mother. She never wanted a career. She preferred staying home with the kids and being a full-time mom. Once the kids started school, she took classes in sewing, gourmet cooking, decorating and various crafts.'' He chuckled. ''Friends used to tease her that they knew what kind of class she was taking by the gifts she made.''

Keri heard his words with a sinking heart. There was no doubt Rhyder had had a happy marriage and if he ever looked for another permanent relationship, she hazarded a guess he would look for the same kind of woman—one who cooked perfect meals, kept a perfect house and chaired all important school committees. Whereas Keri's ambition was to own her own fitness club and build up her clientele. Most of the time she didn't dust her furniture until she could write her name on the surface. She cooked only because she believed in proper nutrition, and as for any kind of crafts, she could sew on buttons and repair hems; that was all she felt she needed to know. She reminded herself that while she might not be the Suzy Homemaker type, she was the one with him now. She had a dark suspicion Veronica would have been only too happy to find someone suitable for Rhyder. But then, knowing Veronica, she would probably find him the housewife from hell, too. She ducked her head to hide her smile.

''What's so funny?'' he asked, noticing her smile after all.

''I was thinking of Veronica finding you a suitable woman,'' she explained. ''I can see her now. She would wear all the right designer clothing, play tennis at the club, have lunch at the club and head all the committees at the club,'' she said. ''Let's see. What else could she do at the club?''

''Sleep with the tennis pro,'' he muttered.

At the moment he spoke, Keri was sipping her wine and promptly choked.

''You liked that, did you?'' Rhyder said dryly.

She nodded as she finally got herself under control. ''You are very bad.''

''I try, I really do,'' he murmured, lifting his glass in a toast. ''Turnabout is fair play. What about your love life? And remember, you are under oath.''

''Good thing I didn't take one,'' she muttered. She decided to enter into the game. ''Well, there was a great guy who regularly ran marathons. The man had incredible breath control,'' she confided.

Rhyder blinked as if he was trying to figure that one out.

''Then there was this adorable man who ran a health-food store. We had a wonderful relationship until he found a candy bar in my purse. It was never the same after that,'' she said sadly. ''He felt I'd betrayed him.''

Rhyder narrowed his eyes. ''Why am I having trouble believing this?'' he demanded.

She looked her most innocent. ''I have no idea. Would you like me to go on?''

''Yes,'' he said flatly, although he was less than convincing.

''Then there was another trainer who believed workouts in the nude kept the pores in excellent condition because the skin was able to breathe fully.''

''Wait a minute!'' He held up his hands. ''No way.''

Keri smiled. ''All right, one of the three is not true. It's up to you to decide which one. A high-powered attorney like you should be able to figure out the truth.''

Rhyder stretched his legs out in front of him, his hands

pressed together with the forefingers forming a steeple he tapped against his chin.

"Health-food store owner would naturally go nuts over a candy bar," he mused. "Marathon runners would have great breath control." He glanced at her sideways. "I can't imagine any trainer preferring to work out in the nude."

She shook her head. "Then you never met Klaus. He was a champion bodybuilder in Europe and when he came over here, he decided he wanted to be a freewheeling American. He also did believe in working out in the nude any chance he got."

"Are we talking about one of those hulking bodybuilders?" he asked.

She smiled. "Oh, yes."

He shuddered. "Not a pretty picture."

She laughed. "He tried to get some of his clients to believe in his philosophy, but they weren't as enthusiastic about it. He finally joined a 'clothing optional' club and goes around to their various resorts working as a trainer."

"Is there anyone normal in your circle of friends?" Rhyder asked.

"Of course not. It's not allowed." She lifted her wine in a toast. "Can you top that, counselor?"

"I doubt it." He thought of Brianne's story. Her starting out in life as Allie, a coffee-shop waitress, until one night when her boyfriend killed her she ended up in the body of Brianne Sinclair who was accused of murdering her fiancé. It would easily top Keri's stories, but this particular tale was Brianne's to tell. One day, he just might introduce the two women. Meanwhile, he was rapidly tiring of all this conversation.

"Why don't you come on over here and sit on my lap," he suggested. "We can indulge a couple of carnal appetites."

She was sorely tempted. "And what if your kids show

up at an inopportune time? I don't think they'd see it as two almost-relatives getting to know each other. Not a good idea, buddy.''

He muttered a few choice curses. "I should have known those kids would turn out to be trouble." He stilled when he heard rustling noises from the side of the house.

"Hey, what's up?" Jake called out at the same time he and Lucie walked up to the back porch. "Grandma said Ferd told her you guys went for a walk, but we figured you were hiding out here. Aunt Sylvia told Charles he doesn't seem to do very well with women and maybe she should find a woman to handle her portfolio. He about had a stroke when she said that. Man, it was great. His face got so red." He chortled as he dropped onto the top step.

Lucie shot him a dirty look as she stepped over him. "No, please, don't get up," she said sarcastically, just narrowly missing his head with her foot.

"If you're getting a Coke, get one for me, too," he called after his sister.

"Get your own, microbrain," she retorted, letting the screen door slam behind her.

Rhyder shared a momentary personal look with Keri. "I see what you mean," he muttered.

Jake looked from one to the other. "So what's up?"

Rhyder's gaze slid slyly toward Keri. "Not what I'd like," he murmured for her ears only.

Chapter Eleven

Keri was up early in hopes of catching Kim at the hotel. She mouthed silent prayers as she listened to the hotel operator's greeting and request as to how she could help the caller. She quickly gave Kim's name and listened to the phone ring again.

"Jean Paul?" Kim asked in a breathless voice.

"No, this is your sister," she hissed, keeping her voice low. "And why the hell aren't you on your way back here?"

"Keri? How's Stuart feeling?"

"You'd know how he's doing if you were here," she countered. "He's getting better and you need to be back before he's out of bed because I'm only going so far as his fiancée."

"But Jean Paul isn't back from Nice yet!" Kim protested.

"I don't care if he's in the next room, Kim. Your place is here, not tracking down that idiot." Keri started pacing back and forth. She could feel a headache coming on. "We can't continue this. It isn't right." Especially when she wanted to be with Rhyder openly instead of sneaking around. The past two days had been difficult for both of them. Last night, Lucie had suggested they all do something today and before Keri knew it, Frannie had come up with the idea of a family outing. Rhyder had shot her a wry smile and listened to his mother's planning.

"I know what you think about Jean Paul and he isn't my favorite person, either, but if I tell him by mail or phone he's going to say I was too afraid to tell him in person because I still love him," Kim explained. "This way he'll know I mean it."

Keri rubbed her forehead with her fingertips. "Look, I'll send him a very detailed letter stating exactly what you think of him and what a wonderful man you're marrying. Just come back here. Please! I have a job to get home to!"

"Two days. Give me two days," she pleaded. "Then I'll fly back and call you to arrange a switch. Please, Keri. It wouldn't look right if I suddenly left there. You told me how well it's going. Please don't do anything to ruin this big chance for me."

Keri wanted to argue, she really did, but what if this *was* her sister's big chance? She could feel her headache getting worse. She heaved a deep sigh.

"All right. Two days. Just remember to say you're Keri."

"I will," she said, exasperated as if it was something she wouldn't forget. "By the way, how much did you charge on my Visa?"

Keri now had an excellent reason to smile. "You should be proud of me, Kim. I spent the way you do on one of your wild days."

"*What?* What did you do?"

"Two days, Kim. Do not forget." She hung up on her sister's sputterings.

Keri set the phone down. "If she wants me to play her, she'll have to expect me to spend like her," she said with great satisfaction.

"DO YOU THINK KIM'S sister is anything like Kim?" Jake asked Lucie as they washed the car.

Lucie adjusted the water flow coming from the hose. "Kim said they're twins, so I guess they look alike."

"Yeah, but what about personality? You know, Kim's pretty hot," he said slyly. "And if her sister is anything like her, maybe Dad'd have a chance to get a woman of his own instead of having to hang around Uncle Stuart's. I have to say it's pretty pathetic for Dad. He really needs to find a woman of his own."

"You act as if he can't even get a date," she protested.

"Dad and dates aren't exactly compatible words," he observed.

Lucie turned off the hose and walked over to the porch, retrieving two cans of cola. She handed one to her brother.

"He'll probably think we're trying to get rid of him." She chuckled.

"I call it finding him a companion so we won't have to look after him in his old age."

Lucie looked reflective for a moment. "You know, we might have forgotten something," she mused. "What if she has a man in her life already?"

Jake had just tipped his head back to drink deeply. He promptly choked.

"I could ask," Lucie offered, as she helpfully pounded him on the back.

"Great idea." Jake pointed his can at his sister. "That will be your assignment," he droned. "If you choose to accept this mission, Ms. Carson, you will find out from Ms. Putnam if her sister is consorting with a man and if she is, if she would be willing to drop him in favor of a well-known criminal attorney. Be prepared for hazards as you endeavor to gain the information we need so badly."

"I will not only accept the assignment, but I will succeed," Lucie declared with her head held high and dramatic fervor in her voice.

"What's going on here?" Rhyder asked as he stepped outside. "I think all this fresh air has softened your brains."

He ducked too late as a sopping-wet rag hit him squarely in the chest. In no time, a water fight was going on, fast and furious. No one called a halt until all three were soaking wet and weak with laughter.

"That's the last time I'll let you two wash the car," Rhyder declared after the battle was finished.

"Then we've accomplished what we set out to do." Jake jumped, pumping his arm up and down in the air.

"I'M SORRY YOU WON'T BE able to join us today," Keri told Stuart as she stood in the safety of his bedroom doorway. She noticed that the spots on his face and bare chest were lessening and guessed he was getting better. She prayed Kim had listened to her and would be back in time.

"I know I'll be glad when I can get out of here," he admitted with a grumpy expression. "This virus should be limited to kids. They can handle all the itching better."

Keri smiled. "I don't think they'd see it that way. I guess I should have picked up some coloring books and crayons for you when your mother and I went shopping," she teased.

Stuart looked at her quizzically. He shifted in the bed, pulling the covers up a little higher.

"What's wrong? Did my mascara smear?" she asked with mock horror. "Please don't tell me I have lipstick on my teeth."

He shook his head. "You've changed, Kim."

She stiffened. "What do you mean?"

He stared at her for a few moments. "I don't know what it is exactly, but you don't seem the same."

She leaned forward. "It's the clean air. My brain doesn't know how to act anymore," she said lightly.

Stuart didn't react to her lighthearted comment. "No, it's not that," he said finally. "I don't know. Maybe it's because I've been locked up in here for so long that I'm seeing things that aren't there. Have fun today. I'm glad you're doing so well with my family. I know they aren't all that easy to take at times."

She arched a disbelieving eyebrow. "Easy? Such as Veronica?"

He offered her his best sympathetic expression. "You'll know what to do if she gets out of hand."

"Yes, I do know what to do, but I believe it's illegal," she murmured, backing away.

"WE SHOULD HAVE TAKEN the boat out," Frannie fretted, as she directed the men in the setup of the picnic table they'd brought along. "It's such a lovely day to be out on the water."

"Oh, but this is so nice," Keri said hastily, not even wanting to think about going out in the boat again.

"No, dear, it would be better over near those trees," Frannie called out to Stu. An errant breeze raised the full skirt of her dress and she quickly clapped it down. "I knew I shouldn't have worn a dress," she grumbled.

"Is this better?" Stu called out.

She nodded. "Yes, dear, that's much better."

"If I end up with bird crap on my head I'm not going to be happy," he groused, as he unfolded the table legs.

"Then just keep your hat on," she advised gaily. To Keri, she said, "I always did hate that cap of his, so hopefully a bird will do me a favor and ruin it so he'll have to throw it out."

"Is that what you call the path of least resistance?" Keri asked.

The older woman nodded. "With Stu, it's the only way. I am so grateful the boys took after my side of the family. Although there are days when I could swear Charles is just like Stu's Uncle Leon. I swear, the man didn't have one humorous bone in his rigid body. The last words he uttered on this earth were to tell the doctor what an idiot he was. That he'd die when he was good and ready. He passed on right after he said that."

Keri looked to Rhyder who only smiled and shrugged as if to say "That's my family for you."

She wanted to tell him she liked his family, idiosyncrasies and all. Her family seemed so tame compared to his. She couldn't think of one relative that could bring a broad smile to her lips if she just thought of them.

"DAD, DO LUCIE AND I really have to stick around for this?" Jake asked, sidling up to his father. His sister stood next to him, her expression hopeful.

Rhyder kept his eyes on Keri even as he answered, "Yes, you do have to stick around for this. And you might even try to pretend to have fun."

Jake's shoulders slumped as he heaved a deep sigh. "You're asking an awful lot of us."

"Just consider it practice for the time your kids are begging you to let them take off because they're bored with their ole granddad," he replied, wrapping his arm around Jake's neck and pulling him toward him.

"Oh, sure, wait until Aunt Sylvia finds out the teapot holds real tea," Lucie muttered, walking away. "She won't be happy at all."

Rhyder groaned. "Oh, hell."

KERI HAD DECIDED she liked the water best when she watched it from a comfortable spot on dry ground.

"Do you mind if I sit here with you?"

She looked up to find Lucie standing over her. "Pull up a patch of grass," she invited, patting the spot beside her.

Lucie sat and stretched her legs in front of her. She idly plucked a blade of grass from her dark pink plaid cotton shorts. Her short hair was fluffed by the wind.

"I guess you're wishing Uncle Stuart had told you the truth about us, huh?" She inclined her head in her grandfather's direction where he stood waving a golf club as he argued a point with Charles. For a moment he looked as if he would break the club over his knee. Instead, he threw it to one side.

"Not really. I like surprises, and your family seems to be full of them." She chuckled. "Your grandfather is serious about his golf the way my dad is serious about tennis. It's always nice to know someone else has relatives with that passion for sports."

Lucie seemed to stare off into space. "What about your sister?"

"What about her?" Belatedly she remembered that Lucie was actually asking about *her*.

Lucie kept her gaze averted as if the boats skimming over the water were just as important as their conversation. "Does she have a guy in her life? Someone she's serious about?"

Keri only had her profile to study. "Not lately."

"Maybe you should ask her to come up here when Uncle Stuart is feeling better," the girl suggested. "I bet Dad wouldn't mind showing her around so you and Uncle Stuart can be together."

Keri fought to keep her expression neutral. How easy Lucie made it sound!

"It would depend on whether she could get away from her job," she said carefully.

"Maybe you could tell her that there's this good-looking guy up here who would like to meet her," Lucie said just as carefully. "She doesn't mind children, does she?"

"Not at all," she answered truthfully. "Although she hasn't been around a lot of them."

She brightened. "Then why don't you call her and ask her to come up? You could tell her how much fun you're having. Didn't you say she doesn't know Uncle Stuart? It might be a good way for her to get to know him."

"And get to know your dad at the same time?" Keri asked with a knowing smile.

Lucie shifted uncomfortably. She ran her fingers through her hair, disarranging the short waves even more.

"Jake and I are getting older. Our lives don't include Dad as much as they used to," she explained. "Before we know it, Jake and I will be out of school and on our own, which will leave Dad by himself."

"And with the two of you out of the house you envision your father sitting home alone at night," she guessed.

The girl nodded. "Dad's a great guy and he shouldn't live out his last years alone."

Keri looked away as she fought her smile. "That's very thoughtful of you, Lucie," she said, still struggling not to break out in laughter. She wondered if Rhyder had any idea what his children had in mind for him.

"Dad worries more about us than himself, so we want to make sure he'll have someone to be with him during his old age," she agreed, oblivious to Keri's battle to keep her composure.

Keri's humor drained away as she remembered Rhyder talking about his wife. She wondered if Lucie realized that if he were going to look for another relationship, he would naturally look for another woman like Ellen. She doubted he would want someone like Keri, who would never achieve the title of homemaker. She opened her mouth to subtly point out that Keri Putnam wasn't anything like Ellen Carson and how would Lucie feel about that, when she noticed Rhyder walking toward them.

Lucie followed the direction of her gaze and grimaced. "Oops, busted."

"Why is it when I see two women sitting together I feel as if they're planning something against the male sex?" Rhyder bantered as he dropped onto the ground next to Lucie. He draped an arm around the girl's shoulder and gave her a brief hug.

"Now why would we want to discuss such a mundane subject when there are so many other fun things to talk about?" Keri said in a bright voice.

Rhyder didn't look convinced. "Such as?"

Keri's smile should have warned him. "Oh, you know, girl talk. For instance—"

"You don't need to tell me any more!" Rhyder held up his hands in self-defense. His expression was that of a man completely out of his depth.

Lucie's eyes were dancing with laughter as she got to her feet. "Thanks for the advice, Kim," she said lightly. "There are times it's so much easier talking to a woman who can understand these things."

"Anytime, Lucie," Keri said solemnly.

Rhyder watched his daughter walk off. "Damn. I still remember the day she took her first steps and her first day at preschool. She cried because she was afraid we'd forget to pick her up. She had no idea it hurt us more than it hurt her. Now she's growing breasts and walks with a hip swing that makes other boys turn around to watch," he groused, with the weariness of a parent who couldn't cope with the idea of a child maturing before he was ready for it. "I can't handle this."

"Sure, you can," Keri told him. "Dads are flexible when it comes to their daughters. Our dad survived."

He tipped his head to one side and eyed her. "So, tell me, what were the two of you really talking about?"

Keri shifted around so she could face him. She didn't want to miss the slightest change in his expression when she related the conversation.

"Nothing all that important, really. Lucie asked me if I'd call my sister and invite her up here to meet you," she said with a perfectly straight face.

"Call your sister?" he repeated. "Why would I want to—?" He suddenly stopped. "Kim's supposed to call Keri and invite her up here?"

She nodded. "Yes."

"So we could meet and maybe get to like each other," he continued.

She nodded again. The barest hint of a smile touched her lips.

He pulled up a blade of grass and ran it between his fingertips. "Lucie and Jake want you to do this because they don't want me to end up a lonely old man. They're hoping Keri and I will hit it off. Then they won't have to feel responsible for me," he mused. Rhyder smiled and shook his head at the idea of his kids caring so much about him. "Any time I'd think about punishing them they'd do something so nice that I'd honestly think twice about discipline. Now I'm not sure if what they want is a compliment or an insult—as if they're afraid I can't live on my own."

He grinned. "Maybe this time I'll only ground them for one week instead of two. I'd consider a plea bargain but the sentence won't be completely set aside."

"They *were* making a very sweet gesture," she said, resisting the urge to reach out and touch the dark hair-dusted skin of his bare leg. When he'd sat down, his navy shorts had hitched up to show the deeply tanned, long lean thighs of a runner. Keri always prided herself on understanding specific muscle strengths. And enjoying

Rhyder's muscles was a nice little perk of the day. She silently resolved not to look too ecstatic about this masculine picture of perfection.

At the same time, she reminded herself she really didn't have the right. While the kids seemed to think Keri would be good for their father, she knew he would want another woman like Ellen. A total opposite of herself. It hurt, but she was adult enough to admit that was just the way it was sometimes. Still, she decided it wouldn't harm anyone to be selfish and to accept what she could for now.

It didn't take her long to realize that while she was admiring *his* legs, he was doing an excellent job of studying *hers*. To better enjoy the warm day, Keri had chosen a sleeveless black-and-white polka-dot romper. A black webbed belt cinched in her waist and black sandals completed her outfit. In keeping with her image as Kim, she had pulled her hair back into an intricate braid and secured it with black and white ribbons.

Rhyder stared at her as if he was mentally cataloging what he saw.

"Too bad the kids crashed our way so early last night," he said.

"They didn't crash. They were escaping, too," she protested, remembering how the four of them had sat on the porch talking about nothing in particular. Keri had enjoyed listening to the mildly insulting banter between brother and sister that would sometimes even include the adults.

Rhyder's gaze heated up. "They could have escaped somewhere else. I'd hoped we'd be alone."

Keri was suddenly aware of the proximity of the rest of the group. She was powerless to respond to his words the way she wanted to and she read the same frustration in his eyes. She kept a bland smile pasted on her lips and hoped that his family only saw two people having a friendly chat.

"I don't think that would have been a good idea, Rhyder," she said softly.

"What I had in mind seemed like a very good idea," he said just as softly. "Such as starting out by pulling you onto my lap."

She could already feel the heat building inside her body. "Rhyder."

"Then I would have to kiss you, of course," he continued in a low, throbbing voice.

The temperature kept rising. "Rhy—"

He kept his gaze on her face. There would have been no missing the red creeping up her throat or the dazed expression in her eyes. "And you'd naturally kiss me back. Which you do very well, as I can attest from experience. And something I'm sure you'd enjoy a hell of a lot more than, say, playing around with a barbell, which couldn't be half as satisfying," he said in that same low voice that continued to throb with emotion. "This isn't like me. You have to believe that. But there is something about you that inspires some pretty interesting fantasies. I sure wouldn't mind finding out if truth is just as good as fantasy. Something tells me it would turn out to be even better."

She noticed he deliberately didn't say her name— probably because he didn't want to take the chance of saying the wrong one. She wasn't about to chance telling him he had inspired some pretty good fantasies for her, too.

"Are you sure it's a good idea to talk about this now?" she murmured, hoping she still looked cheerful and unconcerned to anyone watching them. The effort to keep her expression neutral was worth it, since Veronica kept looking their way. "We're under observation."

"Then it must be Ronnie," he guessed correctly. "She

hates it when she doesn't know everything that's going on. Once her daughter hit puberty and shut her out of her life, Ronnie's been mad at the world.'' He didn't take his eyes off her. ''So, tell me, Kim. Are you going to call Keri and ask her to come up here? I'm sure my mother wouldn't mind having another guest.''

''I think Keri might accept. I just hope you understand that we are identical twins. It's very difficult to tell us apart when we're in the same room,'' she teased.

He didn't smile. ''Believe me. I'd know.''

RHYDER'S WORDS STAYED with Keri all through lunch. He sat across from her and two places down, so she couldn't look directly at him while she ate. She was grateful for that, since she knew looking at him would greatly interfere with any attempt at eating.

''Kim, dear, Lucie said something about asking your sister to come up for a visit,'' Frannie said as she passed the coleslaw. ''I just want you to know she's more than welcome to join us. We have plenty of room and I'd love to meet her.''

''Thank you, Frannie.'' Keri munched on a strawberry. ''I'll give Keri a call and see what she can arrange.'' Her mind was spinning with possibilities. She could meet Kim at the airport and they could easily switch clothing there. No fuss, no muss. It would work even better that way. She would have to try to get hold of her sister before she left Paris. Keri would want her to stop in San Diego and pick up some of her own clothing first. ''I know she would have to rearrange her appointments, so it would take a couple of days.''

''I'd be curious to meet your sister,'' Rhyder spoke up. ''It's always interesting to see how alike siblings are.''

Keri smiled sweetly. ''Considering we're twins, we're very much alike.''

"Twins!" Frannie enthused, clapping her hands. "How wonderful! When you talked about your birthdays, I'd never realized you meant the same year. Now, why didn't Stuart ever mention your sister is your twin?"

"We try not to think of ourselves as twins," Keri replied. "We live such different life-styles that we have been able to consider ourselves true individuals."

"I'm sure when you were children you enjoyed changing places to fool people," Veronica said.

"Of course," Keri replied swiftly. "We considered it an elaborate game and I'm afraid took ourselves seriously back then. Naturally, after we got out of school we realized it was no longer a good idea."

Veronica leaned forward. "Oh, really? Why not?"

"Would you want your sister to pretend to be you on a date and end up with your boyfriend?" she asked.

"Twins seem to enjoy fooling people," Sylvia pronounced. "Rhyder, would you pass the iced tea, please?" She smiled at her great-nephew.

"Our grandfather is a twin," Keri explained.

"Good Lord, I'd hate to think of two Stuarts running around," Sylvia said bluntly. "One's been more than enough."

"Bet you can't tell that Uncle Stuart isn't one of Aunt Sylvia's favorites," Jake said in a low voice.

"The boy has no manners," his great-aunt stated.

"Aunt Sylvia, that's me as a boy you're thinking of, not Stuart," Stu told her as he reached for another corn muffin.

"I'm not so old I can't tell the difference," she snapped. She turned to Keri. "Don't have boys. They're nothing but trouble."

"I'll do my best to have girls only," she solemnly promised.

Rhyder watched Keri treat the older woman with respect and admired her for it. At the same time the idea

of seeing her pregnant brought a strange pang to his
stomach. For a moment, he forgot who she truly was and
thought of her in her role as Stuart's fiancée, instead. The
idea of her ripe with Stuart's child didn't strike a pleasur-
able chord inside him. Yet, when he thought about it, he
couldn't see Stuart as a father. Admittedly, just because
his brother was so curt with other people's children didn't
mean he wouldn't be a good father. Rhyder remembered
only too well that he had learned the hard way.

Lucie's comment about wanting him to meet Kim's
sister was a surprise to him. He knew the kids had been
urging him to start a social life, but he had held off. It
had been a long time since he had taken a woman out on
a date and even back then, he hadn't felt it was something
he did very well. Given the choice, he would prefer ques-
tioning a hostile witness to taking a woman out to dinner
and making conversation.

Still, when he thought about inviting Keri out for a
romantic night of dining and dancing, the idea of dating
didn't sound so scary.

Chapter Twelve

"Do you realize what time it is?" Keri whispered fiercely. The insistent tapping at her bedroom door had intruded on her pleasant dream. When she threw open the door she was fully prepared to punish whoever dared disturb her sleep.

"Trust me, I know," Rhyder whispered back, dropping a kiss on her lips. "Get dressed and we'll sneak down to the gym."

Should she? She hesitated. This might be her last chance.

"Let's go play, Keri," he murmured against her slightly parted lips. "Whaddeya say?"

"Give me three minutes." She closed the door in his face. Before he could react, she opened it again. "I'll meet you down there."

Rhyder knew he was in trouble the minute Keri walked in. Her hair was pulled up into a ponytail under a navy baseball cap. Her navy bike shorts and navy-and-pink crop top were molded to her lean body. He uttered a low whistle of appreciation.

"Have you started warming up?" she asked.

He gazed at her. "I'm warming up just fine."

Keri shook her head. "Onto the treadmill, big boy," she instructed.

"I do belong to a fitness club," he told her, stepping onto the treadmill and studying the display. "Stu got a new one, I see," he murmured, starting to walk at the same time he hit the Enter button. When nothing happened, he tried something else.

"Rhyder," she began to explain when he hit a third button. The treadmill suddenly gave a violent lurch and he flew backward, landing on his butt.

"Damn!" he swore.

Keri crouched in front of him. Her lips quivered as she endeavored to hold back her smile.

"Hey, captain, I said *warm up,* not *warp speed,*" she told him, finally losing her battle with her grin.

"Ha, ha, very funny," he grumbled, slowly getting to his feet. He approached and boarded the demon machine with a glare that should have melted all its circuits.

"Okay," Keri said, following him. "Get back on and I'll fire her up."

Rhyder watched as Keri stepped up onto the small rail in front of the treadmill and her fingers began to fly over the display. "How did you know my weight?" he asked.

She grinned. "Trade secret. After five minutes I'm going to up the incline and speed a bit," she warned.

"So this is what you do, huh?" he asked, breaking into a slow jog while enjoying the sight of her standing in front of him.

"This is only part of it." She studied the display and increased the speed. "You're doing fine. Don't stop."

Rhyder hadn't realized how long it had been since he'd taken a good morning run until Keri put him through his paces. A small smile curved her lips as she stood watching him. He could feel the sweat start to pop out of his pores.

Before he realized her intention, she leaned forward and kissed him, lightly flicking his lower lip with her tongue.

He gulped.

"What's that for?" he choked.

"It's just a test," Keri murmured, adjusting the controls again. "The best way to find out if a person is working at their peak is to see if they can talk while exercising on an aerobic level. If they can't talk or are gasping for air, they're at too high a level. If they can state their name and address, they're just fine. In fact, I think you can handle a little more."

"I never knew running on a treadmill could be so fascinating," he managed to get out.

"Just another way of finding out how fit a person is." She ran her fingertip down the front of his shirt. The cloth darkened against his sweat-dampened chest. "I must say, you're doing very well." Her finger stopped at his shorts' waistband.

During the next hour, Rhyder decided exercise took on a whole new light when Keri was in charge. She had him using the free weights and, once she'd seen what he could do, was continually increasing the weight. By the time they finished, his body was covered with sweat, his clothes clinging to him. He lay on the weight bench, positive he couldn't move.

"And people pay you to do this to them?" he gasped, allowing his arms to flop down.

Keri sat cross-legged on the floor next to the bench. "Yes, they do." She handed him her sports bottle.

"Then they're nuts." He drank deeply and returned the bottle to her.

"What exactly do you do at your club when you find the time to work out?"

Rhyder had to think for a moment. He began to wonder if he had lost oxygen flow to his brain.

"Treadmill or bike for fifteen or twenty minutes, different equipment for upper or lower body, depending on my mood. Sometimes I'd run on the track they had on the roof or use the pool,'' he told her.

Keri shook her head. "And you probably spent no more than an hour there and felt you were doing good. No wonder you don't have a lot of stamina. I'm amazed you're in as good shape as you are." She handed him a small white towel so he could wipe his face.

"Some of us don't have the time," he said, irritated.

"You can make the time or you can organize it better." Unperturbed, she uncoiled her legs and stood.

"No wonder some people call you trainers torture experts," Rhyder grumbled, finally managing to sit up.

Keri glanced at the clock on the wall. "Guess I'd better get upstairs and change for breakfast. Are you staying?"

"Just bury me here." He rotated his shoulder, grateful to find that it still moved. "You should work with Jake. He deserves this kind of misery."

"I'd be happy to work with him," she replied.

Rhyder pushed himself to his feet and snagged Keri around the waist, pulling her toward him.

"You enjoyed all this, didn't you?"

Keri grinned and nodded.

"You were showing off, weren't you?" He slid his hand along her back.

"Maybe a little," she confessed, looking not the least bit guilty.

Rhyder didn't care that he was sweaty as he pulled her against him, and he noticed she didn't seem to mind his condition. She wrapped her arms around him and kissed him with the same hunger he displayed.

"We're living dangerously," he murmured, sliding his hand under her crop top. Her breast fit perfectly inside his palm.

"Not if someone remembered to lock the door," she said in a breathless voice, running her hands down his spine while she nipped at his lower lip. "Too bad you didn't get me up earlier."

He locked his fingers at the base of her spine as he leaned back, keeping their lower bodies in close contact.

"It would have been easier if I'd only had to roll over and nuzzle you awake."

Keri's hands stilled in their exploration.

Rhyder studied her, gauging her response.

"It would be the only natural outcome from what's happening between us," he said quietly.

"An outcome that can be a positive or a negative," Keri countered.

"Now that sounds like a lawyer's statement." His expression turned somber. "I want to make love with you, Keri."

The stark declaration hung like a challenge between them.

"You don't make it easy, do you?" she said, once she could catch her breath.

"I've never been one for beating around the bush when it's much easier to just say what's on my mind."

She turned away, grateful he'd released her without an argument. "Nothing about us has been normal or predictable," she said. "We only met because I came up here pretending to be my sister."

"We would have met eventually if they go through with the wedding," Rhyder argued. "Who says the attraction wouldn't have been there then?"

"Maybe we saw it as forbidden fruit, maybe—*what do you mean if they go through with the wedding?*" She whirled to face him. "Has Stuart said something to you?"

"No, but his record speaks for itself. He's been engaged six times in the last four years. So far, none of them has gotten to the 'I do' part. But the ladies walked away with a lovely engagement ring. I was surprised you didn't have one.''

"Kim said they were flying to New York to look for a ring there," Keri explained.

"Have you talked to her?"

"I left a message at her hotel. She should be here by tomorrow if she knows what's good for her." Keri walked over and flipped the lock. She glanced over her shoulder. "There is one thing, Rhyder," she said in a soft voice. "As long as a boat wouldn't be involved, I would like to make love with you, too." Then she pulled open the door and walked out without looking back.

"The woman never ceases to surprise me," he muttered to himself.

Rhyder dropped to the bench feeling as if all the air had been let out of his lungs.

"I SAID I WILL BE THERE and I will," Kim insisted in an aggrieved voice.

"Even if you haven't heard from Jean Paul?" Keri asked, not wanting to believe her sister would finally give in.

"Even if I haven't. He isn't back yet, so I'm leaving a note at his office," she replied. "Amazing. It took me three pages to tell him what I thought of him. And don't say it's what I should have done in the beginning!"

"I won't." Keri relented when she heard the distress in her sister's voice. She knew Kim had cared a great deal for the man, but he had never seemed to return that deep affection that could easily have turned into love. She only hoped Kim found what she needed with Stuart. "I can meet you at the airport and we can change clothes there."

"I don't know what flight I'll be on. I'll check into a hotel and we can make the switch there. You can say you're going into town for some shopping."

"All right." Keri thought for a moment, then came up with what she felt was the perfect idea. She made a note of the name of the hotel. "If there's anything else, you can call Rhyder, but only talk to him." She gave her Rhyder's phone number.

"What exactly is going on between you two?" Kim asked.

"Not what I'd like, thanks to having to pretend to be you," Keri grumbled.

"I really can't wait to see him," her twin said coyly.

"If I were you I'd worry more about your fiancé," she said bluntly.

"I am worried about him," Kim protested. "You said he's doing better."

"Yes, he is. And pretty soon he will no longer be contagious, which is why you need to get here. What I'll do is take over your hotel room and hide out there for a few days before I show up here as myself."

"I'll call after I check into the hotel, so we can make the switch. Keri..." Kim paused. "Thanks for helping me out."

"Don't worry, you'll be suffering under my tutelage soon enough," she said lightly.

Keri ended the call feeling a combination of relief and sorrow. She was relieved the deception would soon be over, but she was going to hate to have to leave here, even for a few days.

After she left the gym, and before speaking to her sister, Keri had showered and changed for breakfast.

"One of the last times I need to act like Kim," she murmured, leaving her room.

She stopped at Stuart's door and tapped lightly. When she heard his voice, she opened the door.

"Hi there," she greeted him. "Ah, fewer spots, I see." *And he's wearing another pair of silk pajamas. How many pairs does he have?*

He nodded. "No blistering, so I'm not contagious." He lifted his cheek, silently inviting her kiss.

Keri would have preferred to hear that announcement from a doctor.

"I don't think I'd better step inside until your mother releases you," she teased. "Frannie wouldn't be pleased with me if I went against her orders."

"She looks and acts like a cream puff, but on the inside she's pure steel," he agreed. "Okay, I'll tell her I need some of your special TLC."

"That might not be a good idea, but I'll see if I can deliver your tapioca to you."

Stuart pushed back a stray lock of hair that had flopped over his forehead. Keri watched the gesture. She felt as if he'd done it more for effect than because the hair was bothering him.

While she hadn't seen very much of him, she felt she had learned enough about Stuart to know that while he was good-looking, personable and a great catch for any woman, she was more than ready to give him back to Kim. They were a perfect match. With that in mind, she gave him an even brighter smile than usual. Stuart sat up straighter.

"I've missed you," he said huskily.

"And you've been missed," she told him. "I'm going down for breakfast." She started to turn away.

"Kimmy?" She turned back. "You haven't fallen for my brother, have you?" he asked lightly.

"Kim and Rhyder," she said out loud. "You know, it just doesn't sing. Oh, he's very nice, but that's all."

If she didn't know better she would have sworn disappointment swept across his face.

"Glad to hear my brother hasn't been trying to steal my lady," he said.

She sensed he had more to say but even her standing

there another moment didn't prompt him to continue. She smiled again and left.

She had almost reached the breakfast room when she saw Rhyder walking down the hallway. She looked both ways, made certain no one else was around, grabbed hold of his shirtfront and literally pulled him into the powder room, kicking the door shut after them.

"I had no idea you were so eager to see me again," he murmured, leaning back against the sink. "I also never realized you had such a forceful side to your personality."

"Just tell me one thing," she said between clenched teeth, still gripping his shirtfront in her fingers.

"Anything."

She put her face near his. "What do you sleep in?"

The question threw him off balance. "Come again?"

"You heard me. What do you wear to bed?" She pulled on his shirt so forcefully there was a slight tearing sound.

Rhyder was afraid she would think about strangling him next. "Underwear or nothing."

"No silk pajamas?"

"Not a one." Then it dawned on him. "Stuart sleeps in silk pajamas."

She released his shirt and stepped back. "You gave the right answer."

"That I don't sleep in silk pajamas?" he clarified.

Keri nodded.

"I'm glad to hear it."

She looked around and grimaced when she realized where they were. "I guess I overdid it a bit. Kim will be here in the next twenty-four hours."

Rhyder stiffened. "And?"

"And I'll go into Seattle for a few days to hide out, then return here as Keri," she explained. She wondered what he would say if she told him perhaps it would be best if they ended their relationship now, before things went too far.

"Lucie and Jake will expect me to show you around." He moved closer to her.

"I hope it won't put any imposition on you." She fisted his shirt again to keep him where he was.

"I'll bear up."

They tensed when they heard voices on the other side of the door. Without moving away, Rhyder reached around Keri and flipped the latch.

"No talking," he murmured, before his mouth found hers.

Keri couldn't have talked if she tried. She doubted her brain could have formed one coherent word if her life depended on it.

The voices on the other side of the door were barely audible although Keri thought she heard her name mentioned. Frannie's slightly high-pitched voice sounded like a baby bird's twitter, while Charles's deeper voice overwhelmed his mother's words. Over it all, Keri heard her ears ringing.

"Is someone going to pick up the damn phone or just let it make that blasted bleep forever?" Stu's voice roared.

"Are you sure you want to sit down to breakfast with them?" Rhyder murmured against her lips, which he dotted with tiny kisses.

Dazed, she could only bob her head.

"As much as I'd like to be a gentleman and allow you some time to yourself, I think it's going to have to be the other way around," he told her. His arms dropped to his sides as he stepped back a pace.

Keri's gaze dropped below Rhyder's waist, then skittered back up. Her cheeks burned.

"You're right," she whispered, quickly turning around and fumbling with the doorknob.

"Keri."

She looked over her shoulder. Rhyder, still smiling, turned her to face him, then reached up to adjust her blouse and refasten her buttons.

"I don't think we need to give them anything to talk about, do you?" he said in a mock whisper. The backs of his fingers lingered against her bare skin above the lace of her bra.

Keri felt ready to sink to the floor in a huge puddle of embarrassment. It was bad enough she had literally kidnapped the man and then demanded he tell her what he wore to bed. As if that wasn't bad enough, they had taken a chance of being caught in the bathroom in a compromising position. Judging by her disheveled appearance and his obvious arousal, she doubted they could convince his family they were in there looking for a leaky pipe!

"I have not seen you today," she muttered, opening the door a crack, peeking out to make sure no one was about, then slipping out.

"Yeah?" he murmured to himself, leaning back against the counter. "Then I can't wait to see how you'll explain that smudged-lipstick look of yours."

Chapter Thirteen

After that, there was no way Keri could concentrate on breakfast. Frannie greeted her with a bright smile and the news that it appeared Stuart was no longer contagious, while Veronica gave her usual poisonous smile and suggested she try a lipstick pencil to get a more even line.

Keri wasted no time in escaping to the powder room. As she repaired her lipstick, she forced herself to ignore what had been going on in there not all that long ago. When she returned to the table with an apologetic smile, Rhyder merely grinned.

But Lucie and Jake noticed something was amiss. A look passed between sister and brother that could have spoken volumes.

"Sherie and I are taking the ferry over to do some shopping," Lucie announced. "We're not going to be home until late afternoon."

Rhyder looked at his son.

"I'm going over to the Willoughbys'," Jake explained. "Dave and I figured we'd shoot some hoops, then maybe take the ferry over to town."

"Frannie and I have hair and nail appointments today. You're more than welcome to come with us," Veronica invited Keri with a patently insincere smile. "I'm sure Simone could find the time to fix your hair."

"Thank you, but I think I'll just laze around the house, if you don't mind," Keri replied. "I put a call in to my sister, so I'm hoping to hear from her today," she lied without batting an eyelash.

"You just tell her there's a guest room ready any time she can make it up here," Frannie said. "I just feel so bad leaving you here all alone." She glanced at her husband and sighed. "I'm sure Stu and Charles will be battling it out at the golf course again."

"Please, don't worry on my account," Keri insisted as she drank her coffee. "I'll be fine."

"Then if no one minds, I think I'll make some calls this morning and find out how my office is doing after all this time," Rhyder said, once he'd finished his meal.

"I'm sure your new partner is doing just fine without you," Frannie told him.

"Yes, but how is he handling Sonia?" he murmured, thinking of his secretary, who had once been a woman with much more varied talents before she decided a day job was much safer than a night job where she rarely knew the person she was dealing with.

Frannie giggled. "It's like a murder mystery. Everyone has announced where they'll be as if they're setting up an alibi." She looked around the table. "Now we just have to guess who the victim will be."

"I can easily suggest someone," Veronica drawled, sipping her juice, and slicing her gaze in Rhyder and Keri's direction. "Perhaps even two someones."

"Usually the victim is a poisonous character no one can stand," Keri commented, looking from one to another. "So, whom shall we choose?" she asked brightly.

"I'm taking the Fifth on that question," Rhyder announced, getting up from the table. He didn't look at Veronica, but the fury written on her face told her she knew exactly what he meant. "If you'll all excuse me, I'm going back to the cottage."

Not long after that, Lucie and Jake made their escape. Before Keri knew it, she had the house to herself. She quickly looked in on Stuart and found him asleep.

She stopped by her room long enough to snag a book. A stop in the kitchen netted her an insulated pitcher filled with iced tea, a glass and a plate of cookies to take outside to the patio with her, even though she had protested she was still full from breakfast.

"This way you won't come in here and bother me while I'm busy watching my soaps," Reba said bluntly, pushing her out the door.

I guess she considers me a part of the family. Keri chuckled to herself as she carried her booty out to the patio. She arranged the chaise longue in a sunny spot and settled down with her book.

It didn't take her long to realize the book wasn't holding her attention the way it should. Not when she was thinking about Rhyder—alone and not far from her.

Just a short walk, the voice in her brain told her. *You know the way.*

She tossed her book to one side. At this rate, she doubted she would be able to read a word!

"It wasn't all that good a book anyway," she muttered, gathering everything up and heading indoors—and straight into Ferd.

"The sun wasn't too hot, was it?" he asked in his expressionless voice.

"No, it was just right, but I think I'll do some girl things in my room and relax," she told him. "I won't care to be disturbed."

He nodded. "Of course not."

Keri escaped upstairs, positive the man could read her mind.

Then she was stuck with the problem of what to wear. She surveyed her clothing choices. Should she be obvious with something filmy and frilly? Or should she look casual in cotton and denim? Perhaps she should choose something in between.

It wasn't until she crept out of the house, feeling guilty as hell, that she asked herself if Rhyder would be happy that she showed up. And, even more important, would *she* be happy?

She decided there was only one way to find out.

"YEAH, I'M DOING FINE," Rhyder said, twirling a pencil between his fingers. He sat on the couch with his feet propped on the coffee table and the phone nestled between his chin and shoulder. A legal-size notepad lay on his lap, but so far he hadn't written anything on it. One foot impatiently tapped the air. "No, I'm still planning to come back at the end of the summer. The kids want a few weeks to settle before school starts and I'll need to get myself geared up for the grind."

The trouble was, the whole time he spoke, his mind wasn't on what his secretary was saying, but on a woman staying a short distance away.

He couldn't believe it. Everyone was gone. She was alone. He was alone. Didn't that mean anything to her? Couldn't she take a hint? Answer a man's prayer? Couldn't the lady have picked up on the very strong vibrations? Especially after their unexpected meeting in the powder room? He'd been so hot he could have made love to her right then and there. And he had already told her how he felt about her.

Rhyder frowned as he stared at the blank television screen. Beau was in his cage, happily breaking open walnuts and muttering to himself.

"Rhyder, honey, are you there or not?" Sonia shouted. "'Cause if you're not, I'm hanging up this phone. I have better things to do than listen to you act like a dirty old man who gets a kick out of calling someone up and breathing heavy."

He quickly returned to the present. "Sorry, Sonia. And here I thought I could give you a thrill," he teased.

"Trust me, it wouldn't be a thrill. Are we finished here?"

"Is anyone home?" A familiar feminine voice drifted through the open front door.

Rhyder snapped to attention and looked toward the doorway. What he saw promptly dried his mouth and shut down his brain.

Keri stood on the other side of the screen door looking like the answer to his prayer. She wore the same bikini she'd worn the day they went sailing but she'd draped a sarong around her waist that dipped below her navel and knotted over one hip. Oversize sunglasses covered her eyes and her hair was piled haphazardly on top of her head.

"Bye," he said into the phone and hung up on Sonia's sputtering. He slowly rose to his feet and walked over to the door.

"Hi," Keri said softly. "Are you busy?"

He simply stared at her. The only thought that came to mind was that the woman standing before him was surely every red-blooded male's fantasy in the flesh.

"May I come in?" she asked tentatively when he still didn't speak.

"Uh, sure." He jumped forward and pushed the screen door open. "Come on in."

When she walked past him, he detected a hint of her perfume. No coconut suntan lotion for this lady!

"Have a seat," he invited, taking a quick look around. It had been Jake's turn to clean the living room. Luckily, he'd done his chores because there weren't any newspapers lying around and Beau's cage was clean. "Would you like something to drink?" he asked, staring at the rise and fall of her breasts as she seated herself on the couch. The sarong parted to reveal her shapely legs as she crossed them.

"Anything cold is fine," she replied.

"Don't blow this, Carson," he muttered to himself as he went into the kitchen and poured two glasses of iced tea.

He carried the glasses back into the living room and handed one to Keri.

"Now if you had worn that outfit this morning while putting me through my paces, I'm sure my heart rate would have hit the max in no time," he told her in a low voice as he seated himself on the coffee table so he would be across from her. His knees lightly touched hers.

Keri looked down and blushed. "Believe me, this is not something I wear on a regular basis." She sipped her tea. Her tongue emerged to blot her lips.

Rhyder watched a bead of condensation drip down the glass and plop onto Keri's upper chest. He was positive sweat was popping out all over his body as he watched the droplet slide down her skin and disappear into her brief top. He would have killed to follow that drop.

Keri noticed his fixed gaze and glanced down again. "You are one very sick man," she said softly.

"No, just a man."

She looked up and met his eyes. "I realized that sunbathing was very boring. Especially when my book wasn't holding my attention."

Not sure what she wanted him to say, he settled for a nod.

"Stuart's asleep and Reba didn't care for any company," she continued, rolling the glass between her palms in a nervous gesture. "We won't even discuss Ferd."

Rhyder took pity on her and plucked the glass from her fingers and set it to one side. He covered her hands with his, stilling their restless motion. She smiled briefly.

"Maybe I shouldn't have come." She started to rise but his hold on her hands tightened, gently forcing her back onto the couch.

"Yes, you should have." He kept his voice low and soothing, in hopes she wouldn't be spooked again.

Keri smiled. "Fate."

"On the contrary," Rhyder said lightly, "it took a great deal of time and effort to make sure everyone would leave today."

She seemed to relax. "What did you do to accomplish such a feat? Sell your soul?"

"Hey, you forget something. Lawyers don't have souls. We're obliged to give them up our first day in law school." Rhyder stood. With his hands still holding hers, she stood also. Their bodies were so close, even the act of breathing set them brushing against each other.

Keri tipped her head back. She closed her eyes when he gently ran the backs of his fingers down her cheek, stopping when he reached the hollow of her throat.

"Are we crazy to even think about this?" she whispered, opening her eyes.

"No," he murmured, allowing his lips to follow his fingers. "It's very right. It has been from that first day when you kissed me."

A hint of a smile curled her mouth. "That was some kiss." She looped her arms around his neck and slowly drew his face down to hers. "Hi there, I'm Keri Putnam," she teased in a low voice just before her lips touched his.

Their kiss should have been gentle, but they were too hungry for each other to be gentle. The tension had escalated during the hours they had spent together, when they'd had to pretend not to truly know each other, although they wanted to; when there could be no touching but an accidental brushing against each other. This was a chance neither wanted to give up.

Rhyder's mouth was as hard as his body against Keri's, but she gladly received him. His arms enveloped her, bringing her flush against him. His denim cutoffs provided a pleasingly rough contrast to her silky skin as she nestled between his legs.

Neither of them had any memory of getting to Rhyder's bedroom, but they shared an unspoken agreement that they didn't want to be found on the living-room couch, and the bedroom was the best choice.

Rhyder pushed aside the covers and turned back to Keri. He reached for the knot in her sarong, then paused and looked up at her for confirmation. She nodded silently. The silky coral fabric pooled around their feet before the barely-there top and bottoms joined them. His cutoffs soon dropped on top of them.

"No underwear," Keri murmured as Rhyder followed her down onto the bed. "You have a daring nature." Her smile was mirrored in her eyes as she looked up at him.

He rolled onto his side, nestling one arm under her neck.

"Maybe hopeful would be a better description." His lips traced a path along the curve of her cheek. "Hard to believe, but I'm a regular terror in the courtroom."

"Then perhaps it's a good thing we're not in the courtroom now."

Keri turned her head in his direction. She was ready to give as much as receive and did just that as she used her fingertips to trace the shape of his ears and along his jawline. She slid her hands into his hair, relishing the silklike texture and the way the dark strands wrapped themselves around her fingers. She brought his face close to hers. She smiled at the feel of his clean-shaven cheeks, the faint hint of lemon on his skin and the way he tasted as she ran her tongue along his lower lip, then dipped between the seam. She recognized the faint hint of tea as she explored the dark, moist cavern. Their tongues tangled in the love play their bodies would soon follow.

Keri moaned softly when Rhyder cupped her breast in his hand and dipped his head to caress the nipple with his mouth. Her moans grew in intensity when he gently blew on the surface, drying the skin he had just moistened before he rolled the dark rose-colored nub between his fingers.

"Rhyder," she gasped, gripping his shoulders, digging her fingers deeply into the skin.

"Like that, do you?" he murmured, transferring his attention to her other breast. "Good, because I intend to do it again."

"If you didn't, I'd probably murder you," she moaned as she arched up against his openmouthed kiss.

"Not a good idea. You wouldn't have a good lawyer to get you off, then."

Keri's shocked laughter ended in a throaty moan as Rhyder rested his open palm against her abdomen, his fingers spanning the narrow area. When he dipped below he found her moist and welcoming, her inner muscles tightening around his fingers. He took a deep breath and wondered if he would be able to last. As he looked down at her flushed face and lower to her body angled so invitingly toward his, he prayed that he could.

Rhyder discovered Keri was a tiny bit ticklish under her arm and that stroking the curve of her breast brought about another reaction. A reaction he liked a great deal.

But it was kissing her, tasting her unique flavor, that brought him the most enjoyment as he savored every inch of her body until she was pulling him back to her with an insistence he didn't want to ignore.

Rhyder reached for the nightstand drawer, removed a square packet and returned to Keri as quickly as he could. When he settled himself between her thighs, he looked down at her face, memorizing the look in her eyes.

"Don't worry, counselor," she drawled, arching toward him. "I'll still respect you in the morning."

With one thrust Rhyder was buried deeply within Keri. Nothing had ever felt as right as this did. If he wanted to take it slow and easy, his body had other ideas. It had been too long since he had made love with a woman, and someone as responsive as Keri drew him too swiftly into the sensual vortex.

There was no worry he would leave her unfulfilled. With each thrust, she rose to meet him, matching his desire. At one point, she trembled so violently, he felt her explode in his arms. He immediately deepened and increased his rhythm until she climaxed again. When Rhyder felt his own release, he shouted her name, and she quivered in his arms yet again. Her inner muscles tightened around him, pulling him more deeply into her, until he was certain they were truly one.

After a long moment, Rhyder thoughtfully rolled over onto his side to spare her his weight. "I think I died," he said with a huge sigh. Keri's hair was fanned out around her head and he could smell the citrus fragrance of her shampoo mingling with the tangier scent of their lovemaking.

"So that's what a multiple orgasm is like," she murmured with a broad smile on her lips.

He perked up at that. "Sweetheart, you definitely know how to make my day." He leaned over and presented her with a smacking kiss.

Her laughter was music to his ears and he kissed her again. What began as a lighthearted kiss immediately heated up.

"Wait a minute, big boy," Keri said. She rose to her knees and placed her hands on his chest. She pushed him back onto the covers with little effort. "Breath control is very important in an exercise program," she whispered, nibbling on his ear as she straddled his hips.

"Breath control? I'm having enough problem now remembering I even have lungs." His eyes were fastened on her breasts, displayed invitingly in front of him.

"That's right," Keri coaxed, moving against him. "Just as I explained to you in the gym."

"Sweetheart, at the rate you're going, I'll be lucky to remember my own name." Rhyder closed his eyes in bliss as she guided him into her.

Rhyder's predictions were right. Breathing was the last thing he remembered to do, and he couldn't have recalled his name if his life depended on it.

KERI SLEPT BETTER THAN she had in a long time. Snuggled up next to Rhyder, she pushed her head deeper into the pillow and murmured his name. One of her arms was thrown across his waist and one leg was crooked across his thighs while he lay on his side with his face buried against her throat.

She wasn't sure what prompted her to open her eyes, but something alerted her. She froze when she saw a large lump under the covers moving toward the head of the bed.

"Rhyder," she whispered hoarsely, tapping his shoulder.

He muttered her name but barely stirred.

"Rhyder, wake up!" This time she punched him.

"What?" He half sat up and blinked owlishly as he tried to waken. "What's wrong?"

Keri pointed to the lump that still moved. She looked as if she was ready to leap out of bed at any second. "What is that?"

Rhyder tipped his head back and stared at the ceiling. "Beau."

"Beau?" She stared at the lump. "The bird Beau?"

"Yep."

"Why is he here?" Keri hadn't taken her eyes off the moving lump.

"Rhy," a raspy voice called from beneath the covers.

Rhyder lifted the sheet and looked under it. "Beau, you are supposed to stay in your cage."

The macaw waddled up to them and looked from one to the other. Keri reflexively lifted the bedclothes to cover her breasts.

"This is one of those times they mean three's a crowd." Rhyder slid his hand under Beau's claws until the bird clutched his fingers. With the macaw resting proudly on his wrist, Rhyder climbed out of bed and headed for the doorway without even thinking that he didn't have a stitch of clothing on.

Keri settled back under the sheet, content with the view of Rhyder's bare backside.

"I always knew I was a tush woman," she said with a sigh, crossing her arms behind her head.

"SHE'LL CALL ME WHEN she arrives at the hotel and we'll make the change then," Keri concluded her explanation of her talk with her sister as she and Rhyder relaxed with glasses of iced tea. As much as they both would have liked to lie in bed and explore more possibilities with each other, they sadly acknowledged it wouldn't be a good idea. Not without knowing when Lucie and Jake might show up. They had assembled the makings of a late lunch, which they enjoyed while sitting on the back porch.

In deference to Rhyder's self-control, Keri wore one of his dress shirts over her bikini, but she had buttoned only the two middle buttons, which left a great deal of skin showing.

Right now, they sat on the floor facing each other with their legs stretched out in front of them and intertwined, as Keri explained her and Kim's plan to switch places when Kim arrived in Seattle.

"You're sounding as if you see it all falling together," he said, spreading peanut butter on a graham cracker and handing it to her.

"Don't make fun of our plan," she scolded, waving her cracker at him. He laughed and playfully snapped at the wafer, biting off a corner. "It will work, Rhyder."

He shook his head. "Kim came up with the idea of you pretending to be her, and what happened? You were found out in no time."

"I wouldn't have been found out, as you so eloquently put it, if a certain person hadn't decided to invade my privacy and have me investigated and my fingerprints checked," she informed him with a mock glare. "Which I'm sure was something very illegal."

"A mere technicality." He waved his hand in dismissal. "Still, you should have been prepared for any eventuality," Rhyder argued. "You needed to have a contingency plan."

She shook her head. "Only a lawyer would think we needed a contingency plan. And no matter what you say, it wasn't a total washout," she corrected him. "The important person in this deal—namely, Stuart—is still in the dark about me."

"Sure, he hasn't figured it out yet—he's been stuck in bed. And since you're not allowed to get too close to him, he hasn't had a chance to notice any differences," Rhyder observed.

"And you're saying you noticed?" Keri painted another cracker with peanut butter, then added a dollop of chocolate frosting on top of that. She started to bite into it, but good manners took over. She held it out to Rhyder.

"No, thank you," he said with a pained grimace. "How can you eat that combination?"

She nibbled on her cracker. "It's very easy." She

washed it down with iced tea. "Tell the truth. You had no idea I wasn't Kim."

"No, I didn't," he admitted. "But, I don't know your sister at all. Stuart does. However, I *did* sense Kim wasn't all he said she was. *And* I proved to be right," he pronounced smugly, reaching for the bowl of strawberries and popping one into his mouth.

"That would be much better if you dipped it in the chocolate icing," Keri suggested, holding the frosting can out to him.

Rhyder reared back. "No, thanks."

She shook her head, looking disillusioned. "You have no sense of adventure."

"If I didn't have a sense of adventure, I wouldn't have let you torture me in the gym." Rhyder picked up another piece of fruit.

"You need to work on your muscle tone." Keri looked through the strawberries and finally selected one, ignoring his muttered, "They're all the same, Keri." She carefully coated the berry with chocolate frosting before she began nibbling on it. Rhyder made a face. "And whether you like it or not, your middle is starting to get a trifle soft, but considering your age…" Her voice drifted off.

He sat up straight, sucking in his maligned middle at the same time. "I may be over forty, but that doesn't mean I'm falling apart."

Keri reached across and patted his cheek in a way he might have called patronizing if she hadn't punctuated it with an airy kiss. "Don't worry, Rhyder, I can ensure that won't happen."

"What won't happen?" asked a third voice.

They both looked up. Keri glanced over her shoulder while Rhyder gazed straight ahead at his son. Jake stared back at them with a knowing expression.

"Hi, Jake." Keri's voice came out more high-pitched than usual. "Your dad invited me over for lunch."

He shifted his gaze from the shirt she was wearing to what little she wore under it, then looked back at his dad. Jake was only sixteen, but he registered the intimacy of the scene.

"Is there something here I should know about?" he asked finally.

Keri looked back at Rhyder.

"I told you a contingency plan was a necessity," he said. "Even my kid can figure out things are not the way they should be."

Jake glanced from one to the other. "If there's something you need to tell me, I think you'd better do it before Lucie gets here. She can't keep a secret worth a damn."

Rhyder decided to show as well as tell. He reached over and took Keri's hand in his.

"Well, son, it all began with fingerprints," he drawled. "And this lady's didn't match the name she gave us."

Jake burst out laughing. "I knew there was something off about her!"

Rhyder rested his chin on top of Keri's head. "I told you so. You didn't plan it well enough."

Keri narrowed her eyes as she gazed at the boy who was still grinning. "All right, sport, here's the deal," she said in a soft voice. "You keep our little secret and I'll show you how to build up those shoulders to be the best the football team will ever see."

He jumped up and pumped his fist in the air. "Yes!"

Chapter Fourteen

"Well, I'm here in Seattle," Kim announced to Keri. "I hope you're happy now."

Keri hugged the phone tightly to her ear. She didn't want to believe what she was hearing.

"You're two days late," she accused.

"Jean Paul arrived as I was getting ready to leave, so we were able to have our talk," she explained. "He refused to believe I had found someone to replace him."

"So now he knows what you think of him."

"Yes."

Something about Kim's answer didn't quite ring true, but Keri was grateful her sister had finally left Paris to be where she should have been in the beginning. Especially since Stuart was getting up and about now.

"All right. Are you at the hotel yet? I'll come over so we can make the switch."

Kim gave her the suite number.

Keri checked her watch. "I can be there before one."

What she regretted most was not being able to tell Rhyder right away since he had taken the kids out sailing and had planned to be gone the entire day. Rhyder had told Keri privately that he knew she wouldn't care to go and she agreed without hesitation. She decided she could call him that evening and tell him what was going on.

For now, she had to get ready to go into town and take back her life.

Funny thing was, Keri wasn't all that certain she wanted her old life back.

"I KNEW I WAS RIGHT ABOUT you needing to take this time as a vacation!" Kim crowed after hugging Keri. She stood back and studied her. "You look so relaxed. I ordered lunch for us." She gestured toward a table filled with serving dishes.

Keri stared at her sister's head with a mixture of horror and fascination. Her twin's hair couldn't have been more than an inch all over and glinted with pale blond streaks. Keri still felt a little queasy after the ferry ride and now, seeing Kim's hair, she was sure the wild style was upsetting her stomach even more.

"What have you done to your hair?"

"Isn't this great?" Kim preened, turning one way, then the other. "Don't worry. I'll just say I was in the mood for something different and got it cut while I was over here."

"At least I won't have to get my hair chopped off like that," Keri muttered. She walked over to the table set by the window, digging through her purse at the same time. "I made a floor plan of the house for you, listed names and descriptions of the family members." She placed the sheet of paper on the table.

Kim glanced at it. "I'm sure I'll be fine." She grimaced at Keri. "You couldn't have chosen something else for me to wear?" She gestured for her sister to sit down.

Keri looked down at her navy shorts and bright pink T-shirt. "It's your outfit, so don't complain."

"I just never wore them together."

The sisters sat down and had lunch while Keri filled Kim in on everything that had gone on during the past

week and a half. Kim asked a few questions to clarify
something in her mind but otherwise didn't seem to have
a problem remembering the important points. All she left
out was the way Rhyder kissed and made love. She decided those were details Kim didn't need to know. Once
they'd finished eating, she suggested they change clothes.

Kim went into the bedroom and walked over to her
open suitcase. "I picked up a few things for you in
Paris." She held up a sheer, cream-colored blouse.

"Aren't you going to ask about Stuart?" Keri asked,
setting her shirt and shorts to one side. "Or how he's
doing?"

"You said he was getting much better and I'll see him
in an hour or so." Kim loosened her robe.

Keri took one look at her sister's bright lingerie and
hazarded an accurate guess that she had bought new
clothing for herself from the skin out.

"Kim, are you sure you want to marry Stuart?" Keri
asked the question she'd dreaded asking but felt needed
to be brought out in the open. "All this turmoil with Jean
Paul and the way you seem to have avoided asking about
Stuart has me wondering if you have true feelings for
Stuart."

Kim pulled on the shorts and T-shirt and took her sister's sandals. She walked over to the mirror and fluffed
her hair. "Stuart and I are perfectly suited for each other
and we decided it was time to get married," she said
bluntly. "Then, after we talked more about getting married we realized we did love each other. He admitted he's
introduced other women to his parents, but he knew I
would be the last one. We thought a fall wedding would
be lovely." She reached for a lip-lining pencil and lipstick and began adding color to her lips.

Keri experienced an uneasy feeling deep down in her
stomach. She remembered the last time she had felt like
this. It had had to do with Kim.

"I'll call you in a couple of days and then you can arrive on the scene," Kim said, taking Keri's purse and refilling it with her personal items. There was a sly smile on her lips. "So Stuart's in the adjoining room, you say?"

Keri nodded. "But he thinks you're respecting his parents by not letting him near you."

"Then perhaps I'll let him suffer awhile longer. It will be good for him." Kim looked around and shrugged as if she'd decided she had all she needed. She walked over to Keri. "I know I come across like an uncaring bitch at times, but I really do appreciate you doing this for me. The closure with Jean Paul was just what I needed to get on with my life." She hugged her.

Keri hugged her back. "Just as long as you're happy."

"Enjoy the hotel and just keep up with your vacation," Kim said. "I'll talk to you the day after tomorrow."

When she swept out of the room, it seemed the energy went with her. Keri picked up her twin's robe and slipped it on. She settled on the bed and leafed through the hotel directory.

"At least here I won't have to sneak around to go to the fitness center," she mused.

Keri thought about the last time she had worked out and knew it wouldn't be the same. She wasn't sure it was a good idea to think about Rhyder. At least, not in that way. She had thought this time alone might be a good way for her to truly come to terms with her feelings for him. Deep down, she feared they weren't meant to be. The distance between their homes and businesses. The distance between their life-styles. Was there enough between them other than sex for them to pursue the relationship further? Or would they be better off ending it now, before one or both of them were hurt?

RHYDER WAS SUNBURNED and tired by the time they docked the sailboat.

"Think Grandma will mind if we just clean up for dinner?" Jake asked as he tied off the lines. "I don't want to have to take a shower and change clothes. I'm starving!"

"You're always hungry," Rhyder replied. "Hard to say what she'll let you get away with. We all look as if we need a hose to wash us off."

"Too bad Kim didn't want to go with us," Lucie said, as she gathered up towels and the picnic basket. "It would have been fun."

Rhyder exchanged a look with Jake.

"Yeah, well, she wanted to go into town for some things," he said noncommittally. He had to admit he missed Keri, but considering the last time they had gone out on the boat, he figured it was better that she stayed behind. He'd enjoyed being with Lucie and Jake, but now he was looking forward to seeing Keri. He couldn't wait until her sister showed up so Keri could arrive as herself and he would have a better chance to be with her.

"Hey, Mom, what's up?" he called out when he noticed his mother walking toward them.

"Stuart will be joining us for dinner tonight," she said excitedly. "I thought we should make it a celebration. Kim arrived back about an hour ago and she agreed it was a wonderful idea."

"Please don't say we have to dress up!" Jake groaned, slumping forward.

She surveyed her grandson in all his windblown glory. "Normally I would say yes, but because all my babies are with me tonight, I'll settle for you washing up." She kissed him on the cheek. "We'll sit down to dinner in a half hour," she said before walking back up to the house.

"I don't care, I want a shower," Lucie insisted.

Rhyder grinned. "Go."

She didn't hesitate in disembarking and running off toward the cottage.

"I'll hose off the boat, Dad," Jake offered. "Maybe if you're lucky, you can see a certain someone before dinner," he teased.

"That's an offer I won't refuse." Rhyder clapped him on the back. "And just for that, I'll make sure Aunt Veronica doesn't start talking about that prep school for you again."

"Great!"

When Rhyder entered the hallway, he could hear voices coming from the front of the house. He brightened at the sound of Keri's voice. He waited in the shadows until he heard his mother leave the room. Hoping Keri was still alone, he made his way to the family room. Luckily, he found her still there.

What in the hell? He stared at her, unable to believe she would allow someone to cut her hair so short.

"Hell, your hair's shorter than mine," he burst out.

Keri turned around. For a moment, he just stared at her, then he sauntered over and looped his arms around her neck. The moment his lips touched hers, Rhyder knew he wasn't kissing Keri. He dropped his arms to his sides and stepped back. "When did you get into town, Kim?" he murmured.

For a moment he thought she was going to argue with him, but she seemed to feel it wouldn't do any good. She walked over to a chair and sat down, crossing her legs and swinging her foot back and forth.

"No one has ever been able to tell us apart before," Kim told him, eyeing him speculatively. "What gave me away? The hair?"

He shook his head. "You might look and sound alike, but you don't taste alike. Where's Keri?"

Kim smiled. "Interesting answer. As for Keri, she's

staying in my hotel suite. We decided I'd call her day after tomorrow and she'll arrive as herself then.''

Rhyder nodded. "Care to tell me which hotel?"

She obliged him with the name.

"I'm sure Stuart will be glad to have the real Kim back. I know Keri had to have been glad you finally came back," he told her before he left the room. "And now to find out why Keri didn't tell me you two were switching places today," he muttered as he went in search of his mother. It looked like Jake would be on his own with Ronnie tonight.

"HONESTLY, KIM, WHERE did you think I'd wear this?" Keri murmured, examining the sheer blouse her sister had brought back for her. She had spent the rest of the afternoon unpacking and hanging up the clothing Kim had brought with her.

Funny, though. After wearing some of the wilder clothing Kim had, Keri found herself liking the new side of her personality that had been evolving over the past two weeks.

She turned when she heard the phone ring.

"Yes, Kim, I'm having a party and charging it all to you," she drawled, before picking up the phone. "Yes?"

"Want some company?"

Her heart skipped a beat at the sound of the familiar voice. "Where are you?"

"Downstairs in the lobby. I was tempted to come up and knock on your door, but I figured you wouldn't answer it. So what do you say? Have you had dinner? Want to go out?"

She wanted him. Oh, God, how she wanted him! But was it a good idea when she had been thinking about breaking it off? Still, who was she to turn down the chance of creating some lovely memories? Oh, she was weak. Very, very weak.

"You come up and I'll call room service," she said softly.

"Sounds even better." He hung up.

Keri figured she had five minutes, tops, to decide what to wear. She tore through the mixture of her and Kim's clothing and finally settled for honesty. She chose a deep teal silk robe of Kim's and pulled it on. She had just enough time to run a brush through her hair, pull it up into a loose knot on top of her head and add a touch of lip gloss before she heard a tap on the door.

She knew her efforts were more than worth it when she saw the widening of his eyes as she let him in.

"You're right, room service is just fine," he muttered, kicking the door closed and gathering her into his arms in one smooth motion.

They could have been separated for days instead of hours.

"I'm glad to see you didn't cut your hair, too," Rhyder told her as he pressed hard kisses against her lips.

"It was a surprise to me, as well," she murmured, feverishly pulling his shirt out of his pants waistband. "Is that how you could tell us apart?"

"I told her while you two looked and talked the same, you definitely don't taste the same."

Keri reared back. "Excuse me?" She prided herself on keeping her temper in check, but she didn't like what she was hearing. "You kissed my sister?"

Rhyder wrapped his hand around her nape and pulled her against him again. "It was a natural mistake. I thought she was you." He gently bumped his forehead against hers. "To be honest, she's not as good as you," he confided. "Ouch!" He rubbed a spot along his waistline that she had pinched.

"Flattery will get you nowhere," she informed him, pulling free and stepping away.

"Nice place," he commented, walking around the parlor. He opened the minibar and inspected the contents. He picked up the hotel directory and studied the room-service menu. "As far as anyone's concerned, I'm in town to see an old classmate. If you're willing, you've got me for the whole night." He flashed her a sexy grin.

She grinned back. "Oh, I'm willing, all right."

Keri sat on the couch and adjusted her robe around her. She stared at Rhyder and wondered when it was she had fallen in love with him. She felt certain it was that very first moment when she kissed him, believing he was Stuart. Just thinking of that moment brought a smile to her lips.

Rhyder looked up. "You look cheerful."

"Maybe it's the company."

Keri stood, her movements fluid as she crossed the room. She took his hand and pulled him toward the bedroom.

"Late dinners are always nice," Rhyder agreed amiably as he allowed her to lead him inside the room.

It didn't take them long to fall onto the bed while clothing was tossed every which way.

"*Deltoid,*" Keri murmured, running her parted lips across the front of Rhyder's shoulder.

They had left the lights off and the drapes open so they still had plenty of light coming in from outside. Rhyder lay back against the pillows while Keri leisurely explored his body in a way that was setting him on fire.

She caressed the inside of his shoulder. "*Supraspinatus.*" Then on to the top of his shoulder near his throat. "And right here—" her fingertips lovingly traced the front inside of his shoulder at the same time she tongued his nipple into a hard copper nub; she could feel his breathing grow labored "—is your *pectoralis major.*"

"Let's hear it for those pecs," he said in a raspy voice.

"*Levator scapulae,*" she whispered as she moved

downward to the front of his upper thigh. *"Vastus inter-medius."*

"Mmm, I love it when you talk dirty," he muttered hoarsely, shifting under her loving hands. "Don't feel you have to stop on my account."

"I don't intend to." Keri rolled him over and stroked her mouth across his shoulder. *"Trapezius."*

"Oh, yeah," he moaned.

Keri smiled. "Oh, my, here we are at your *gluteus medius.*" She laid her palm against the top of his behind and slowly moved it downward. "Do you know you have a very sexy *gluteus maximus?* Along with an outstanding *piriformis* and *quadriceps femoris?*"

Rhyder rolled over. "I never knew Latin could get me so hot," he said huskily, pulling her into his arms.

Keri obligingly straddled his hips but only lightly brushed against his erection with her center. He groaned at the sensation of her moist heat caressing him.

"You are making me very crazy," he told her in a raw voice that sounded as if he was rapidly coming to the end of his rope.

"That was the intention," she whispered, grazing her teeth across his earlobe. "You know, counselor, I have to admit acting the part of a sexpot can be very addictive." She tickled his ear with the tip of her tongue.

Now Rhyder knew he was about to go insane. Every brush of her body against his sent shock waves throughout his system. He had his hands braced on her hips and now he trailed them downward and inward. He palmed her mound, carefully inserting one finger, then two. He found her moist and welcoming as she clenched her muscles around him.

"What are you going to do? Try to seduce me with Latin?" she murmured as she touched him in return.

"Habeas corpus," he muttered as he arched up and thrust deep inside her.

Keri's cry was one of joy as she gladly accepted him. She stretched out, kissing him in the same wild rhythm their bodies already shared. She dug her fingers into his scalp, holding his head still for her ravaging kiss. Rhyder gloried in her seduction techniques.

With the light streaming through the window and creating silver patterns on their twisting bodies, they appeared like an erotic living sculpture on the tangled sheets.

As the tension rose to the breaking point within Keri, she moved more quickly still. Rhyder thrust upward, fast and furious, until they both exploded.

When she collapsed onto Rhyder's chest, she was slick with sweat. She moved her face, feeling the salty film covering his skin, as well.

Rhyder's chest rose and fell in a deep sigh as he wrapped his arms around her back.

"I think you definitely killed me this time," he said finally. "I've been taking inventory and so far no one has answered."

"Hmm," she murmured in a skeptical tone. Her eyes closed as she breathed deeply to calm her racing heart.

"All right, if I'm not dead, you have definitely wrung me out to dry." He ran his hand down the back of her head and lower, along her spine. She quivered under his caress and he could feel the jumping aftershocks of her climax under her skin's surface.

Keri laid her cheek against his hair-roughened one, content to be stroked in slow, easy movements. Now she knew why a cat enjoyed being petted.

"And here I felt bad because I didn't have a chance to tell you Kim was in town and we were going to switch," she said softly. "I guess I shouldn't have worried. Although—" she raised her head and snapped her teeth at him "—I didn't know it would take kissing my sister for you to find out where I was."

"And I told you, it was an honest mistake," he said lazily.

"Ah, yes, and you said we didn't taste alike." She looked suspicious.

"You taste like heaven." He showed her by pulling her up for a leisurely kiss. "She doesn't."

Keri could feel her entire body softening under his kiss. She should have been worn out by now, but all she could think of was making love with him again!

"No, sweetheart. Food first," he told her, as one arm snaked out in the direction of the phone. "I think I'd better order some red meat for myself. Something tells me I'll be needing it."

Keri adjusted herself so she lay prone over him. "You're a very perceptive man."

THEY HAD NO IDEA WHAT time it was nor did they really care. The drapes had been left open while they lay intertwined in each other's arms.

"I've decided something," Rhyder said suddenly.

Keri, who had been drowsing, moved her head so she could better see him. "What did you decide?" Her voice was husky.

He stared up at the ceiling as he spoke. "I have an idea that even when I'm ninety, you'll be able to surprise me."

She grew very still. "When you're ninety," she repeated.

He nodded. "Of course, I'll probably be this doddering old man who will still want to chase you around, but my walker will only allow me to go so fast. I just hope you'll be up to it when I finally catch you. Especially if you've had a new hip by then." He caressed said part of her body.

Keri smiled. "If I were you, Rhyder Carson, I'd worry

more about being *up* to it yourself.'' She likewise caressed said part of his body.

He groaned. ''Damn, woman! Sex, sex, sex. Is that all you think about?'' he asked theatrically.

''Just think of it as my giving you plenty of memories to savor when you're ninety.''

KERI LEARNED THAT sharing the Jacuzzi tub with Rhyder was an experience she could quickly become addicted to. Bubbling water, soft music in the background and Rhyder were a winning combination to her senses.

''I'm going to have to go back today,'' he said, his expression filled with regret that their stolen moments were almost at an end. ''I told the family I'd only be gone overnight.''

She felt her euphoria burst like a bubble.

''I know,'' she said slowly and understandingly.

Rhyder groaned a pithy curse and pulled her into his arms.

''I feel as though we're still sneaking around,'' she said with a sigh.

''Yes, I guess you'd have to say we haven't exactly had any conventional time together except that day on the other side of the island.''

''The boat ride from hell doesn't count.'' Her words were muffled since her face was nestled against his shoulder. ''Oh, God! I'll have to ride that horrible ferry again.''

Rhyder gently pulled her head back and dropped light kisses across her face. ''You'll do fine,'' he assured her. ''Just remember to take the seasick pills an hour before you board.''

''Just don't let the whole family show up. Please?''

''No one can stop Mom, but I'll do what I can with Ronnie,'' he promised her.

When room service brought their order they sat on the

floor with their breakfast plates in their laps and shared nibbles of each other's food. Keri didn't want to think about Rhyder having to leave, even if they would only be apart for twenty-four hours.

Later, as he pushed his wallet into the back pocket of his jeans, Rhyder looked over at Keri, who was curled up in a chair wearing a black cotton tunic sweater and a long black-and-red skirt that left only her feet bare. She had piled her hair on top of her head again, and he wondered what she would do if he told her she looked adorable.

He walked over and crouched in front of her, taking her hands in his.

"I'll see you soon," he told her.

She nodded but didn't smile. "I'll call Kim later on and let her know what time I'll be showing up."

Rhyder felt as if something had shifted in the past half hour, but he wasn't sure what. As was his usual way, he just asked.

Keri hesitated. "I wondered if it might have been better if we had taken this break as a hint."

"A hint of what?" he asked, confused.

"That it might be better if we just remained friends," she said softly. "If, when I arrive, we definitely stay apart."

"Friends." Rhyder repeated the word as if it had an evil connotation. "You can say that after last night?"

She held out her hand in hopes he would understand. "Think about it, Rhyder. You live in L.A. and I live in San Diego."

"With a pretty damn good freeway going both ways," he said with a smile. "It's not as if we live in different states."

"And we also have two entirely different life-styles."

He nodded as if it had finally come to him. "My kids."

"No!" she hastened to assure him. "It's not them at all. I think they're wonderful, but aren't you going to be looking for something else? We were thrown together because of a crazy situation, and we've gone headlong into something that seems to have spiraled into a wild time, but it might be only a brief affair." She bit her lower lip when she noticed him flinch as the last word hovered in the air.

"An affair," he repeated, then uttered a curse that had Keri flinching. "I can't believe what I'm hearing. How do you know what will happen unless you give it a try? It sounds as if you aren't willing to find out. Or was all this merely a diversion to keep me off guard while Kim was in Paris and you were playing her?"

"It was never that!" she protested.

"You know, Keri, if you're scared about us, fine. But be an adult and say so," Rhyder rasped. "Give us a chance to talk things out and get to know each other better. Don't just write us off without giving us that chance."

He stood, pulling her to her feet at the same time. Then he kissed her, which rapidly heated up until they stepped apart, both breathing hard. Keri's face was damp with tears.

"All right, you have your wish. I'll act the part of the perfect future in-law and offer to show you the island." His tone was cool and distant.

She silently nodded.

Rhyder looked as if he wanted to say more, but he settled for turning away and heading for the door. It closed soundlessly behind him.

As he descended in the elevator, he realized he'd forgotten one very important thing: he hadn't told Keri he was in love with her.

KERI KNEW SHE COULD sit around the suite all day and feel plain miserable, but she refused to allow herself to do that. She decided it might help if she got out of the hotel and walked around the city.

As she stood up to go into the bedroom to change, she thought about what she had really wanted to tell Rhyder. She had wanted to tell him she was in love with him.

She had just reached the bedroom doorway when she heard a knock at the door.

Her hopes rose instantly.

"I knew you couldn't stay away," she teased, throwing open the door. The moment she caught sight of her visitor, she wanted to slam it shut.

"You're right, *chérie,* I couldn't stay away," Jean Paul declared, throwing his arms around her and pulling her toward him.

Chapter Fifteen

"So you and my sister have something going, do you?" Kim asked Rhyder. Just the two of them had come to the dock to meet Keri at the incoming ferry the following day.

He looked down at her. He couldn't imagine that no one could tell the two sisters apart, even without the haircut. Stuart was up and about now, which relieved Rhyder to no end since he wouldn't be expected to keep Kim company. He privately admitted the first Kim was a hell of a lot better than this one—even if he was still smarting from Keri's words of the previous day. He vowed they were going to have it out once she was here; the lady wasn't going to be given a chance to break it off between them.

"I'd say what Keri and I have going is between Keri and me," he said flatly.

She shrugged, clearly not offended by his rejection. "Keri is a very serious person. She doesn't go into an affair lightly."

Rhyder wished the ferry would hurry up and dock. He could see it chugging its way toward them, but it wasn't going fast enough for him.

"Neither do I. If I were you, I'd concentrate more on you and Stuart," he groused.

"Oh, we've settled all that," she said lightly, waving her hand in dismissal.

Rhyder ran his hand through his hair. "Kim, you're nuts."

"No, Keri's the serious sister and I'm the flighty one." She slanted him a sly look. "But when it comes to coming up with a hot new advertising campaign, no one can match me."

"It's always nice to meet a humble person," he muttered.

As the ferry made its way closer, Rhyder imagined he could see Keri—then reminded himself she wouldn't be standing upright.

"I can't imagine she actually went out on a sailboat," Kim mused aloud. "I swear she can get seasick in a bathtub."

"It wasn't one of her better days." He craned his neck for a clear view of the passengers. Then he spied her near the railing. She didn't look all that happy. His spirits started to take a nosedive. Then he noticed the man standing next to her. The man with his arm around her waist and looking at her possessively. *What the hell?*

"It can't be," Kim whispered, lifting her sunglasses to the top of her head as if to get a better look. She then abruptly dropped them back in front of her eyes again as if they would mask her identity.

Rhyder took one look at Kim's shocked features and Keri's stiff ones, which he could see better now, and easily hazarded a guess who the man was.

"Jean Paul?"

Kim nodded jerkily. "What is he doing here?" she asked between stiff lips.

"Hell if I know, but something tells me tonight is going to be better than anything on TV." Rhyder stepped forward when the ferry bumped to a stop. "All I know is if he doesn't take his hand off Keri I am going to break it."

"Why can't I get someone so primal?" Kim grumbled, following him along the dock.

"Tell him, Kim," Keri said as she marched down the gangway with a set, albeit-green, expression on her face. "Tell this idiot I am not you."

The man close on Keri's heels was dressed in tan pleated trousers and a cinnamon-colored silk shirt that complemented his dark, Gallic good looks.

"*Chérie?*" He looked from one to the other. "Why are you two playing this joke on me?" he asked.

"I'm Rhyder Carson." He held out his hand. "I'd just like to say that you're standing with Keri and Kim is standing here and from what I've heard about you, you're not entitled to either one of them. And you're especially not entitled to Keri."

"Kim, darling!" Jean Paul ignored Rhyder's outstretched hand and embraced Kim. "How could you leave me the way you did?"

"*Me* leave *you?* You were the one hiding out in Nice! *You* were the one who was so upset I'd come all the way to France to see you, and *you* were the one who agreed with me we were better off with someone else," she stormed. "If you have any brain at all, you will climb back on that ferry and go back to France." She glanced at her sister. "Did you have to bring him with you?" Without waiting for an answer, she stalked off.

"But I love you!" he declared, quickly following her.

Rhyder turned away from the scene that was rapidly attracting attention and looked instead at Keri.

"May I welcome you to our island, Ms. Putnam?" he said formally.

"Oh, shut up," she retorted, roughly shoving her suitcase against his stomach. "I've wanted to throw up for the last half hour and I've had to listen to Jean Paul's idiotic ramblings that he wished I'd just put him out of his misery and admit I'm Kim.'' Her lower lip trembled. ''Not to mention I have a horrible headache that refuses to go away.'' She bumped her forehead against his chest. For now, it seemed, any thought of her keeping her distance had been put aside.

''Poor baby.'' He set the suitcase down and brushed a kiss against the top of her head as he put his free arm around her shoulders. ''All right, let's get you up to the house. Although, if there are any fireworks going on, you might not want to stop there.''

''If there are any fireworks, you have my permission to kidnap me and carry me off to wherever.'' She heaved a deep sigh. ''I feel like hell.''

''When did lover boy show up?'' He kept his arm around her as they walked.

''Not long after you left. I thought you had come back and instead I got Jean Paul begging me for forgiveness. He refused to believe I wasn't Kim. After she left Paris, he called her office and her secretary gave him the hotel phone number. My idiot sister had called her office to check for messages and told her secretary where she was. I swear it was almost as if she hoped Jean Paul would follow her. Which he did.'' She grimaced. ''I had to literally kick him out of the suite. Then he ended up tagging along today. I didn't feel like fighting with him about it, but I told him Kim wouldn't want to see him and he was the one who was going to have to explain to her why he was here.''

''After what Kim's put you through, you shouldn't have to do it,'' he agreed. ''That should be her problem.''

As they got closer to the house, they could hear voices raised in anger.

''Shall we just sneak over to my place?'' Rhyder suggested.

Keri closed her eyes. She looked defeated. "No, we have to do this right."

Jean Paul's shouted "Kim, I love you!" drifted toward them.

"I told her not to go to France," Keri muttered, trudging forward.

They found everyone gathered on the outside deck, observing the scene before them with varied expressions on their faces. Frannie and Stu stood in the background, with Frannie looking confused and Stu looking put-out. Stuart hovered behind Kim with a bewildered expression on his face while she looked as if she wanted to kill the overly dramatic Jean Paul.

Keri didn't miss Veronica's malicious smile as she surveyed the turmoil. At least someone wasn't all that unhappy over this turn of events.

Kim turned as Keri approached with Rhyder behind her.

"Keri! I am so glad you're here," she said brightly, trotting over to her and hugging her tightly. She dragged her away from the group so they couldn't be overheard. "You have to do something about this," she whispered fiercely.

"Why?" she whispered back.

"You brought him here! You get rid of him."

"Kim, I have battled Jean Paul and a headache for a day and a half. You're on your own in this. If you can handle all those corporate types, you can handle him." Keri stepped back.

It was difficult for her to feign she was meeting Frannie and the others for the first time. Especially since she felt so horrible. But she kept a smile pasted on her face and did her best.

"Damn, you two look alike," Stu pronounced, pumping her hand up and down. "But I do see a little difference."

"Then you're a very astute man," she replied.

"What is going on here?" Stuart walked up to Keri and Rhyder. "Why is *he*—" he jerked his thumb in Kim and Jean Paul's direction "—here?"

By now Keri felt she'd had enough. "You must be Stuart," she said in a loud voice. "I'm Kim's sister, Keri, and as for Jean Paul, you'll have to ask him why he's here. Believe me, I didn't invite him to come along."

Stuart stepped back at her acerbic tone. "Fine," he said quietly. "I just don't care to have Kim upset."

"Then why don't you go over there and protect your interests," Rhyder suggested with a decided bite in his voice.

Stuart looked from Keri to Rhyder. "You two look awfully chummy for just having met."

"The lady hasn't had a good day, Stuart," Rhyder interjected, quickly looking toward his mother. "Mom, what room are you putting Keri in? I think she should go inside," he said, ignoring Keri's muttered protest.

Frannie immediately bustled over. "Oh, my dear, aren't you feeling well?"

Keri managed a sickly smile. "Any kind of boat and I don't get along very well."

Frannie slipped her arm around Keri's shoulders and guided her inside. "You come with me and we'll have you fixed up in no time. Rhyder—" she looked over her shoulder "—I thought I'd put Keri in your old room."

"Sounds good to me," he muttered, picking up Keri's suitcase and following them.

"We've so enjoyed having your sister here," Frannie went on. "Although she has changed in the past few days. I think it has to do with Stuart having been sick," she confided.

Keri tried to nod, but couldn't find the energy. She remembered her last ferry ride and the queasiness involved. What she was feeling now seemed even worse.

She wanted nothing more than to crawl into bed and sleep for a week. She knew Rhyder was looking at her with concern but she didn't even have the energy to look at him. She wished she hadn't even come here again. She wanted nothing more than to be back in San Diego in her own bed where she could die in peace.

"Here you are, dear." Frannie guided her into a bedroom. "Why don't you have a rest until dinner? Perhaps take a nap. We won't be eating until six-thirty." She looked around, assuring herself everything was in place. "In fact, I'll send up something to settle your stomach."

"That would be wonderful," she said gratefully, sitting on the end of the bed.

"Good idea, Mom." Rhyder had ushered his mother out of the room before she realized what was happening. He closed the door and turned back to Keri. "The ferry ride wiped you out that much?"

Keri dropped backward onto the bed. "Kim, Jean Paul, the ferry. You name it," she moaned. "I just hurt all over. Thank you for bringing up my luggage. Now please, go away."

"Poor baby." He walked over and climbed onto the bed, kneeling behind her. He propped her up against his chest and began rubbing her shoulders. She drooped against him.

"If you think this is going to lead to anything, you've got another think coming," she told him, too sick to protest—not when it felt so good.

"Believe me, I know better than to hope even if you're not feeling well." Rhyder took a deep breath. It wasn't the moment he'd envisioned, but the lady felt, and looked, like hell. Maybe he could help her feel better with his confession. He had opened his mouth when they both heard a tap on the door and saw it opening.

Reba entered, carrying a tall glass, and took in the scene with her usual aplomb.

"Decided to come back, have you?" She handed Keri the glass.

"You must be thinking of my sister, Kim," she corrected. "I'm Keri."

"Honey, I don't care if you're Sharon Stone. The twin out there isn't the one who was here in the beginning. Now drink this all down and your stomach will be put to rights in no time. Just like the last time."

Keri couldn't do anything but obey. She gagged once after swallowing the foul-tasting liquid.

"That was disgusting." She handed the empty glass back to Reba.

The older woman shrugged. "But your stomach feels better, doesn't it?" She glanced at Rhyder. "Be careful about all that testosterone showing when you're with her. Your family's not all idiots, you know."

"How did you guess?" he asked, already feeling defeated.

"Wasn't all that difficult if a body just had a good look at you two." She walked toward the door. "See you at dinner."

Rhyder and Keri just stared at each other.

"Busted," she pronounced.

He nodded. He climbed off the bed and looked down at her. He was glad to see the slight green tint in her skin was gone. He framed her face with his hands, his thumbs brushing at the weariness in the corners of her eyes.

"It's all right. Take a nap," he murmured, kissing her lightly. "I'll see you at dinner."

Keri was vaguely aware of Rhyder walking out. She took the time to slip out of her clothes and into bed before she fell asleep.

"KERI? ARE YOU READY for dinner?" Kim seemed stunned to see Keri in bed. "What happened?"

She sat up and brushed her hair out of her eyes. "A

much-needed nap, although I'm not sure it did any good," she muttered wearily. "What time is it?"

"Oh, you have plenty of time to get ready for dinner. I just wanted to talk with you privately." She dropped into the chair by the window, and looked around with interest. "A little too masculine for my taste." She shrugged. "Why did you have to bring Jean Paul with you?"

Keri could feel her headache returning. "Kim, I already told you he wasn't invited by me. You're the one who insisted you had to see him in person and tell him it's over. Obviously, you didn't do it very well, so he decided he'd fly out here and tell you he really does love you." She rubbed her temples. "I don't want to talk about this anymore. In fact, do me a favor and tell Frannie I won't be down for dinner. I feel like hell." She slid back under the covers and burrowed her face in her pillow.

"You look awfully flushed. I'm going to call Frannie."

"Just let me sleep," she groaned, but it was too late. Kim was already gone.

Keri had just drifted back to sleep when she felt a cool hand on her forehead. She opened her eyes to find Frannie bending over her. The look on the older woman's face was one of pure bafflement.

"This is very strange," Frannie said. "If I didn't know any better, I'd say you were coming down with the chicken pox."

Keri felt the bottom fall out of her world. "No," she moaned.

"You've never had it, then?" she asked. "I know your sister hasn't."

Keri shook her head. She glanced at her arm and saw the rising blisters. "This is not fair."

"Now, don't you worry about a thing," Frannie

soothed. "After all, you're almost family. I do admit it's strange. Here, we were worried your sister would succumb, since she was exposed to it, and instead, you come down with it." She adjusted her covers. "I'll bring up some soup for you in a little while."

"Chicken pox," Keri groaned after she had been left alone. "It can't be true." But the red spots that seemed to be erupting at light speed told her another story.

KERI WANTED TO INDULGE in self-pity, but it appeared that wasn't to be allowed.

"Room service." Rhyder popped in, carrying a tray.

"Go away," she ordered.

"Mom said you're to have soup," he told her. "Better I'm here than her." He sat on the side of the bed and settled the tray in her lap. He spooned up some of the soup and held it in front of her lips. "Open up," he coaxed.

Keri's suggestion was more graphic and a lot more pungent. Rhyder didn't turn a hair.

"You need to eat," he said.

She looked as if she wanted to cry. "I look like a connect-the-dots puzzle, my hair is standing out in twenty different directions and I itch. I want you to go away."

Rhyder smiled. Feminine vanity made sense. "Look at it this way. We've seen each other at our worst."

Due to her illness, her glare lost some of its potency. "I haven't seen you at your worst."

"Then it's something for you to look forward to, isn't it?" He managed to get her to take some soup.

"People are going to wonder why you're so willing to help a perfect stranger," Keri said, now sipping the soup on her own.

"Mom likes family members to chip in and help. And there wasn't any way I'd allow Stuart in here." He grinned. "Although he has more than enough going on since Jean Paul has been invited to stay for dinner and to spend the night.''

Keri shook her head at the idea of the fiasco going on downstairs. ''I'm better off sick.'' She shifted uncomfortably in the bed. ''But this itching is going to drive me crazy.'' When she started to scratch her arms, he grasped her hands in his to stop her.

''You'll regret it if you scratch.''

She jerked her hands away.

''Out.''

''Keri, don't worry.''

If it hadn't been for the red blisters on her face, she would have looked fierce. ''Get out.''

Rhyder slowly got up.

''Good thing I'm immune.'' He dropped a kiss on top of her head and walked out.

FOR THE NEXT FEW DAYS Keri cared little about anything. She was so miserable she could only lie in bed and wish she would die.

She requested that she not be disturbed. Because of her earlier story of Kim never having had the chicken pox, her twin wasn't allowed any closer than the doorway. As it was, Kim and Stuart spent most of their time on the boat. Keri didn't mind one bit. She preferred to be miserable. And while she adored her sister, she never thought of Kim as the nurturing type. Rhyder tried to stop in several times, but each time, she refused to see him. Finally, he just stayed away.

She told herself she preferred it that way.

She knew she was lying.

''YOU HAVE NO CHOICE BUT to come back.'' These were words Rhyder didn't want to hear, and he wasn't above saying so.

''He's convinced he'll go to jail unless you defend

him,'' Sonia told her boss. ''You know this case has been pending for some time. We just didn't expect it to come up so fast. But we've got everything up-to-date for you.''

''I hadn't planned on coming back until the beginning of fall.''

''I guess fall fell earlier this year,'' she replied.

He swore. ''All right, I'll book a flight and get down there as soon as possible. Call Frank and set up an appointment with him day after tomorrow. That will give me time to reacquaint myself with the case.''

''Will do.''

Rhyder hung up. He paced the room trying to catalog his thoughts. The thing was, they all came back to Keri.

He wanted the chance to talk to her! He understood she felt like hell. He understood she didn't like him seeing her at her worst, but dammit, he loved the woman!

And now he was going to have to return to Los Angeles early before he could settle things with her.

That this turn of events would be a surprise to his family didn't matter to him. All that mattered was Keri.

''Do we have to go back right away?'' Lucie asked when he broke the news.

He turned to his daughter. ''I do, but there's no reason why you and Jake can't stay up here. But,'' he added when he saw the pleasure in her eyes, ''you'll have to move up to the main house.''

Lucie wrinkled her nose. ''You really know how to ruin a girl's fun, don't you, Dad?''

Rhyder headed for his bedroom. Luckily, he could pack light since all his suits were still in Los Angeles.

''Rhy!'' Beau shrieked from his cage.

''You're taking him with you, aren't you?'' Lucie called after her dad.

''He can go over to the main house with you.''

''Oh, goody.''

Rhyder called the airport and booked a flight for that

afternoon. He wanted enough time to shower and change his clothes, then stop by the house to see Keri before he left.

"I thought you had planned to stay until the end of summer," Frannie commented when Rhyder later gave her the news.

"I had until this came up. This is actually a case that began a couple of years ago and it's now come to a head," he explained. He glanced at the ceiling. "Any chance I can drop in to see the patient?"

"She hasn't wanted much in the way of company," Frannie replied. "Stuart and Kim spend a lot of time on the boat but I'm afraid they're arguing more than anything. Every time they come back they act so stiff toward each other." Her shoulders lifted and fell in a deep sigh. "This is not what I expected, once Stuart felt better."

"Kim's old boyfriend showing up didn't help matters any." Rhyder was privately pleased to see the man leave on the morning ferry the day after he'd arrived with Keri. "I'll go up and say goodbye." He kissed his mother on the cheek and left the room.

When he walked into the bedroom Reba was just setting a tray on the bedside table.

He felt sorry for Keri when he saw she was covered with nasty red blisters. She looked so thoroughly miserable that he wanted to gather her into his arms and not let go.

Keri looked over at Rhyder.

"This isn't fair," she said, uncaring that they had an interested audience.

"I'd stay to let you tell me about it, but I have a flight back to L.A. this afternoon. An unexpected turn with an old case," he explained.

"My cue to leave," Reba murmured, edging her way to the door and closing it after her.

Keri stared at Rhyder. "Have a good trip."

Rhyder smiled. "Oh, no, that's not enough." He walked across the room until he stood by the bed. Without another word, he pulled her up toward him, blisters and all, and kissed her as if there were no tomorrow. By the time he gently put her back against the pillows she looked as if all the breath had been sucked out of her. "Now *that* is something you can take to the bank," he said, holding her gaze with his own. "Are you going to give us a chance?"

Keri just stared at him, not saying a word. Eventually, he took her silence as her answer.

Without another word, he walked out. Keri could only stare stupidly at the door. She thought about calling him back, but purposely kept her mouth shut.

She took several deep breaths to calm her racing pulse. It didn't help.

It wasn't until a few hours later that she realized she hadn't felt the itching since Rhyder had kissed her.

Chapter Sixteen

"Do I really have to do this?"

"Yes."

"But Stuart and I aren't getting married. It's over." Kim appealed to her sister. Dressed in fuchsia crop top and bike shorts, she looked the part of the fitness buff, but the apprehension on her face as she stared at the varied equipment she equated with torture showed that she wanted to be anywhere but where she was. "So I really don't need to do this, do I?"

Keri's crossed arms in front of her chest told another story. Then she took her sister's arm and led her over to a computerized bicycle.

"This has a fitness-test capability, so I'm putting you here first." She adjusted the seat to the appropriate height, then gestured for Kim to climb on. "Now, start pedaling." Keri's fingers flew over the display board.

Kim's face soon grew shiny with sweat but Keri gave her credit; she didn't stop—until she finally collapsed against the display.

"That's it. I'm going home." She started to climb off the bicycle, but Keri held her back.

Her smile was that of a master torture expert. Or a fitness trainer with a mission.

"Oh, we're not finished yet."

"But Keri," Kim whined, as Keri led her across the room. "Stuart and I broke up. Jean Paul and I are back together again."

"The deal was I would pretend to be you and afterward, you would come in here so I could help you shore up those sagging glutes." Kim automatically twisted her head to look at her behind in a nearby mirror. "I did my part of the deal. Now it's your turn."

"Have you heard from Rhyder?" Kim asked as Keri instructed her to lie down on a bench for the hamstring curl. "Wait a minute! It's too much weight!"

"Try it first before you start complaining," Keri told her crisply. "And no, I haven't heard from him."

Kim groaned as she slipped her legs under the pad and bent her legs back at the knee. "It's been going on for more than six weeks. I've seen news reports on the trial. He looks so tired."

Keri already knew it had been six weeks since she had seen Rhyder—since that day he had walked into the room and kissed her until her toes curled up and told her she could take his promise of commitment to the bank.

Well, sometimes deposits got lost.

"Now do two more." Keri looked away from her twin.

The past six weeks had been hell for her. She'd been positive she would never recover from the chicken pox. The itching and the fever had been hell for her. And the memory of Rhyder's kiss had been another form of hell. It hadn't helped with Frannie smiling at her as if she somehow had figured out what had been going on all along. But she understood why the woman seemed relieved, once things were straightened out for Stuart. Kim and Stuart announced they had talked it over and realized marriage wasn't a good idea. Kim enjoyed the challenge of her work too much and Stuart enjoyed playing too much.

And he didn't like the idea that there would be times

when his favorite playmate might not be available to play with him. Kim's supposedly broken heart was immediately mended when Jean Paul reappeared on the scene and pledged his heart to her. He was even looking for a position in the United States so he could be closer to her.

Kim had remained with Keri until she recovered. But Keri couldn't leave without telling Frannie the truth. Frannie had laughed and hugged Keri, telling her she was so pleased that Rhyder had found someone to love again. Keri hadn't had the heart to tell her that she didn't think she was the right woman for her son.

So she'd returned to San Diego and the club. It had been easy enough to bury herself in her work as she filled her schedule with training sessions. The first name she penciled in was Kim's and reminded her she had a promise to keep.

The only word of Rhyder she received was what she saw in the newspapers and on television as he defended his client. She knew Kim was right. He did look tired when she saw him on TV, but she stood by her conviction that there was no reason he couldn't make one quick phone call. No wonder she felt as if he'd forgotten about her. *She* elected to forget that she had pretty much told him to stay out of her life. He hadn't listened to her before. Why should he listen now?

But every night when Keri dragged herself home and crawled into bed, her body wasn't so tired it didn't remember that night in the hotel and that day at Rhyder's. More than one night she called herself a wimp for feeling like crying herself to sleep.

"Keri." Kim pulled herself upright and touched her sister's arm. "You're in love with him, aren't you?"

Keri looked at her and saw something new in her normally self-centered twin's eyes—concern mingled with understanding.

"Yes, but he was married to a woman who knew how

to make a home. The ultimate housewife, and you know that's not me," she said sadly. "Oh, well. As they say, I have the memories."

Kim looked down at herself and wrinkled her nose. "I'm sweating. This is so disgusting. How can you do this every day?"

"It's good for you." Keri pulled her over to another piece of equipment. "Someday, you'll thank me for this."

"I don't think so."

Keri grinned. Now, that was the sister she knew and loved. Kim loved Kim best and worried about Kim more than anything else. Self-centered, yes, but Keri had to allow there were those times when her twin allowed her better self to surface, as she had a few seconds earlier.

By the end of the half hour, Kim looked ready to drop.

"You could try an aerobics class," Keri suggested, watching Kim mop her face with her workout towel and gratefully swig water from her sports bottle.

Kim's expression said the exact opposite. "I promised you three half-hours a week and that's all you're going to get." She winced as she stretched muscles she probably had had no idea she owned.

"You did great," Keri said sincerely.

Kim grinned. "There must be a little of you in me." She looked past Keri's shoulder. "It looks as if your next appointment is here."

"I don't have anyone for another hour...." Keri's voice drifted off as she turned around.

Rhyder Carson was the focus of all female eyes.

Keri had thought him good-looking in casual clothes, but when the man wore a charcoal-gray suit and burgundy-and-gray tie, he was devastating. He stood there looking as if there was nothing unusual about a man wearing a suit in the middle of a fitness center. His hair was neatly combed, his face clean-shaven and he looked tired. But he was physically there, and had come without a word of warning.

Her sister now forgotten, Keri walked toward him.

"Quite a nice setup you have here," he said.

"I like it." She could only stare at him. Was this merely her imagination having a field day with her?

This Rhyder was unfamiliar to her. This was the high-powered attorney she'd read about in the newspapers and seen on television. This wasn't the man who had taken her sailing, teased her unmercifully and made such exquisite love to her.

Then he grinned.

"You know, you look pretty hot in that outfit," he told her. He glanced around, taking in the men and women pretending to work out but very curious about the visitor who had Keri's attention.

Her gaze flickered over him. "Why are you here?"

He was unperturbed by her less-than-gracious question.

"You knew I'd show up."

"Really? How would I know that?"

He grimaced. "All right, I get it. I didn't call. I didn't write. But dammit, you didn't make it easy for me the last time I saw you. You acted as if you wanted me gone for good." His features darkened with frustration. "I decided I could work you out of my system, but I should have known better. Instead, I worked twenty-hour days to get the case settled so I could come down here and pound some sense into your hard head." He looked around. "Do you have an office or anything? Cubicle? Corner of a room where we can talk privately?"

She was determined not to make it easy for him. Not after what she had been suffering these past weeks. "We're fine here."

"Hello, Rhyder," Kim sang out.

He didn't take his eyes off Keri. "Kim. I see you're paying your debt."

"Keri's getting even for all the horrible things I've done to her over the years." Kim walked forward to stand next to Keri. "I gather you won the case."

"Yes, I did."

"How's your family?" she asked brightly.

"Kim," Rhyder said, still keeping his eyes on Keri.

"Yes?"

"Go away."

Kim wrinkled her nose and grinned. "I'm gone." She walked off, wiggling her fingers at Rhyder over her shoulder.

Keri turned back to Rhyder.

"Frannie sends her love." He smiled. "She said she liked you more as Kim than Kim as Kim. And Reba wrote out her lime-cookie recipe for you."

Keri softened at the mention of the cook's name. "She's very special."

"We all think so. It seems to be busy here."

"It always is." She silently vowed she wasn't going to make it easy for him. No way. No how. He was all on his own. And if the man dared walk out without saying what he must have driven a couple of hundred miles to say, she would kill him.

He thrust his hands into his pockets and for the first time, looked a little uneasy.

"It seems this case showed me I still tend to throw too much of myself into my work," he said quietly. "I guess I need someone around to remind me there's more to life than the law."

She wasn't going to hope. She didn't dare hope. "I thought Lucie and Jake were doing that."

"It's not the same." He smiled, his eyes warm with emotion. "All right, I'll lay it on the line, shall I?"

She swept her arm out. "Please do."

Rhyder nodded slightly. "At first, I thought I would buy into the club and put it in your name. You know, help out the little woman." He saw that flare of temper flash in her eyes and knew he was hitting the right nerve. "But I also knew it would be the biggest mistake I could make and your murdering me would be the least of my worries. So I came up with another idea. If you want to save up your share, it might help if you had a roommate, or I guess I should say three and a half roommates. Expenses would be lower for you."

She didn't say a word. She just stared at him. That gave him faith that she wasn't just going to throw him out without listening to him first.

"Of course, there would have to be another stipulation to this new arrangement." His gaze bored into hers. He wasn't going to miss one bit of her reaction. "We'd have to get married first. For the kids, you understand. But even more for me," he said quietly. "We're made for each other, Keri. You're not going to ignore that, are you?"

For a brief second Keri's face crumpled, then it seemed to change into a frozen mask.

"How can you do this?" she demanded in a tortured voice that fairly throbbed with fury. *"How?"* She spun around and walked swiftly away.

It took Rhyder a second to realize she was leaving him. He rushed after her.

"Keri!"

She didn't stop. Quickening her stride she made her way into the women's locker room, not realizing Rhyder was right behind her.

"Hey!"

"Get out of here!"

Women in various forms of undress hurriedly covered up and backed away from open locker doors.

In his peripheral vision, Rhyder saw only the woman slumped on a bench.

"Could you excuse us, please?" he asked the women.

Kim, who had been pulling a shirt over her clothing, took in the scene and easily figured out what was going on. She went from one woman to the other, whispering to each. As a group, they moved into the shower area.

Keri looked up. Her eyes were bright with tears.

"This is the women's locker room," she told him.

He nodded as he glanced around. "Very nice. Not like the locker room I use at my gym. We don't have the hair dryers or the makeup lights. And it definitely doesn't smell like perfume." He straddled the bench so he could face her. He picked up one of her hands and laced his fingers through hers. "Do you want to tell me why?"

She stared at the floor. "How could you ask me to marry you?" she demanded in a shaking voice.

"It was easy. I love you. I have a pretty good idea you love me. I can either move my practice down this way or we can find a place in between. There are commuter flights into L.A. all the time," he said simply, as if he didn't see any problem with his decision. "I figured you wouldn't mind Lucie and Jake since they're housebroken. And I'll make sure Beau is securely locked in his cage every night."

She shook her head.

"You make it sound so simple and it's not," she whispered. "Cooking is not one of my specialities. We live two different life-styles." She argued as if she felt she had to.

"So we take turns with the cooking and we blend the best of both life-styles."

"My apartment is dusty more than it's clean."

"That's why there are cleaning services."

She took a deep breath. "I'm not like Ellen. I can't even sew on a damn button!"

Comprehension flooded his features. He picked up their entwined hands and turned hers so he could kiss the center of her palm.

"Keri, yes, I did love Ellen and she was a good wife and mother," he said quietly. "But I love you a great deal and I want you to be my wife. I'm not looking for someone to cook my meals, clean my house and darn my socks, but someone who's willing to be my other half. Ellen had no desire to do anything outside the house unless they were activities related to the kids' schools. You have a life beyond the home and I respect that. I know we can have a great life together because I know we can meld those two lives into one wonderful one. Besides—" his eyes twinkled "—Reba said she'll poison me if I don't do the right thing by you."

Keri hiccuped as she tried not to cry.

Rhyder continued holding her hand close to his lips. "You have to say yes, Keri," he murmured. "Where else am I going to learn the Latin terms for muscles?"

Tears and laughter collided. She threw herself into his arms.

"You *are* that sure we can do this?" she asked.

He nodded. "I knew it after that first kiss. Just think of it. Our kids will be healthy, brilliant and great-looking."

Keri trailed her hand along his inner thigh. She smiled when she felt his immediate reaction to her caress.

"*Adductor magnus,*" she whispered in his ear.

He took a deep breath. "Something tells me we need to take this somewhere more private."

"Excuse me?" A voice came from the shower area. "But I need to pick my daughter up from school in half an hour. If you two have figured out marriage is what you want, could you please leave so we can finish dressing?"

Keri burst out laughing. She hopped up and reached